REVIEWS

"*The Severed Cord* is the second book in a trilogy; the first being *The Veiled Thread*. It is the story of three Australian brothers who joined the Light Horse brigade to fight in Palestine during the first world war from the perspective of the part aboriginal half-brother and culminates in the Charge of Beersheba and pursuit of the vanquished Turkish army. There are flash forwards to episodes in the life of the grandson of the main character in the first book and conveys the lasting effects transmitted through his family from the violence and psychologically damaging experiences of young men sent to foreign wars.

While set in a history of an Australian victory with Australian command and superb horsemanship it is not a celebration of military glory, rather it serves to inform of the terrible price young men pay when sent to kill other young men, whom they are taught to hate, on the initiative and motives of their elders and governments. This story is not entertainment; it is a reminder that when we condone an act of war that we are, and will be, responsible for the destruction of many young and innocent lives that will take generations to absolve, whether the war is won or lost. The final chapter plumbs the depths of understanding and compassion that one traumatised soldier feels for another.

The book is well researched and written with descriptions of places and relationships that tell of influence from personal experience. Tension, anxiety, and foreboding are woven into the events

i

– the reader, however, is spared the worst because there is strength in the story through the quality of the aboriginal half-brother with his feel for nature and intimate communion with his horse.

During these times of an existential threat of another great global conflict, this story serves to remind us that each of those we send to war will bear the burden of the trauma and that it will affect their families for generations to come. This is an Australian story that applauds the individuals trapped in the collective influence of forces beyond Australia. While revealing the best and the worst in human nature responding to violence, the reader is spared some of the pain by their survival and sustained by an ever present and enduring search for love.

— **Michael Lawrence-Brown** is an Australian emeritus consultant vascular surgeon in Western Australia. He is a co-inventor of the Zenith family of endovascular stentgrafts that are used in the aorta for traumatic and aneurysm disease and a pioneer in the endovascular revolution to minimise the invasive procedures in vascular surgery.

Born and raised in Kenya as a fifth-generation British colonial with a safari guide for a father, he studied Medicine in Sydney. Michael has worked with scientists, engineers, academics and other doctors in the Universities of Western Australia, Perth's teaching hospitals and CSIRO Melbourne, leading them to global recognition."

"Choose any page from this new novel, *The Severed Cord*", by Stephen Twartz, and you will experience a lesson in superb literature. It is easy to step into the lead character, Jimmy's world – *"the sunlight glanced off crystal in the rock, through the thin cold air." Every page continues to course with images – "...thunder....smacked at the senses.......mad rush.... splintered the fabric of everything."*

The elegance of the environment is pitted against Jimmy's language – *"Fuck me,"* he thought. *"The bloody mongrel survived."* Jimmy an aboriginal stockman has to survive in *"The ghost ground of his people"*, leading up to joining the Light Horse to protect the sons of his boss in Egypt and Palestine in World War One. Jimmy does not want to go to war – *"the silly buggers are killing each other for nothing."* The minding of the sons, becomes part of an invisible cord that binds him to a family by means he never really understood. Years later the descendants of one the sons, Harry, finds the link and is able to sever it. This is such a powerful story. Jimmy and Horse will stay with me.

I highly recommend this book. You will not be able to put it down until you have finished it."
— **Judith Flitcroft**, author of *Walk Back in Time*

"Stephen Twartz offers us a story about connections, or rather a lack of them. From Jimmy, a competent and skillful indigenous bushman and ringer on a cattle station, who stands caught between his ancestral past and his modern day reality. To Eiric, his white half-brother, who likewise is lost to his family connection owing to his experience in war torn Palestine during WW1 and his love for Jimmy. Then there is Harry the present day grandson of Eiric, whose life is constantly falling apart, because he can't find a connection to his past. Or is the real reward for us the discovery that Jimmy makes in a remote cave in Palestine, when he stands in awe of the cave paintings left by people who inhabited the land eons ago. In Jimmy's own words, 'we're all the same, mate, the same people, try'n t' survive.'"
— **Kenneth N. Price**, author of *Broken Lives*

"In *The Severed Cord*, Stephen Twartz takes us on a journey where we are introduced to how the fallibilities of one generation are manifested in subsequent generations. It is set against a backdrop of the harshness of farming life on unforgiving lands in regional Australia; the harshness of engagement in Palestine in World War 1; and the harshness of the tribulations and constraints of broken family relationships.

This story is also about resilience. Resilience of the human spirit, one way or another, to survive in a very challenging circumstance. Sometimes those circumstances are beyond our control, while in others the past determines how we confront the future.

Stephen Twartz has created characters who are very relatable. The more you read, the more you want to read. A story of many truths."

—**Ray McMillan** spent thirty years as a business consultant in business development, marketing and organisational development, working across multiple industries but predominantly mining and wine. He was the CEO of Busselton Chamber of Commerce for nearly ten years as well as holding numerous Board positions with various preforming arts companies. A graduate of UWA in Commerce and with Post Grad qualifications from Curtin University in Finance and Administration.

"At the end of the first book (*The Veiled Thread*), I wanted to know more about Jimmy and his experiences. *The Severed Cord* provides that, taking us on the same journey as the first book, but from Jimmy's perspective.

I found the novel exposed the difficulties that Jimmy had to face as an Indigenous Australian during the period prior to WW1. The injustice and cruelty to our indigenous community was laid bare, hunted like wild animals, no rights or privileges, *"abandoned to extinction"*.

Prior to his enlistment into the Armed Forces (The Light Horse), Jimmy felt a sense of hopelessness and despair. His only sense of purpose was to protect his family. This was the trade-off for his agreement with Angus to enlist and protect the boys he grew up with. Angus guaranteed that his family would be protected on the farm.

Jimmy's cultural connection with country (environment and nature) was highlighted throughout the novel. In particular, the beautiful close relationship with his horse. These traits were to become the fundamental tools for survival during the war.

An extremely difficult agreement, Jimmy was responsible for not only his survival, but the boys' safety and survival. It was a wonder anyone survived physically, given the horrific and murderous battles described in the novel.

As with the first novel, we were subjected to the overlapping of two main characters Jimmy and Harry (Eiric's grandson) based in the present time.

After surviving the war and returning home, we see the true mental effects of PTSD begin to surface with Jimmy. At the time this was an undiagnosed mistreated disease and the effects were felt by not only the returning troops, but their families and future generations. The novel clearly explains these phenomena referring to Harry's difficult life journey, *"The Veiled Thread"*.

I found the novel easy to read, the descriptive language helped formulate a specific imagery that made the story easy to follow. *"I felt that I was observing a movie of the story"*

It followed an interesting and at times a sad period in Australian history, the injustices of our indigenous people and the futility of war. The format of short chapters was refreshing, allowing the reader to stop and reflect. This was particularly useful when jumping from one time period to another.

The family secrets exposed overtime in this novel whet my appetite for more home truths. It kept me interested in the outcome of the story.

There were plenty of highs and lows within the novel and I refer to the final parting of Jimmy's relationship with his horse. This was the saddest section of the novel, the unwillingness of the Australian Defence Force to repatriate these wonderful heroes, was unforgivable.

In reflexion of my own life journey, the novel opened up old wounds of the past, related to my family and extended families dealing with PTSD. As a Baby Boomer, our fathers returned home from WW2 experiencing the same physical and mental afflictions expressed in the novel. Undiagnosed and mistreated it had disastrous effects on my family and their future offspring.

On a final note, the recent Anzac Day Services held 25 April 2022 was a long overdue recognition of the contribution of all Indigenous Australians who served in the AIF. My thoughts were with Jimmy and his family.

Congratulations Steve a wonderful read (a great movie or TV series)."

— **Darryl Kelly**, Self-employed medical professional, established Spinal Cord Injuries Management WA (SCIMWA), involved in its management from 1997- 2014.

THE SEVERED CORD

STEPHEN TWARTZ

Published in Australia by Sid Harta Publishers Pty Ltd,
ABN: 46 119 415 842
23 Stirling Crescent, Glen Waverley, Victoria 3150 Australia
Telephone: +61 3 9560 9920, Facsimile: +61 3 9545 1742
E-mail: author@sidharta.com.au

First published in Australia 2021   This edition published 2022
Copyright © Stephen Twartz 2022
Cover design, typesetting: WorkingType (www.workingtype.com.au)

Stephen Twartz
The Severed Cord
ISBN: 978-1-925707-79-3 pp344

ABOUT THE AUTHOR

Steve is a 6th/7th generation Australian, of Irish-English/German heritage, with training as a biologist, geologist, engineer and environmental manager, working over many years, across four continents. He has been based in Western Australia for over 25 years and currently resides in Dunsborough, Western Australia.

Steve has maintained a deep interest in the creative arts for many years as a writer and also as an artist, mainly focused on the history, people and landscapes of Australia, but also those in South Asia, Europe and the UK.

He lives with his partner, Susie, in Dunsborough, has a son and regularly surfs the large south-west Australian waves.

Other books by this author
The Veiled Thread

*To Marion, who selflessly gave to myself and others
so much of her time, creativity and inspiration.*

ACKNOWLEDGEMENTS

The Australian Light Horse Association – the Keeper of the Flame.

Susie, my ever-present and patient sounding board.

First Peoples everywhere who have endured incredible hardship and have shown unbelievable resilience in the face of almost overwhelming odds.

TABLE OF CONTENTS

Prologue

The Australian Alps
– South-Eastern Australia

His fingers folded about the reins. The fingers of his left hand felt slightly stiff in the morning cold. He hoisted himself lightly into the saddle. It smelled of oil. The world always looked slightly smaller from up here: people scurrying about their yard duties, horses avoiding inevitable capture. The dust of the stock-yard formed a billowing film just above the ground, veiling the hooves of the animals despite the bright dawn sun. It was the chaos in the yard that struck him the most. He could almost see himself entangled in its cords, pulled every-which-way to its rhythms and its discords.

After a while, the pandemonium dissipated. He didn't see its beginning, but it seemed to melt away. He gently pulled the reins to the side, heading to the gate. One of the men, finishing the final tightening of a girth, looked up at him and nodded. He smiled and angled his head in the direction of the waiting herd. The light green of the paddock against the dense-packed bush of the hills pulled him forward.

They followed as the herd, strung out for almost a mile, rose through the mountains towards thinner pastures. The trees were shorter now, squat and bent amongst the wiry, long-stemmed grass. A light, chill breeze blowing up the narrow valley had scattered the remnants of the previous days' snowfall across the exposed, pink granite slopes and spalled boulders. The cattle tarried only briefly to sample the sparse greenery; plumper, sweeter pickings were promised across the range. They had made this journey before.

He watched the winding column for a while from the top of the pass; they were warriors trudging towards some unknown, unsuspected foe. Their mottled hides blended well with the landscape, comforting in a way he couldn't understand or wouldn't be able to explain, but – he suspected – a possible salve for his battered soul; immersion into the land, transparency, was, after all, what he wanted most.

His horse suddenly moved nervously sideways. He knew horses found their sense of the land in the same place as himself, but it always seemed more acute, and he wondered to what depths they delved into the earth. He put his hand out, felt the greasy mane and slid his fingers down the horse's warm neck. The horse settled, but he felt tension still; perhaps the memory of friends neglected, violated, abandoned.

He smiled; the thought of old friends, remembrance tinged with regret. He recalled the yawning expanse of a dry land where there was a merging of friend and foe. But he couldn't remember when it all ended.

How he had wanted to be part of the army's camaraderie; to create a history, and forever tell of the journey. He had loved the inclusion, the brotherhood with its jokes and laughter, loved the naïveté of their lives, loved the destruction, loved the way their survival rested upon such thin circumstances, and loved as well the orders that reinforced the minimalism of their existence. You could always trust that stupidity would outrank sense; their infallibility was a given. You had to be in their shoes, he supposed, to feel the weight of decisions that brought so much loss, before remembrance carried any burden, before forgetting was a welcome release.

It was no ordinary achievement, they said, but victors record history, inscribe the tombs of their dead, crush the graves of the vanquished. An allusion of the approaching misery, a preview of universal grief, came with those souls flung away in their mad rush to ruin. No matter how often it occurred, he could not reconcile his part in it all.

But how could he have avoided his share? He had struggled with intractable characters, tried so hard to show the way, made mistakes, allowed the gradual domination of a malign perspective that took hold of all their lives, heard still the condemnation, '*You stood by while it all went to shit. You let it happen.*'

His wife didn't agree, preferring to see all the destruction, the instability, the flux of their lives as merely a procession of events beyond any control. And he saw the sense of her part. She came from the earth, deeply embedded in the fabric of the land; an old line that was rich in the lore, an irresistible beacon that muted the madness threatening to flood his mind.

He reached forward to stroke the horse's neck and readied himself for the move back to the trail. Mid-afternoon. The herd would need water soon, slowing to a crawl no matter the encouragement they gave and risking an extra night within these barren hills. He smiled again, the tantalising thought of a visit to the sacred places at the high pass, but then realised he was looking directly at Jacko. Jacko, his most reliable hand was the one who could carry forward without him; a short, square man, almost glued to the saddle, with a deadpan face.

He took a deep breath and repositioned himself in the saddle.

'Jacko,' he said.

The man remained silent, implacable. Behind him, he could see down the road, into the tight V-shaped valley, the tail of the herd disappearing around a steep promontory of the pink granite, almost at the crest. The sunlight glanced off crystal in the rock, through the thin, cold air.

'Time to go, Boss,' said Jacko.

'Yeah, nice view from here.'

'The bloody cows need water.'

'Yeah.' And he remembered foam-streaked horses, at the last of their endurance, labouring slowly up yet another dune, the probability of yet another desperate fight over the crest. Where had the years gone? Where was the praise, the respect, the gratitude for all their suffering? Where was the completeness that had kept them all together; sane, safe and committed?

He shook his head, turned the horse to leave, walking towards yet another desperate column of beasts.

'Water at Eucumbene. Only a few miles now.'

The day was turning cold; short with the lowering sun. He

headed the horse downhill towards the rough road – just a path really – into the shadow of the mountain where the small patches of hard, icy snow, remnants of the previous cloud-soaked week, survived, to eventually feed the creeks and rivers of the lowlands. There was a chance there, a chance of redemption, despite all the damage done, a hope that the tide would reverse, where he could savour once again familiar places, his kin, the truth.

'Better hurry,' he said over his shoulder. 'Dark soon. No time to waste.'

1

THE RIVER – NORTHERN NEW SOUTH WALES

Summer 1914

Jimmy rode along the bank of the river, his back to a rutted, muddy dirt track. The storm surged, water heaving, buckling like a writhing python, gouging at the soft walls of the river channel, undermining the world, carrying its solidity away. The earth began to shift; deep, fathomless fissures in the land, propagating rapidly beneath and past the horse's legs. Fractures suddenly everywhere. At the base of the bank, he saw a spurt of sand erupt into the watery maelstrom; he fell towards the watery grave.

Jimmy never really felt fear. There was no need. A waste of time when you accepted your part in it all. It was hard to understand, but it usually made sense. And Horse, he knew, had a similar attitude. They had worked together long enough to understand each other.

Twenty feet in two seconds. The trick was to stay together, stay upright, close your mouth, have a plan, a simple plan they could both use. The plan? Head for the other side. No plan, really, just survival. How could you make worthwhile plans here amongst these mountains of water?

The turbulence tugged and pulled at them, threatening to upend them, spin them to oblivion, but he found a tenuous equilibrium amongst the floods and eddies, submitting to the rush downstream. He felt the flood abate for a second, almost spilling from the saddle, a faltering of the current. Horse lurched forward, grabbing at the gravelly bottom, heaved, lurched again, rose from the water with herculean strength. Land! The far bank?

Amidst the rushing water, an island!

Horse stood on firm land, breathing heavily. Nothing was dry. Rivulets of water coursed across the landscape like veins across a hand, the roaring tide threatening to devour the edges; the diminishing dry land boiled with a mountain of desperate rabbits. They bustled about Horse's legs, seeking dry ground, fleeing their doom as the flood rose.

Jimmy urged Horse forward after a brief recovery. No time to waste, the island would soon be overwhelmed by the torrent. They had one more narrow channel to cross before reaching solid ground, scoured deep, full of churning, fractured water. Horse pushed through water-sodden rabbits, plunging fearlessly into the race, and was immediately almost carried away by a careening log, missing his nose by inches, threatening to return for a second try in a tight eddy, churning water and logs, floating rabbits, a drenched horse and rider and only a few feet to go! It seemed almost impossible amidst this chaos.

He felt the grab once again, the rise from the water, the ascent onto dry land at last. Breathing hard, Horse stood and trembled, that slight shake of the legs and shivering of the withers that indicated a close-run thing.

'You made it, mate,' said Jimmy.

A bark.

Jimmy turned in the saddle. 'How the fuck did you get here?' The dog answered with an additional bark. The channel, it seemed, was a step too far.

'Well, y'got this far, now y'gotta give this bit a go!'

The dog hesitated, rabbits careering about it, oblivious of one who loved a bit of rabbit.

'Come on!'

Again, the dog barked, turned a circle and charged into the stream. Jimmy watched as the current swept the dog away; it went under, amidst a deluge of boiling debris. He saw only a faint ripple where the dog had been.

He sat for a moment.

Good dog, that one, he thought. *Plenty of guts and bloody good with them cows.* Life could be hard but they all took their chances, the outcome perhaps not always equal to the effort.

He walked Horse up along the river bank towards the ford where he had fallen, glancing back as he went, hoping the dog had survived. The island had vanished and with it, its burden of rabbits. *He would need to renew soon*, he thought, *his commitment to the ways, gratitude for their survival and support for the teachings of the ancients.*

A flicker of light lit the sky above the mountains. Jimmy looked up and sniffed the air.

The faintest smell of ozone, then a deep rumble of thunder. The vibration washed over him, unsettling Horse.

More flashes of light, closer this time. These summer storms moved fast and could be vicious. Thunder rolled directly overhead – a hard smack at the senses – and it seemed the river lingered a moment in its mad rush; a hiccup that touched the universe, splintered the fabric of everything.

Jimmy stopped: a bird caught in flight, leaves on the trees motionless, drops of icy rain suspended above the ground. Horse unmoving, with questioning eyes, stopped like a movie when the projector stops, an image frozen to the screen.

He bent forward, suddenly nauseous. He felt like throwing up.

There was a time when the world burned, not with fire, but with ice. Jimmy knew this. It was told in the songs, the chants, the campfire tales: grey hills, ice walls, the hunt for water, food, blackened remains of great forests, life clinging to bare slopes, a time of hardship, perhaps even misery.

When it was dark, his uncle would point to a place in the southern sky: 'The abode of their past, they said, where those people who had endured until the world's blossoming, now lived.'

He had learned gratitude from those storytellers, appreciation for the bounty of their lives; and the earth seemed to take the opportunity at the oddest times to remind him of his part.

He looked about him, searching for meaning: a bird in flight, rolling clouds, raindrops that seemed to connect the whole universe. Soundless. Jimmy could not see the pattern. But then, that was hardly surprising. His uncle always despaired of his grasp of the obvious.

Then he saw it.

The dog.

Fuck me, he thought. *The bloody mongrel survived.*

The sound of the river suddenly roared back into his ears, the brutal water once again devouring the world, clouds reaching out to grip the earth, to deliver their flood in hard, stinging clumps. The mongrel raced to him, ears back, tongue floating with the breeze. Horse lowered his head in greeting as the dog arrived. They were in this together, that was obvious, but he had no explanation for what had just happened. He felt the blood flowing within him, a tightness in his head, and finally remembered the reason why he was here.

The herd. Surely the boys wouldn't drive them across the river now. Jimmy peered through the curtain of rain to the other shore. Another flash seemed to diffuse through everything. A clap of thunder clawed again at his senses, so close it drew strength from his legs. A test? Surely this was a trial. How was he to know?

Jimmy peered again at the far bank. Nothing. Just a disintegrating shore, an empty muddy trail leading to the hill crest. No doubt the boys had steadied the mob to wait out the storm; an hour and it would be gone. The river would subside as quickly as it had grown.

As he watched, the first head showed above the crown of the hill. The bloody cattle were in full flight towards the water, riders in their midst, powerless to stop the charge! For a moment, he thought the swaying horns would impale one of the horses, but the horse deftly sidestepped the weapon. No chance to stop the mob now, just save yourself!

Jimmy watched as the beasts poured over the bank. He thought about all the dead washed downstream. What a waste! He saw them all. Bodies caught in flood debris, stagnant pools, dried channels, dead piled high against weirs, floating in dams, creeks, billabongs, bloated and stinking in the summer heat as the water receded. There was no acquittal, no release. He was witness to extinction, the rending of life's fabric.

And yet?

The first of the cattle surfaced, swept rapidly downstream, but striking out instinctively for the far bank. Maybe there was a chance? The beasts weren't about to easily succumb to a watery grave. He had underestimated their craving for survival, how tenacity can rise in adversity. Jimmy looked downstream, hoping to see survivors clambering ashore. He thought he saw several beasts emerge from the turbulent waters.

'Time to go, Horse,' he said. 'Looks like we've got some lucky fighters.'

Jimmy swung into the saddle and cantered towards the wet fugitives, the dog keeping pace. There was no doubt. He felt that a message had been delivered and finally understood. He looked forward to life's renewal.

2

KEMPTON HOMESTEAD – NORTHERN NEW SOUTH WALES

Summer 1914

Jimmy went through yards to the stables, a structure big enough to hold all the horses, visitors, occasional hands and the odd, additional buggy or two. The old man had done well. He picked up Horse's blanket, still wet after the battle with the river as the rain had persisted all the way home. He held it lightly and sniffed at it.

A strong smell of damp wool. A deeper breath. Horse. Not just any horse. Horse.

He walked past the stalls, onto the outer covered verandah, and laid the blanket over the rail – better airing here – looked across the yard to the house and saw the neat, cut hedge, carefully trained bougainvillea; the heart of old man Angus' realm. Shire president for how many years? Probably too many. Proud, determined, stubborn, narrow-minded, openly intolerant of anyone's judgment except his own, and no real talent for farming; but Jimmy was thankful for the work and time with the old man's boys, especially Eiric, a dreamer with a chance at a real connection to the land.

Angus was on the verandah: an aggressive pose, legs apart, hands resting on hips, broad, sweat-stained hat jammed down tightly exposing a torn peak. The hedge partly blocked Jimmy's view, the veil of rain adding an ethereal edge to the old man's form. Jimmy considered turning away, pretending ignorance, or other more pressing duties.

Angus waved. An imperious summons into his presence. Too late now for any withdrawal from the fate that beckoned.

Jimmy stepped from cover into the downpour and breathed out sharply as his boot sank ominously into the yard mud, his heart unsettled by the promise of a lecture from the old man. The pale grey of the day gradually gave way to the brilliant pink and red of the bougainvillea. His heart steadied; impassivity meant survival.

'What the hell happened out there?' asked Angus. Jimmy felt that the old man's mouth enclosed enough loathing and disgust to cross a lifetime.

Jimmy stood in the rain, beyond the roof's extent, regarding the house. He thought he saw Doreen submerged in the shadows beyond the fly-screen door. He recalled how incensed Eiric became when he witnessed the humiliation of his mother. 'The old bastard uses her to do his washing and cook his meals,' he often said, 'and then heads off to one of his women in town.' Jimmy's wife, for all her submission to the will of the family, would have used a length of timber on him when he least expected it, just on suspicion of infidelity. Doreen just didn't have a way out of defeat and Eiric didn't have an answer either. They were all afraid of the old man.

'They panicked,' said Jimmy. He stepped back slightly, further into the rain, water draining from the hat brim.

Angus regarded him; firm mouth, nicotine-stained teeth prominent through the tight hole of his mouth.

'The cattle,' said Jimmy. 'It was a cracking storm. They couldn't hold 'em.'

The deluge intensified. The rain clattered on the tin roof, the ground about his boots turned into a pool. He wasn't invited to take shelter.

Angus said, 'They should have kept them well away from the river.'

His solutions were always simple, obvious, and, to him, enlightened.

'It moved very fast,' said Jimmy. 'The storm ...'

'And where were you?'

'The river ... it came up really quick. The bank gave way; I had to swim for it.'

'Really?' The sarcasm wasn't lost.

'Nothing I could do, just swam for it, me and Horse ... to the other bank.'

'Damn fool. You could've headed the bastards off before they got to the river!' Anger was rising now. Jimmy knew there was no point in defence, but he had to try.

'They were on the run. Me, Horse and one of the dogs rounded 'em up.'

Angus wasn't listening. 'Should've been with the mob! Should've stuck with Ted!'

Jimmy saw the rage in the old man. Angus bent forward, his long, angular body and prominent nose thrust forward in defiance of everything, hands moving in crossing circles, scattering the focus of his fury. Yet, Jimmy knew he had faith in Ted, the eldest, and arguably the most competent of the brothers.

'None lost, Boss,' said Jimmy. Agitation abated, tension remained, the downpour intensified.

'What?'

Jimmy pointed. The distant yards were full of sodden cattle.

'You can't be sure!' Angus was not to be convinced.

'Counted ... me, Eiric, Ted.'

A sneer. 'Ted gets lost after five, Eiric's more interested in that shit you teach him.'

'None injured either.'

Angus looked over Jimmy's head to the yards, doubt in his eyes. He half-turned to go, swung back to face Jimmy and stood silent for a moment.

Slowly, he raised his arm, pointing at Jimmy.

'Keep your arse there,' he said. 'I'll get my coat. We'll take a look at this miracle.'

Jimmy shuffled his boots in the slurry that had built up around his feet. 'Ted's re-count'n 'em now.'

The old man disappeared inside the house with a bang of the fly-screen door.

Jimmy had come to Kempton as a young boy, in the care of no one in particular. 'Didn't have parents, couldn't remember any siblings, was embraced by the local people, aunts and uncles,' they said. He still wasn't old, in his early thirties. The old man saw things in him: loyalty, a way with horses, a shrewdness that seemed to ease the passage in a hard world. But he was a blackfella, which meant he counted for nothing in the old man's eyes: useful, yes;

trustworthy, maybe; close, no.

'Righty-o, Boss,' he said.

He regarded the old man's anger with a detachment, a strategy he used every time, avoiding making sensible suggestions that would only further the derangement. *Standing in the rain isn't so bad*, he thought. A gentle, warm breeze came with it. He could hear the soft rhythm of rain on the ground, feel and smell the release of the earth. The river had been hard: the whirl of the storm, icy water, grit that lodged in his trousers, in his crutch, boots, even under his hat.

'Hello, Missus,' he said. A figure had appeared at the screen door.

Doreen stood for a while. *The screen door*, he thought, *is like a shield against any distress.*

'Is everyone safe and sound?' she said.

'All safe, Missus.'

Doreen nodded. 'Saw Eiric as he came in,' she said. 'He looked pretty done-in.'

'All the cattle in good shape too.'

'How are Ted and Joe?'

Jimmy thought for a moment, about the fear the brothers had for the old man's sour moods.

'Missus, all good,' he said finally. 'Bit wet, though.'

'Angus was worried about the storm.'

'Yeah, came right over us. Lotsa lightning.'

Doreen frowned deeply, showing the lines of worry despite his reassurance. She suddenly faded away from the door, a ghostly image, evaporated to nothingness.

The old man flung open the door and strode forth, face furrowed with grim determination.

The rain beat at them as they skirted the worst of the mud, walking through the slush towards the yards, to the rail where Ted and Eiric were perched, absorbed in a count.

'Where've you been!' Angus marched forward, with Jimmy forgotten now.

Jimmy veered towards the stables. He'd seen performances like this before. No need to be a witness, a veil of rain quickly forming across the confrontation.

'And you! ...' The stable wall and the clatter of the rain on the roof muted the remainder of the old man's invective.

Jimmy walked cautiously through the wet ground. Time to see to Horse, get free of these wet clothes.

'Well, that was inevitable.'

Jimmy turned. Eiric, breathless, smiling.

'He was worried,' said Jimmy.

'About his cattle and what any damage might do to his profit margin,' said Eiric.

'You boys could've gone under in that river.'

'It wasn't that bad.'

'We should've held 'em back well before the river.'

'Ted's decision.'

'No, we were all part of it.'

The stable interior reeked of horses, wet saddle blankets, straw, and oiled leather. Jimmy felt contentment settle on him.

'We were lucky to get out of it in one piece,' Jimmy said. 'But your father doesn't believe in luck.'

He pulled at his boots, full of water, beginning to hurt.

'What does he believe in? The next sales, keeping the herd safe, his judgement ...?' said Eiric.

'Family is everything, Eiric.'

'Well, you can't convince me he's concerned at all.'

'It's his way,' Jimmy said.

Jimmy felt the intensity of Eiric's gaze. This boy, a young man really, almost twenty, was more like his father than he would admit, yet ... there was something else pushing past the petulant mask. 'He believes the only way is the hard one.'

Eiric remained mute.

'Have you sorted out your horse and gear?' asked Jimmy. Eiric accepted the diversion.

Jimmy, relieved to be free of the rancour, turned towards Horse. Maybe a quiet talk with his companion would dissipate the tension that these people seemed bent on holding close. Jimmy felt the calm attraction of an evening with a dear friend as he approached the stall.

3

THE DAM – KEMPTON HOMESTEAD – NORTHERN NEW SOUTH WALES

Summer 1914

At the dam, Jimmy stood and waited for the old man to arrive. As he waited, he watched his son, Cara, young, lean, lithe like his mother, carelessly skipping stones across the water.

The season wasn't turning yet, though he could sense winter's advance – summer haze abating, deep purple hills succumbing to a gentler mauve, sighing trees at the passing of parched summer months, a faint lightness in the air.

When Angus had summoned him, Jimmy felt the strangeness of the request – another eccentricity of the old man? And here at the dam? Contact usually came as a series of commands from on high relayed through one of his boys or orders shouted across the yards. Jimmy didn't mind; that was the way Angus did things; he had known nothing else in all his time here.

A flight of galahs swooped and swerved its raucous way through a clear, cloudless sky, to trees forming at the bank of the dry creek; confirmation that change was imminent? They descended in a squabbling mass, clutching at branches, tearing, throwing leaves about in their quarrels. *Like these whitefellas*, he thought, *never satisfied, always at odds.*

With Eiric gone bush, Ted and Joe bore the peevish torments of their father. Gone where? His guess was the Black Hills or somewhere to the south, Eiric's favourite spots, for thinking, free from the fractious plague of this place, where the old man was a dark memory.

Jimmy squatted down on his haunches, dug into the ground with his fingers, scooped up earth to fill his palm. Different soil here – thick loam, full of rich clays – good land, but bone dry now after a burning summer, despite the recent rain. The bones of the earth rose to the surface in the hills: unbreakable, crystalline, stoic, faithful, the energy of the world, speaking to whoever paused to listen. The water in the dam moved as concentric rings spread from a large pebble as it skittered across the surface. His son suddenly looking towards him, he detected a change in the calm. He looked behind.

'Rain,' said Angus as he approached. 'But not enough.'

Jimmy discarded the soil and stood facing the old man.

Angus had an unfamiliar softness in his voice – expansive tones.

'The years seem to be getting drier,' he said. 'Can't stock as high as I used to.'

'Runs in cycles, Boss,' said Jimmy. 'Things will improve.'

'And I'm not getting any younger.'

'Hasn't slowed you down.'

'The boys are gett'n there, but they need to be mak'n the right decisions,' he paused to look over Jimmy's shoulder, 'on their own.'

'Pretty good now,' said Jimmy. 'All of 'em, 'specially Ted.'

'The river ... it was a close-run thing.'

Silence.

'They were lucky.' Jimmy believed in luck as a gift from the unknowable forces that governed the earth.

Pause.

'You know how I feel about luck,' said Angus, his eyes straying briefly to the horizon. 'Saying it'll be all right, trust in God. Can't trust it. A fool's way.'

Jimmy saw the river, the storm, how the world, for an instant, had stopped turning.

Angus took a deep breath. 'Jimmy, we've been together for a lot of years, right?'

Jimmy nodded. Silent.

'I need you to fuck off for a while. Give 'em a chance on their own.'

'Boss, they're do'n it themselves already.'

'They turn to you when things are tough, especially Eiric.'

'Fuck off where, Boss?'

'Spend some time with the Kamilaroi. Where are they these days?'

'Coonabarabran, Warrumbungles.'

Jimmy felt a lurch in his chest, a deep fear that he would be banished from here without his family, doomed to wander between camps, forever depending on the largesse of distant relatives.

'Well, take your family and go!'

'Not that easy, Boss.'

'Just fuck off for a while!'

'Need horses, a wagon, supplies. A long way to go.'

'Take what you need. Be out of here before Eiric gets back.'

'He won't be happy, Boss.' Jimmy could feel the old man's rising irritation.

'Where the fuck is he anyway!'

'Don't know, Boss.'

'Ignored me when they arrived with the herd and vanished when I went to see what damage they did.'

'Reckon he's look'n for the gear they left behind at the river.' Jimmy hoped the lie would hold.

Angus paused, perhaps considering Jimmy's words.

'Anyhow, be out of here by tomorrow,' he said finally. Angus looked again over Jimmy's shoulder. 'And tell that young fella of yours to stop pissing in my dam!'

Jimmy turned, saw the boy, pelvis thrust forward, an arch of fluid cascading into the still waters of the dam. Another flock of birds passed overhead, riotous, fractious, a distorted image reflected in ripples as they spread rapidly outward from the impact point.

Jimmy turned back to Angus, but he was gone, striding in his ever-purposeful manner towards some private, personal destination. The old man didn't see it, how the world had intervened to teach them all a lesson, a lesson that if left unheeded would return, he knew, with renewed intensity, until they either accepted its message or were destroyed by it. Jimmy wanted to avoid the mess that would result. The trick, he knew, was to recognise that there was a lesson in the first place.

He sat on the bank of the dam for a long time, eyes tilted to the sky, watching a wedge-tailed eagle wheeling about, so high it was just a speck. How could the bird see to the ground from such a point? To have such vision, perception, would be a gift.

The Black Hills. He felt their weight, the pull of the crags and cliffs, the ancient caves of the people who had lived in this country before the whitefellas changed everything. They would go there first. Eiric would know where to find them. Then there would be a reckoning, compromises that he hoped would reflect learning rather than blindness.

Jimmy thought about his treaty with Angus' boys. He would need to see them before leaving.

*

'I've been fighting with this damn pump for days,' said Joe. 'The bloody thing won't work!'

'It's a test,' Jimmy said. 'To see how much you can take.'

'Reckon I'm there then.' Joe threw the spanner so that it speared into the soft ground.

'Won't suck water unless you get a good seal.' Jimmy was good at these things, but he wasn't going to take it away from Joe.

'Mum's yell'n for water on her garden.' Jimmy couldn't see Doreen yelling for anything.

'You can get one of the stable hands to fetch water.'

'Still, need this pump.'

'Old piece of shit,' said Jimmy.

'Yeah, not wrong there.' Joe rose from a crouch. 'But the old man's decided we need a pump rather than cart'n water.'

'That's progress.'

A trial. No jury, no justice. Jimmy felt the rift as well as the bond, a tie that seemed to bring resentment – approval of the result,

23

dislike of the practice. He could have despised the old man's dismissal, regarded it as a betrayal, and invoked some long-forgotten deity in revenge. He had devoted years to the cultural growth of the boys, enjoyed their awakening to the moods of the land. At times, he had even stepped back from his own family. A test. He *could* see it in those terms – a chance to join with the land once again.

'Reckon it's the fuel,' Joe said.

'Might need to think about it for a while.'

'Na! Gotta be the fuel.'

Joe had always been an inattentive student, the last to grasp the obvious, ready to reach conclusions, keen to launch an offensive. His mind drifted quickly to wanton pastimes.

'The old man's told me to sling me 'ook,' said Jimmy.

Joe's eyes swung to Jimmy. 'What!'

'Told me to get the fuck off the place.'

'He can't do that!'

'Did. And told my boy to stop pissing in the dam.' Jimmy couldn't help a laugh. 'Caught the little bugger at it.'

'With what? Where?' Joe was visibly alarmed. He reminded Jimmy of a brush turkey, clumsy, arms flapping, head going in every direction. 'You can't just up and go!'

'Me and the family, off tomorra.' Joe stood, open-mouthed.

The birds in the trees against the dam were settling now, less unruly as the light waned. Jimmy could hear the distant croak of the first frogs, the faint buzz as the insects rose, the gentle waft of an evening breeze across the water of the dam. Again, he felt a change.

It was time he left.

'We're off to the Black Hills for a while,' he said.

Silence.

'Tell Eiric not to follow.'

'Can't tell him anything,' Joe said.

'He'll understand.'

Joe tilted his head back, for a moment settling his gaze at the sky, the raw, blazing yellows of the sunset submitting to the deep forest greens and blues of the encroaching night. Jimmy wondered if there was any more to say.

'I don't,' said Joe, hurt in his eyes.

'Gotta leave, gotta tell the family we're off, gotta get stuff together for tomorra ...' There was little more that could be explained.

Jimmy turned to go. 'Maybe tell Eiric and Ted you don't know where I've gone. Best that way,' he said as he walked away.

Joe said nothing for a while until Jimmy reached the end of the dam wall. 'He'll beat the shit out of me until I tell him!'

'Mate, you always win.' He meant to be cheerful, but looking back, he saw a stooped figure, rounded shoulders, the aura of the old man's bitterness plain in the dying light. He wondered if Joe was already beaten.

He walked into the setting sun.

'Got a wagon and a couple of horses,' Jimmy said to his wife. 'Need some supplies, enough to get us to the Hills.'

'He's a nasty old bugger,' she said.

'You need to ask Doreen for some food.'

'She won't give it unless the old man says so.'

'He's fine with it, Gurley.'

She moved to him, yielding, dark corkscrew hair brushing his face. 'No excuse for what he's done. After all this time here and there's his boys.'

'He's fight'n for them, Gurley.'

'And we're the victims.'

'Doesn't mean we're gone forever.'

'Time in the Hills ...' She moved closer. 'Our chance together.'

She was slim, muscular, not bony, her submission a design. Jimmy knew she wanted him, wanted the change that the Hills would bring, the conversion that separation from the whitefellas would beget. She pushed him to the bed, pinned him down.

'Y'can't fight me,' she said.

'No.' He didn't want to fight, didn't want to struggle against absurdity, to rest against false ground. The old man would follow the hard path, achieve his aims, risk the alienation of his boys, shift ground when it suited him.

He rolled over, held Gurley to him, embraced the chance given to him – and smiled.

4

THE BLACK HILLS
– NORTHERN NEW SOUTH WALES

Summer 1914

Jimmy rose, the shadowy, flickering light from the fire casting a gloom amongst the overhanging branches. He weaved his way to the light, through the slumbering silhouettes, poked at the dying embers, the sparks fluttering skyward. The earth was quiet, small sounds amplified, the faint crackle from the cinders filling the void, echoing in the slow, dark hours before dawn. On the ground before the fire, his boy, a small bundle, was sleeping, and beside him several other children; Gurley's nieces and nephews, buried beneath a pile of old blankets.

In his face, Jimmy felt the weak, cold draught, the night air clinging to the ground as it filtered up from the river.

It had taken three days to get here, the roads rough, the group of Kempton refugees he led larger than anticipated, the last bit to the start of the Hills difficult with the old, broken wagon. The old man had not been thoroughly generous.

From the old roadhouse back from the river, Jimmy managed to get some more supplies by chopping a pile of timber for the pub's stove, provisions rather than money; he had no use for money now.

Jimmy stood for a moment focused on the fire, writhing flames, tortured shapes, their solidity simply evaporating at the end, a slight wisp of smoke into the nothingness of the black sky. He knew it didn't end in emptiness. There was too much felt, seen, touched, that challenged those thoughts. He wasn't scared of the void; it was just another place the path would cross, where he could look both forward and back to the light.

'Can't sleep?'

He turned. Gurley was wrapped in one of the rough blankets, her brow furrowed with worry.

'The caves,' he said. 'Not sure there's enough shelter for all this mob.'

'They're feel'n a bit guilty about tagg'n along.'

Jimmy reached forward, pulled her to him, the blanket about them both, her head resting on his chest.

'Guilty is the day when they use me and give nothing back,' he said. 'Christ, it's gett'n cold!'

'They're looking forward to real food, bush tucker, stories around the fire, no whitefellas.'

'Eiric will follow us.'

'Yeah. As long as that bastard father of his don't turn up.'

'He'll want us to come back.'

'He's a big boy now. Doesn't need you.'

'Need's not the word, Gurley.' Jimmy glanced back to the fire and wondered what the word really was and what he meant. 'He's looking for a way out.'

'Way out? Of what?'

'The storm ... he just wanted to get away from Kempton when we got back.'

'Everyone wants to get away from the old man.'

'No. He listens to the old tunes, the songs. Can see some of the things ...' Jimmy was grasping for an explanation, 'different.'

'Whitefellas can't see those things, Jimmy.'

'Maybe,' he said, paused and raised his eyes. 'Light's come'n.' He looked to the east, felt rather than saw the difference in the sky, heard the rustling of the rousing birds, the change in the breeze on his face.

'We move'n today?'

'Yeah.'

Gurley said, quickly, 'He mightn't find us. It's hidden up there.' Gurley was the eternal optimist.

'He knows where I'll be.'

'We can tell the kids to be quiet.' Gurley unwrapped herself from around him, stood back and looked directly at his face.

'He'll know, Gurley.'

'If you give in, the old bastard will keep on.'

The eastern light was lifting now.

'I won't give in.' It was a lie. He knew Gurley saw the lie. At these times, she didn't get angry, she just accepted that he had reasons. Her dark, trusting eyes probed him as she turned to the fire.

'We need to get to the Kamilaroi at the Warrumbungles some time. My family will be there,' she said.

'Yeah ...' There was no more to say on the matter. 'Get the kids awake. We'll be off.'

'Some tea, first?'

'Yeah.'

The first, bright rays of sunlight lanced through the trees. He had seen an understanding in Gurley's eyes, an appreciation of things that he wished for himself. Gurley had the nurturing of a strong family; could believe that the Hills could generate a life, contentment without the demands and angst of the whitefella. She could still trust in the power of a place.

'We'll go to the Kamilaroi, Gurley.' She turned, her smile broad and trusting. He marvelled at that trust and understood, at least, that the power of belief *could* change their future, maybe even divert the old man's malice.

'Sulli, or any of those brothers won't stand up to the old man, Jimmy,' Gurley said as she poured water into the billy. 'You'll just get used, like always.'

He didn't need to see her eyes now. He could hear it in her voice; not an accusation but sadness. Jimmy couldn't remember when he wasn't used, now almost a need in himself. Guilt. In its absence, there always seemed to be a thirst for it. He could see it in Eiric, in himself, but not in Gurley. Maybe she was his escape.

'Time in the Hills.' He said it softly, not knowing whether his voice had carried. 'Forget all the other bullshit.'

Jimmy followed Gurley's agile movement around the fire, across to the kids still clinging to the warmth of the blankets on the ground. 'Get this stuffed wagon to the caves first though,' he said. 'Then figure out how to stay away from Kempton.'

He drank his sweet tea in front of the fire, watching as the camp came to life. Gurley went to the kids, carried blankets to the wagon, organising the mob. With the steaming, enamelled cup in his hand, he looked down the road towards Kempton, thought he saw a horse and rider under the trees in the early morning shadows, and startled when Gurley touched his elbow.

'Need to pack that,' she said, pointing at the cup. 'You got to forget that place for a while. Think of y'self and us.'

'Yeah, already do'n that,' he said, though he wasn't sure it had forgotten him.

*

Amongst the tall tree ferns, Gurley walking behind. 'Saw that fella at the roadhouse watch'n us while we packed,' she said. 'Reckon he knows where we're headed.'

'No, just wanted us off his place,' said Jimmy.

'Probably reckons we're on the run from someth'n,' said Gurley. 'Could get the coppers after us.'

Images of men in blue uniform wielding black truncheons clouded his vision; stealers, herding the mob of children into wagons. It forced him to pause. He remembered the screams of distraught women as he lay hidden in the brambles where he had been dumped by an uncle.

'Nah, too busy drink'n to bother with us.' Jimmy looked up towards the ridge line, into the face of unyielding bands of veined rock that burst through the dense vegetation, sullen at the intrusion. 'Over on the right, I reckon.'

Further along the gully, crowded now by the trunks and fronds of grasping ferns that draped above a narrow, gentle stream, the menace of the crags faded, replaced by the cloying humidity of the forest.

'Got noth'n against drunks,' said Jimmy. 'But he'd have trouble point'n the wallopers in here, even if he was sober.'

He climbed the steep path, ducked to the side through low undergrowth, stepping onto the perimeter of a large, clear space, bolstered at the rear by the glowering walls of the scarp.

'And he's never sober.' Jimmy let out a long breath, a sigh that revealed his fatigue. 'Those caves will do us all,' he said, pointing to the cliff base.

'Gotta get everyone up here before dark,' said Gurley.

'Can hide the horses and the wagon in the clearing we saw on the way. Lotsa grass.' He knew the risk, acceptable if he was right about the innkeeper, right about the old man, right about Eiric. *Lots of 'ifs' there*, he thought.

Jimmy moved past a collection of large, head-height boulders, tumbled debris from the cliff. *A gateway to the camp, protection against the outside world*, he thought. *Only problem: Was there clean, fresh water?*

Gurley stood at the margin for a moment, surveying the place.

'I'll go get the mob,' she said suddenly. A rustle of leaves, and she was gone.

Jimmy strolled about the border, the fringing trees dense like a curtain against the outside, gradually edging closer to the dark caverns at the cliff base. He waited for a minute at the entrance to the largest cave, unsure whether he should enter. The smell reminded him of mushrooms; a vague fragrance mingled with damp soil, clean, redemptive, the earth alive, sighing.

Breathing deeply, Jimmy stepped over the fine rubble strewn about the opening. He had seen the tightly coiled etching on the rocks about the entrance. Light from the opening fell across the cavern floor to the far wall, flat-topped rocks, smoothed by generations, rising from a dusty base.

He stopped, looked about. The space closed to below head-height at the furthest point, the floor crisscrossed – the patterns of feet, hands, knees, rituals, lives, left as if inscribed yesterday.

Jimmy moved carefully to the smoothed, stone podium. The blackened ceiling bore the remnants of fire, the ground littered with shards of carbonised wood, the walls a canvas for an ancient palette, a library that preserved the history of a people. His people? He couldn't be sure. Too much time had passed, too much was lost, so much had changed.

Beyond the door, Jimmy sensed, no, heard the arrival of the mob. Gurley appeared abruptly at the cave entrance. 'Brought the kids first,' she said, peering into the dark space. 'The rest are bring'n everything up.'

At the archway, Jimmy glanced back into the cool stillness, heard something, looked intently and saw a cluster of tiny bats shivering indignantly against the roof.

'Keep the kids clear of the caves for the moment, Gurley,' he said. 'Until we can talk to them about this place.'

They walked together to greet the shouting, laughing mob of children and he wondered if Gurley's belief in the power of a place, this place, was indeed right. He breathed the clean, cold air, the thick scent of the tall mountain eucalypts, the undergrowth, leaf litter, a hint of rain somewhere near. The caves would do when the rain came, though he could not use them as a permanent abode. This was a sacred place, a place to be reserved for contemplation, learning, resolution.

A fresh breeze drifted in from the east now. Yes, wet, the rain was not far away. He looked to the sky, the scudding grey clouds, heard the rush of the approaching weather high in the trees, the channelled face of the cliff, obdurate against all tempest.

'They're buried up there,' he said, pointing upward. Shards of bark protruded along the ledges formed by the rock bedding.

'Makes this place special, then,' said Gurley, looking over his shoulder. 'Our people.'

People, past and present. He could deal with them, acknowledge them, respect and include them. He wasn't sure though, what they wanted from him.

Gurley stayed with him as he walked along the cliff base, past the dark hollows. They pushed through light undergrowth, finally confronted with large boulders, smooth, wet. He looked to the clifftop again – a fine spray of water drifted sideways with the growing breeze.

'We've got water,' he said.

Gurley peered skyward. 'A good place, Jimmy. We can stay here forever.'

Jimmy had a surge of hope, the prospect of freedom, of a renewed binding to *thawun* and *mingga*, his country, the ghost ground of his people.

Jimmy and Gurley stood beneath the falls for a moment, fine droplets of water settling on head and shoulder, the air quick with life and the hallowed stature of the ground.

He walked back to the open space below the cliff, his attention drawn to the valley below.

'Better get the mob settled and horses hid, else them wallopers will be here before y'know it.'

They would all be arriving at the camp. The searchers were bound to come, and this place needed protection.

5

THE BLACK HILLS
– NORTHERN NEW SOUTH WALES

Summer 1914

The scent came with a slight breeze. It was a reminder of the life left behind, of muck, mud and shit.

Breathing slowly, Jimmy let go of the smell, turned and walked towards the people clustered about the entrance to the largest cave – like a herd of rabbits, struggling to stick together, without a leader or purpose, confused, adrift, vague, liable at any time to be alarmed, to scatter every way.

'They're wonder'n about the caves and this place. Whether we should be here,' said Gurley as she converged on his path.

Jimmy offered no comment.

'Could tell 'em it's the promised land,' she said, the joke in her eyes.

'Yeah,' he said. 'But I ain't no Moses.' And he certainly didn't want such an appointment.

Jimmy needed a quiet acceptance from everyone that they would live with the mood in this place. The presence of the souls here subdued the clamour of the outside world; it gave him a chance to think, to calm his uncertainty, gave them all the connection needed to make the break from the white man's world.

'They need to be talked to,' said Gurley.

'Yeah, but we got someth'n else to worry about first.'

Gurley stopped short of the crowd, wariness creasing her brow, perplexed.

'What?'

'We got visitors,' he said.

Gurley turned her eyes to the path that led towards the valley. 'What sort of visitors? Coppers?'

'Get the mob quiet. Sit'n down.' He spun on his heel, pushed into the fringing foliage, captured silently by embracing greenery.

The day was warming after a chilly, after-rain wet sunrise, morning damp quickly burning away, birdcall echoing through the tall trees in the valley, a faint crack of branches – someone moving along the trail below – lizards cautiously moving to prey, two-legged reptiles searching for easy pickings. *I've hidden the track leading to the camp*, he thought, *but one of them Anaiwan trackers wouldn't be fooled.*

Jimmy moved quietly down the path, peering as he went through the foliage into the shadow of the valley. Beads of moisture from the dew-laden leaves whipped at his face, his feet disturbing the odour of pungent leaf litter – a tell-tale sign for any experienced tracker. He would need to stop well before the main trail, let it settle, with hope to remain invisible.

Another crack from trampled tree branches. He couldn't tell yet how many people were passing through the valley, along the path beside the stream, the faint watercourse that had its source at the waterfall, an obvious corridor to them all.

Smelling he had learned from one of his 'uncles', that imprecise group of elders that lead any of the young boys interested enough through the maze of totems, dreaming, bushcraft – a natural awareness that seemed to open doors, portals to a universe of colours and shapes.

'Once you open the door,' his uncle said, 'it'll always be there, open wide.'

Jimmy still couldn't see the number of the enemy; they were too far away. But as he sniffed the aethers from the forest, a faint portrait seemed to fix itself in his mind – sure-footed, long stride, the odour of horse and leather.

He perched on his haunches at the edge of the ridge. Trees moved to a light breeze, the distant sound of the waterfall, a crowd of parrots careening recklessly below the treetops, the drip, drip from the last of the night rain, a nearby lizard's rustle, the faint whisper of ants trooping to food discovered.

A sudden loud snap of a branch underfoot. There's movement below. Just a brief glimpse of a dark hat, gone in an instant. He still didn't have a feel for their number.

The valley below was curiously quiet now, the light morning breeze backing off. The steep track, slippery with loose stones, smelled of scuffed soil and crushed lichen.

An errant sound, a stone rolling down the precipitous path, partially muffled by the deep, moist leaf litter. He sniffed acrid eucalyptus, almost alcoholic, cloying, clumsy, disturbed; they weren't trying to hide their presence!

Another thing. He waited as the impression grew. Soap,

perfumed. Jimmy turned towards the main path to the hill. Sniffed again. A woman? Or a man who had shaved recently.

He closed his eyes now, not dozing, instead painting an image of the passage below.

The steep, rocky path led down to the left. Rocky outcrops were marching like troopers up from the creek, moss-laden boulders bursting from the ground, the stone sentinels submitting to leafy hands stretching towards the way, whipping at interlopers, the last desperate defence to intrusion. A bird scattered from the undergrowth perhaps fifty yards away. He felt the flutter of the air from its wings, the alarm, panic, grief, sorrow for generations adrift, a burnt land, ash, a shadow that loomed. A man frowning, puzzled at absent signs, fumbling for meaning, lost in indecision, labouring to comprehend the signs. The footfall showed confidence, but the breath projected intrinsic uncertainty. It was laboured; he could hear it now, recognised its hesitancy, feared the consequence of exposure.

Jimmy opened his eyes.

He stood, torn between retreat and contact; and felt the large hand of his uncle, so often a restraint on his arm, laughing as he advised caution, reflection, delay.

'Want to get bitten?' Uncle Henry said. 'Grab the snake by the head.'

Jimmy smiled at the memory. He felt a brief sting in the decision he was about to make.

He moved, bold now that a decision had been made. Brushing aside the last of the leaves and branches, he stepped into the cleared space of the narrow path.

'*Buralga,*' said Jimmy to the tall, lean, angular man, short of breath, damp from the enfolding foliage. 'Wondered when you'd get here.'

Jimmy moved to the intruder, threw his arm about broad shoulders and wondered whether he had committed himself and his family to suffer; a treaty with powers that could destroy them all.

*

Jimmy handed Eiric a tin mug.

A wafting vapour drifted above the chipped, enamel lip.

'The days are long here,' said Jimmy, 'once y'get into the sway of it.'

'But you didn't need to leave,' Eiric said.

'Yeah, we did.'

He watched Eiric's face contort with anger and disappointment, felt Eiric's distress, but couldn't prevent the consequences. Enough had been said about the old man's decision, the crude, blunt dismissal. Eiric had to look to the future; they all had to embrace hope, a better path.

'My boy shouldn'av pissed in the dam.'

He knew it was a lie; the boy wasn't the cause. But what purpose was there in cursing the old bastard, pulling him down to where he should be. Bitterness only led to more resentment.

Eiric glanced to the side, to the people clustered about the entrance to the large cave.

'They looked at me as if I was an enemy,' said Eiric.

'They thought you were the coppers.' Jimmy paused, considering whether he needed to go further, to the secret place of their fears. 'And they're com'n to terms with our blood in this place.'

'Blood?'

'Our people.' Jimmy hesitated again. 'The ones who used to live here.'

'Here?'

'Long time ago, before anyone can remember.'

'How do you know?'

Jimmy felt a deep stir, sadness, melancholy, a portent of betrayal. 'They speak to us,' he said.

He paused.

'In their own way.'

Jimmy stood, the warming day now alive with loud cicada song and echoing bird call, waiting for Gurley to join them.

'You need to talk to them,' said Gurley as she arrived.

Jimmy looked briefly at a still seated Eiric, touched his shoulder. 'Come and see.'

Gurley looked at Jimmy and doubt clouded her eyes. Determination filled him as he marched towards the cluster of people. They turned to watch as he approached, Gurley at his shoulder, Eiric trailing hesitantly behind.

Jimmy's level voice. 'Reckon you lot all know Sulli,' he said with a casual gesture towards Eiric. 'He's come to see us, make sure we're all right.'

'What difference does him know'n make?' said an elderly man at the back of the group. 'No disrespect, Sulli, but we got things we need to talk through 'ere, private like.'

'Sulli needs to see,' said Jimmy, 'so's he understands, and keeps the coppers and government men away.'

In the crowd of faces, some were still suspicious, others visibly relaxing. Jimmy wanted to get this done, to clear the air of discord, to refute the dread they found in this place. He needed their support, as well as acceptance of Sulli's part. He looked to Gurley. 'Bring the mob. We're all gunna sit in the cave for a while, see the stars, and talk to the emu.'

Jimmy walked to the cave entrance, stood for a moment on the threshold – he felt lost. They all expected a key to solve their problems, leadership he doubted he could provide – a miracle. Jimmy knew the extent of his fakery, tailoring answers and actions to meet his own needs as well as their fears. He couldn't see a clear pathway, the enmeshing of stars, as it was supposed to be, with the earth, the seasons and all those souls. Sulli behind him, he went into the dark cavern, moving to its centre, lifting his arm to point at the ceiling, wondering once again at the portrayal of the heavens.

Sulli, eyes raised to the cave roof, fell into place beside him.

'Emu in the sky,' Jimmy said. '*Gawarrgay.*'

'Shit!' said Sulli. 'Who did this?'

'Don't know whether you should be see'n this,' said Jimmy. 'Folk outside aren't happy.'

'What? 'Cause I'm here?'

Jimmy sat on the smooth, flat, rock bench. 'Nah. It's me. I brought 'em 'ere. Don't remember who made this.'

'My people.' Gurley answered as she moved inside from the entrance, followed quietly by the silent group. '*Dhinawan* changes, see the legs, it's running there. Mother emu. Time to chase men. Make eggs.' She was smiling.

'Autumn. Good food, eggs,' said Jimmy.

'Over there.' Gurley pointed. 'Legs gone. Dad's looking after the eggs on the nest.'

'Winter,' said Sulli. 'June, July?'

'In the stars,' said Gurley, 'man emu looks after the chicks.'

'There.' Jimmy pointing. 'Time for the *bora*, initiation time.' Jimmy said it quietly, the group now gathered to listen.

'The Milky Way. It's how it changes,' Sulli said. There was awe in his voice.

'Waterholes are full when *Gawarrgay's* sitting.'

'Spring. The emu's on the horizon to the south.' Sulli's words were hushed. 'Gone when the waterholes went dry.' Jimmy finally lowered his arm. 'They left us this. Gotta keep it safe. Tell no one.' There was determination mingled with fatigue in his voice.

Jimmy regarded Sulli, silent, the boy's eyes still fixed on the journey of the emu through time, through the Milky Way.

A quiet moment.

'Yeah, I won't tell anyone,' said Sulli finally as he focused on Jimmy, scanning the horizon from Gurley to the assembled group. 'You coming back to Kempton?'

Jimmy studied Sulli's face, the guiltless eyes, the frank expression. A contrast to the old man? So much to doubt there, to hate, to loathe. Yet, he believed the promise this young man had made, trusted his own instincts.

'Like I said. We'll come back,' Jimmy said. 'Just got a few things to sort before we head back to the farm.'

He looked across the gallery, to Gurley. She held his eye, for an eternity it seemed; the deep, hard furrows in her forehead slowly softening, a slight, closed-mouth smile flickering about her pretty mouth, so desirable, so loyal. Could he bear such trust in his choices, such explicit tenderness?

He sat for a moment, eyes closed, deep breathing, felt the burden of their ancestors, touching the calamity that had driven those people from this place and forced abandonment of the stars, severing the ties that bound the earth to the heavens.

Eyes opened, a faint nod, a smile to Gurley.

6

WEST AFRICA

The Present Day

Harry slipped quietly into the room, crowded, the burble of conversation pitched almost perfectly to drown the strains of the lounge music issuing from the ceiling speakers. He stood against the back wall, reluctant to join anyone in the room, watching the false laughter, guffaws in response to some awful joke, earnest faces that wearers hoped would disguise the tedium of such occasions, the obligation of their attendance.

He looked across the room to the podium, his peculiar sanctum at such gatherings, his pulpit, where he would address the great unwashed, preach his version of their future, avoid the personal interactions he so loathed.

A face turned towards him, fresh, alive, fascinating. A slight wink, a flick of the head – he was summoned to her presence, into the folds of her allure. Harry wove carefully through the crowd. She lightly touched his arm, fingers curiously chilled – the residue of the glass of champagne perhaps – and raised a hand to her private audience, stepping back slightly, an invitation for him to join the select group.

'Business done, then?' Teresa said.

'Yeah, they're satisfied with the result.' Harry diverted his eyes from the swirl of her frock, the way it clung tightly to her flat middle, the way it climbed unashamedly to accentuate the swelling curve of her breasts, resting snug at her throat. He wished they were somewhere else, anywhere, so he could hold her, feel her warmth, smell her hair, like sweet, new hay, scented with abandon, free from restraint.

'So they should be,' said the diminutive man facing Harry. He raised his glass in salute. 'A great discovery, success in every sense.'

Though Harry didn't disagree, the man made him uneasy — not dislike exactly, rather it was distrust. This man was a slave to convenience, whatever would curry favour. If Harry fell from grace, he knew he would be abandoned.

Harry smiled, then turned towards the rest of the group. There were smiles all around. He was, it seemed, riding the crest of a wave. The question was: *could he maintain balance, riding through the spray whipped up by the offshore wind, over the lip, into smoother water on the wave's face?*

He hadn't told the whole truth – dark clouds, bumpy waters, hidden reefs had in fact gathered about his supposed victory – a discovery yes, but at a cost.

As he turned to scan the broader crowd, he caught Teresa's eye, knowing, penetrating, calculating. He saw it in the set of her mouth, her lips tightening slightly, no reflection of it about the eyes, except ...

She swung her skirt with a slight bob at the knees, hailed a waiter, replaced her glass, raised her chin, smiling engagingly at the small man.

'There is the matter of the oil price,' she said. 'We don't know what the Saudis are going to do next.'

The close entourage remained silent, the room growing loud, merry under the influence of imported champagne.

Harry scanned the room once again, perhaps searching for a way out, a gap in the crowd he could quietly slip through, away from the disappointment, the limitations of his life.

Teresa placed a firm hand against his.

Harry held her eyes for a moment.

He nodded, climbed to the podium and cleared his throat. A hush descended upon the room.

He began.

'A billion barrels,' he said to the hushed, expectant crowd, 'is no small reserve, you, the team, brought from home with the able, tireless support of you, the wonderful local mob ...'

Harry heard his voice in muffled strains. He knew this speech, had rehearsed its delivery with Teresa's help, eliminating the unnecessary, bolstering the politic. It was a masterpiece, a testimony to Teresa's acuity; yet, it would end in a mess, a muddle that was his life, the tattered threads blown like the trailing edge of an old flag, ripped, torn, vanquished. He mouthed the words, blind to his audience, picturing that beach, the dog, the love he craved, Teresa.

'... the dedication and success of you all will now flow to the next phase, the monetisation of your good work.'

His sight cleared, a sea of faces watching, listening.

'The reins of the project ...' He felt the finality of his existence. '... will be passed to ...'

He fixed his sight on the foreground.

'… to Teresa …' Any further words were lost in the celebration. Harry watched, detached, as the ingratiating crowd gathered about the new monarch, the deposed already forgotten.

The king is dead, long live the queen.

Teresa climbed to the top of the podium. There was a hushed expectancy. Harry stepped left into the shadows.

*

They sat quietly, traces of the evening still playing in their minds, the dissembling, the half-truths. Teresa looked up, fixing Harry with a soft gaze. Harry thought she was about to say something. She moved slightly, re-arranging her dress, pulling its fluffy volume over her knees. She smiled. He tried to remember when he had last seen her look so desirable – those wide, almond eyes, green with slight speckles – and decided it was every time he saw her, every time she looked his way or came into the same room.

'I think that went rather well,' she said.

Harry thought for a moment. 'Do you think they bought it?'

'Yes, mostly, except maybe Bruce.'

'He clung to you all night. I think he fancies you.' Harry looked for a reaction. Teresa only produced the ghost of a smile.

'He'll be happy with the deputy label.'

'He'll want more.' Harry knew there wouldn't be more, not in the personal stakes, though he couldn't prevent a twinge of apprehension. Teresa's smile broadened.

'Are you jealous, Harry?'

'Well, I won't be here to fend off all your admirers.'

'They all want something,' she said. 'And it's not me.'

'Still,' he said. 'I won't be here.'

She turned away, reached for the glass balanced on the arm of the lounge. For a moment, he couldn't see her face, couldn't gauge her mood; it could fluctuate wildly, one instant affectionate, the next acerbic, disparaging.

'We'll be together again, once this project is taken care of.'

'That could take years.'

She pursed her lips. 'Six months, tops.'

Confident as usual, he thought, *such a view, at odds with everything they had discussed.*

'Anyhow,' she said. 'You'll be up to your ears trying to rescue the subcontinent operation.' She smiled again. 'You wouldn't have time for me.'

Wouldn't have time? Was it a challenge or Teresa he needed in his life? He couldn't see the dichotomy.

Harry remembered leaving Sydney, the guilt, the relief at being free, finally allowed to roam the world, he thought, set his own standards, conform to no dictates, to walk an unrestrained path. Teresa was the bonus; beautiful, smart, captivating, available, a temptation he didn't, couldn't ignore.

He felt a stab, as he always did – his infidelity, abandonment of responsibility in Sydney, family, Frances, baby, mother, dog.

She took a small sip from the glass, fixing him with a stare. Would it be caustic or kind?

'Once I've found a buyer and locked them in with a good deal, you know I can be with you.'

Harry looked at Teresa, the confidence, the deep-seated self-assurance. 'A good deal?' he said. 'What's that?'

'Anything that makes money.'

'And tosses all those people to the wind?' He hoped there was no trace of cynicism.

'Harry, you know they're getting you out of here because you would want to take care of everyone.'

'That's not true,' he said, but he knew she was right. She knew him too well, the desires of his heart, his weaknesses.

'Yes, it is, and you know it. And they're right to send you to Dhaka and Delhi, to get that lot on the right track.'

'You'll need to watch Bruce,' he said. 'He can be tricky.'

'You're changing the subject, you always do, when the subject is you.' She smiled, a knowing turn-up of her beautiful mouth. She rose from the couch, came to him, raising her skirt as she advanced, sitting astride his legs, facing him, holding his face in her hands, slowly lowering her face, lips to his, watching him as their mouths came together. He submitted, letting the angst of the evening wash away, his doubts subsiding as he wrapped his hands about her thighs, releasing the shackle of her clothes, pulling her closer, feeling the rhythmic movement of her hips against him and the stirring of lust, the tie that bound them to the path, the inexorable journey. Harry surrendered, rose with Teresa's thighs tightly locked against him, and carried her to the bedroom, the lights burning bright in their wake.

7

Northern New South Wales

Late Winter 1915

'It's a long way to the Warrumbungles, Gurley,' said Jimmy. 'We can take the cart, but it'll be slow.'

'Need to be there,' she said. 'They're expect'n us … at the *bora*.'

Jimmy looked to the dark cloudless sky, the emu, head down, sitting on a nest of stars, a great stream of water flowing past the revered bird, the shape of the emu egg prominent in the southern stars.

'*Bora* in another month, maybe.' He wasn't sure, but he reckoned they had time. 'Need to move soon, tomorra maybe.'

He stood silently, watched Gurley smile, a grin that showed her appreciation of his faith, recognition of a trust he didn't deserve. He felt the weight of Eiric's hopes – a return to Kempton, the inevitable slide into old habits, associations, routine – as well as Gurley's expectations. He tried to remove them from his thoughts.

'We'll be 'cross the river,' he said, 'near Wiradjuri country.'

Gurley smiled again. 'You're a worry sometimes, Jimmy.'

Jimmy remained silent. There wasn't any response to that one – Gurley knew his shortcomings; they were all too apparent.

'Family are com'n from the south too.' *She said it with a laugh, not bitterness*, he thought, *maybe hurt?* 'We don't fight anymore ... not enough of us left for that.'

'No.' He just wanted to move on. He felt all that stuff was other people's business – old feuds, enmities, quarrels, even friendships. He wasn't even sure he wanted to be part of the gathering, the *bora*, wasn't sure where his allegiance lay, his duty fragmented by links he could not contrive, memories difficult to disconnect from his vision of the world. It would be easy to say *no* to this journey, over one hundred miles through rough country, past aggressive whitefella farms, skirting hostile towns, struggling with belligerent coppers, always hoping government men wouldn't hold them, take the children, shatter his family, sever his tenuous hold on the foundations of the past. A return to Kempton would at least provide a refuge, if only temporary, for his family.

'No,' he said again. 'Not sure how many will get there.' *Was he trying*, he thought, *to talk her out of the trek?*

Gurley looked intently at him with clouded brow. 'You don't want to go!' Could he hide nothing from this woman?

He paused, looking again at the dark sky, to the south, saw the beckoning emu, remembered the tales of *Baiame* who lived in the sky beside the great stream of water, the stars that flowed to the southern horizon.

'Yeah, I want to go.' Another lie. 'Need to stay clear of them government men on the way through.' And that at least was the truth.

*

Jimmy squatted beside the small cooking fire, looking forward across the bare patch of ground. Gurley was rounding up the children in preparation for another day on the trail. Jimmy watched them, enjoying the peace before the inevitable commands, the orders delivered to a reluctant, lethargic mob.

'They don't want to move,' said Gurley, tussling with an errant child finally caught.

The trees formed a sinuous line, a thicket across the flat ground, the river to the left, a flooded dip forming a narrow swamp, a billabong, to the right. A high ridge, red, rose behind him, a natural bulwark against the meander of the fast-flowing stream that wrapped itself about the base of the crusty cliff. The small town, Gunnedah, lay to the west beyond the river, a celebration of the whitefellas' creed, fount for those fearful epistles, Sodom and Gomorrah, the Apocalypse, Armageddon; fleeting visions that teased him.

He laughed. There was calamity in everything the whitefellas did.

The morning breeze from the distant mountains had backed off to a thin whisper, stillness, with not even the raucous call of the white cockatoos. A small crowd of people, adults and children gathered, seated quietly about a campfire on open ground, a discrete distance from the nearest trees.

'No one wants to leave this place,' she said. 'They're feel'n the long-ago here.'

'Yeah,' he said. 'Pretty strong, here.'

He didn't understand what the marks on the trees meant: great swirls that drew you forward, pulled you into the womb, back to some ancient place, sucked you onward until you realised the tremors that poured through you came from hands that caressed the carving. Almost all the trees showed some whittled design. Were they hinting at some forgotten state? He couldn't tell, and Gurley could only grasp at a possible meaning. So much had been lost, flung away in the tumult and chaos of the invasion. Jimmy supposed this dilemma wasn't unique in the history of the world, though it left a vacancy in his past, a hole that sought restoration and a need for explanation.

No one with any awareness remained. The path to the river of stars was murky, faded, obscure.

'Uncle Frank told me about this place,' said Gurley, 'said it was called *yammunyamun*. Said this place was special *bora* ground ...' She paused, perhaps tugging at her memory.

'Wouldn't tell me much. Too much secret stuff.' She laughed. A wry tone. 'Boys!'

Jimmy always found intriguing the contrast between Gurley's accord with the old ways and her spirited independence. A foot in both camps? 'Do the whitefellas know about this place?' he said. He turned to look across the flat ground once again, the line of trees beginning to shimmer as the sun sought to focus on the bare earth. He was suddenly aware of the aches in his thighs and forearms, into his neck on the left side – too much lifting, pushing, cajoling this mob.

'Maybe,' said Gurley. 'No trees stolen yet though. Might be too far from Gunnedah?'

'Need to get go'n,' he said, standing to stretch the aches away. 'Tell'em the government man will get'em if they stay here too long.' He looked across the flat to the cart and the horse grazing amongst the meagre grass by the swamp, remembering that he had not thought of Horse for some time. What was it, two weeks, a month or more?

Gurley laughed, a fresh, open chortle, deep in vibrant eyes. 'They won't catch us. We're mov'n too fast. Dodge'n from tree to tree's the trick.'

He nodded. 'Not stay'n too long in one place more likely.' He strode towards the horse. 'And mov'n fast,' he said. Despite her jest, she had a point. They needed to dodge.

*

Jimmy walked ahead, as he always did, looking for problems. Gurley would take care of the tail.

Safely through the flat, cleared country west of Gunnedah, Nombi, Goolhi, threading their way through the stony outcrops south of the Pilliga, Coonabarabran, the next settlement to side-step. He smiled as he thought of the old man and his definition of good luck: *just good management.*

A craggy knoll rose above the trees to his right, Gurley and the mob somewhere behind him, hidden by the infringing forest.

'Take a look up there, Cara,' he said to his boy, pointing to the rocky rise. 'Tell us if y'can see Coonabarabran, yet.'

Without a word, the boy scampered away. Jimmy watched him, lithe, sinuous, athletic like his mother, long, graceful strides, effortless, and still not ten. Jimmy's stockiness kept him close to the ground, sturdy, balanced in a strong wind, his uncle used to say.

He pulled his eyes away from the receding youth, scanning the track ahead. He had just about decided to walk forward when he felt a change. Was it a vibration in the ground, or a bird call from the trees that bound the hills to the north?

He stood motionless, silent, glancing again towards the place his boy had been. Gone, swallowed by the looming rocks.

He felt it again. The sensation was more insistent, rising pressure in his guts, gravity behind his eyes, an ache about the teeth. A cloud darkened the sun. The light, cool breeze fell away. He stood and listened.

Then he sprinted.

He wished the trees were closer, he coveted the anonymity of their broad trunks, glancing towards the rocky knoll once again as he ran. Cara was gone, invisible against the grey of the low ridge. He knew the boy would stay down, blend with the basalt.

Jimmy ran towards the first line of trees, breath now wrestling with the effort. The first horse caught him on open ground, the shoulder of the beast knocking him sideways. Jimmy knew he could withstand the push and shove, could continue to run, would be stable as always, despite the rider's best efforts. He heard more hooves behind, a shout:

'Stop!'

Then he sprawled face down in the dirt.

'Stop right there, you black bastard!'

Jimmy felt the stamp of hooves about his head, lay motionless, arms spread before his head. He spat the dust from his mouth. It formed a gritty slurry with his saliva, pressing fine granules into his teeth, crumbs that reminded him of spoiled flour used to make damper.

Footfall.

One of the riders – there were at least six he guessed – had dismounted. Slow steps to where he lay, a dull tremor through the ground. Jimmy glanced up at a man's shape silhouetted against the sun. A boot prodded at his hip.

'Get up,' said the man. 'Tell us what you're doing here.'

Jimmy rolled onto his back, levering his shoulders off the ground, climbed to his feet, rubbing grazed hands together on his thighs. Four mounted horsemen surrounded him, the fifth on foot, square to him, legs wide as if bracing for a fight. *Could've sworn there were six of them*, he thought.

'What are you doing here?' said the man. 'Where you from ... and all alone?'

Jimmy felt his heart throttle back a few beats. *They weren't aware of Gurley and the mob ... and they hadn't seen Cara! Now, that was luck.* He silently gauged the chance of a run for it. The trees were close now; the horses would be useless amidst the undergrowth.

'On my way to the Warrumbungles,' he said. 'Family get-together.'

'You got work?'

'Yeah.'

'Where?'

'Kempton, near Gyra.'

'Who?'

'Old Man O'Sullivan ... Angus.'

'Yeah, heard of him, Shire President up there.'

'Yeah, real big knob there.'

'A bunch of you lot are coming through for this *get-together*.' Jimmy heard the sarcasm in the voice. 'Don't want you thieving all our stock.'

Jimmy thought it best not to respond to such an assumption. If they were unaware of Gurley and the mob, then his chances of a getaway were good.

The man's tension seemed to abate a little as a sixth horseman joined the host.

'We got a government man here,' the man said, pointing to the latecomer. 'Looking for kids, half-castes.'

Jimmy felt the pull in his chest. *Knew there were six*, he thought.

'None with me, Boss.' Jimmy reckoned it best to sound submissive.

'Yeah, why *are* you on your own?'

'Everyone stayed at Kempton, Boss.' Should he say more? 'Too far to walk.'

'Yeah, that'd be right. Lazy bastards.' *Maybe it had worked*, Jimmy thought.

The man raised a hand to stroke his chin, perhaps pondering what to do next.

'Well, stay out of town,' the man said finally. 'We haven't got time to stuff around here ... and we'll have you if you touch any of our sheep.'

'Yeah, Boss.'

Jimmy watched silently as the horsemen gathered together and headed away towards Coonabarabran. Dust from the withdrawing horses billowed skyward, rising in a freshening breeze, wafting over him, cloaking him in a white veil.

Jimmy turned to the rocky outcrop, signalled, saw a small agile figure emerge from the crenulated basalt boulders, and he wondered how Gurley had managed to evade the mob of whitefellas.

*

Jimmy hurried Cara, who was silently struggling to keep pace, back along the road. The winter sun seemed chilly now, long afternoon shadows from the encroaching forest stretching dark, grasping fingers across the trail. He felt the bite, a nip in the air that penetrated deep into his bones despite his haste. He always expected the best, now he anticipated the worst, predicted misery, feared for their survival, pushed away a rising panic. The horsemen had appeared from Gurley's direction. How could they have missed her? The cart, the horse, the mob!

The road curled back on itself, following the banks of a stream. They came to a crossing, water surging around smooth, black boulders. He was sure the water had risen since that morning when they had all stopped to rest, bathe, and refresh in the cool water from the mountains, when he had left them, abandoned them it seemed now. Perhaps he was wrong – just his imagination?

He stamped into the water, stopped, and turned to check that Cara could manage the tugging flow. He realised abruptly that his abandonment of hope reflected in the stern face of the boy.

'Cara, mate,' he said. 'They'll be hiding somewhere. I mean, there's no sign of them yet, but they'll be somewhere.'

'Yeah, Mum's pretty good at hiding.' Jimmy thought his voice was thin, fearful.

'We'll look for signs,' Jimmy said, turning back to the stream. 'Your mum will have left marks for us to follow.'

The water came to his knees, the boy edging forward, cautious against the flood.

The ground above the water on the far bank was disturbed, scuffed circles printed in the dust where people had rested, sparse grass cropped by equine teeth and the imprint of cart wheels.

He continued to search.

A line of hoof tracks, at least six, possibly seven horses, rose in the east, circling in a confused melee at the entrance to the ford. He could see their exit across the stream.

Seven horses! He had only met six!

Jimmy walked east along the trail.

The sun, much lower now as the afternoon advanced, dipped once again behind growing cloud, the shadows masking any evidence — nothing useful in this direction.

Silence.

The wind was dying away before the evening.

Jimmy recalled the question: *Where you from ... and all alone?*

He most assuredly hadn't met the seventh horsemen.

Back to the cleared area by the ford, this time Jimmy ranged further, walking big looping circles, spiralling away from the epicentre of activity. He stopped several times, bent to the ground, examining a turned rock, a broken blade of grass, a broken twig, then finally standing, quietly looking through the forest, to the north, into the hills of the Pilliga.

'They've headed north, Cara.'

The boy swivelled to look where Jimmy pointed, finally returning his gaze to Jimmy.

'Mum's stay'n in the trees?' Cara said.

'Yeah, but someone's after 'em.' He felt a lurch in his chest. 'On a horse!'

They ran.

It was the pace of hunters, their measured stride meant to last until the prey was exhausted, until the last parcels of energy depleted, until finally brought to bay, their quarry would surrender, glad of the ultimate release, willing renunciation of life itself.

On the rocky path, carrying his hopes, Jimmy passed their cart – broken wheel, absent horses, driven into a shallow ditch, pitiful, a testament to his misjudgment and abandonment of family.

The rocky trail at first resisted him, then he heard Cara's laboured breath behind him, felt the close resilience of youth, and intensified his effort.

8

Bangladesh – Dhaka

The Present Day

Harry watched the ball. A moving ball always captivated him, held his eyes, its motion mesmerising – he had to follow its flight, no matter the game. The bar was empty – all the activity surged about the tennis court, heaving bodies, grunts, the occasional profanity. He watched an errant ball rise, floating carefree over the high, chain-link fence that crowned a sturdy brick wall.

'Another one lost.' Harry followed the missile's flight until it disappeared, dropping towards the clutches of the crumbling street beyond and absolute oblivion. He turned to the voice. 'The beggars wait for them in the street, near the drain at the corner,' said the man.

'What on earth would they want with tennis balls?' said Harry, looking at the tall, gaunt fellow.

'They try to sell them back to the club, but the ball-boys won't take them.'

'What? Even if they're in good nick?'

'The boys reckon they're ruined. Prefer to crack open another pack.'

'Well,' said Harry. 'It is a consumption-driven world.'

'The beggars have minders who dump them at the corner every morning and pick them up every night,' said the man, laughing. 'We reckon there's a warehouse somewhere in Dhaka full of tennis balls from this club.'

'You could make a killing,' Harry said, smiling. 'Find the warehouse, repack the balls, then sell them to all the expat clubs in Dhaka.'

'Too late. Someone's already thought of that, is already doing it.' The man drew a chair back from the table, sat down and waved to one of the bar-boys. 'Our repacked balls end up at the British Club. They are always looking for a bargain over there; not so interested in the excellence of their tennis.'

A shout rose from the tennis court – another ball consigned to commercial opportunity.

The waiter arrived, smiled, looking expectant.

'A Tuborg for me,' said the man. 'You?' He waved his hand at Harry.

Harry thought for a moment. 'Red wine?' he said. 'What sort have you got?'

'Not a good choice, old fellow.' The man shook his long, thin head. 'Been sitting, stewing, for months on Chittagong docks, boiled most likely.'

'Right, what's safe then?'

'They have no concept of wine here. They call all alcohol 'whiskey'.'

Harry winced at the thought of boiled wine. 'No wine then.'

'There's beer,' said the man emphatically. A pause. 'Yes, beer's safe, if you can stomach these international beers long-term.'

'Right, same as you then,' said Harry quickly, not wanting any further stories about the mistreatment of wine, wondering whether his waistline would survive a deluge of hops.

Harry glanced back to the game, a protagonist winding up for a blistering serve.

'Name's Nigel, by the way,' the man said.

Harry tore himself from the contest. 'Harry, Harry Weber.'

'Welcome to Dhaka,' said Nigel. 'Staying long?'

Staying long? Harry reflected on the prospect and decided it was anyone's guess as to how long it would take to sort through this mess, through the restructuring of the company, its finances and its people. Images of his arrival in Dhaka floated in his mind. The shouting, surging crowd at the airport, held at bay behind steel bars, the desperate drive through frantic traffic, the constant bawl of car horns, the heaving mass of people amongst rickshaws, dilapidated cars and trucks exuding clouds of filthy, black smoke. He nearly turned about and bought a ticket home, consigning this place and its problems to someone else.

'A while.' Harry eased himself in the chair – his trousers clinging to his legs in the humidity.

'Well, you'll find the club a welcome relief from the chaos outside,' said Nigel. 'Home, the club and regular trips away to places like Singapore.'

'I'll be travelling quite a lot; Calcutta, Delhi, maybe even Nepal.'

'Lucky you, I'm stuck here, reporting on the charade they call politics here. All I get is sojourns upcountry, witness to yet another bloody crisis.'

A shout. The court was alive with the clamour of victory.

'The locals?' Harry turned away from his examination of the court combatants. 'Much to do with them?'

The waiter delivered the drinks.

'Not with the great unwashed, old fellow.'

'I'll be working with quite a few of them.'

'Bit standoffish really.' Nigel shook his head, fixed Harry with an intense stare. 'Don't get me wrong, there are some nice locals, educated, wealthy, well-travelled. They usually have bolt holes in the UK or elsewhere ... for when things get especially nasty here. But they always want something. Not prepared to deliver on promises most of the time, is my experience.'

Nigel drew a pewter mug from a small canvas bag resting between his feet, decanting the brown contents of the beer can. Harry recognised a cynic, though he thought that prolonged exposure to the subcontinent perhaps could change perceptions, a sort of metamorphosis into pessimism. He looked at his own beer, lifted the can, took a sip – the liquid was already growing limp, tepid in the humidity.

'Your own mug?' said Harry, pointing at the pewter.

'Oh, yes,' said Nigel. 'A trophy from my first weeks here. Hygiene here in Dhaka isn't the best. Open sewers, shit everywhere in fact. Sick as a dog I was. Reckon I caught it from the top of a beer can.'

Harry felt anxious until Nigel looked up from his beer. He could see the amusement in Nigel's eyes. 'Not here!' he was quick to say. 'They're pretty good here in the Australian Club.'

He paused, a slight smile. 'No, reckon it was at the International Club. They let all sorts of expat riffraff in there.'

Harry cautiously resumed his imbibition of the warm fluid. He heard the clang of the gate behind him. The tennis crowd, babbling, left the court, streaming towards the bar, cheerful voices mixed with laughter. Harry turned.

She was amongst the mob, the rowdy collection of sweating bodies gathering together towels, racquets, paraphernalia – not tall, dark, slightly wavy, shoulder-length hair, slim, athletic.

'Hot work,' Harry said. 'Jumping around a tennis court in this steamy weather.'

Nigel looked across at the players, then directly at Harry. 'Only time for tennis is now, before the build-up, the monsoon. The humidity then makes any sort of physical activity impossible.'

Harry watched the group, gear now stored away, as they rolled, haphazard towards the bar.

'Who's the woman, the one in the bright yellow shirt?'

Nigel leant backwards, scrutinising Harry. 'That's Anika,' he said.

'What does she do?' said Harry. 'I mean, does she work here in Bangladesh?'

'NGO stuff. Mainly down by the bay, the Bay of Bengal, at the edges of the bloody Sundarbarn swamps.'

Nigel bent forward. 'Don't go there, old fellow,' he said conspiratorially. 'Taken, fully occupied with someone and her precious NGO.'

Harry lifted the can to his mouth, maintaining his regard of the woman, silent, the longing for answers stirring, the desire for intimacy blooming, for passion, for meaning. The group moved towards them.

'Introduce me,' Harry said.

Nigel sighed, stood and said to the passing group, 'Folks, let me introduce Harry. New to the joint, looking for friends, will be in town for a while.'

Faces turned in greeting, hands shaken, welcoming. 'Come and have a drink, Harry.'

Harry pushed back his chair and stood up. 'Thanks for the drink, Nigel. My shout next time.' He followed the crowd to the bar.

*

Andy's voice was distant, thin down the telephone line from Sydney. The company's guesthouse provided only rudimentary connectivity to the world, limited privacy, marginal comfort.

'They won't be coming,' Andy said.

'What do you mean, "They won't be coming"?' said Harry.

'Teresa's got her hands full. She needs all hands on deck there.'

'So, no competent help here then?'

'Not until she's tied it all up.'

'Andy, I told you it was tricky.' Harry gripped the phone tightly. 'I should be there.'

A pause.

'No, she'll have to deal with it herself.'

Harry heard the frustration, a warning not to argue. He plunged into the fight.

'You know someone else would do the job here better than me.'

'Harry, Teresa needs to see it through, now.' Frustration turning to aggravation.

'I could shepherd her through it.'

Harry heard a low intake of breath.

'Harry, you're thinking with your dick. She'll handle it on her own.'

Andy was right, Harry knew it.

'Get that operation there stabilised and then take some time off,' Andy said.

Harry was silent, saw the sense of it, but couldn't admit to the need.

'You did wonders in West Africa.' There was a new severity in Andy's voice. 'Take time off. Go see Frances, that sprog of yours, the bloody dog.'

'They're getting on great without me,' said Harry, though he recognised it as a lame excuse.

'You've got six months. I want it sorted and you out of there.'

Harry felt a dryness at the back of his throat, sensed his life was turning about this moment, sensed a diversion from the desires that had so far guided him, couldn't see a path to change.

'Teresa,' Harry said. 'She's expecting an assignment here next.'

'No, Harry, she isn't.' Harry felt a lurch, a wrench at his heart. 'We've got other things lined up for her.'

'Does she know that?' Harry knew the answer.

'She's known for quite a while. She's headed elsewhere, Harry.'

Harry looked at the faded wallpaper as he ended the call, the ancient floral design, the slightly embossed pattern, the dilapidated hues, thinking of the forces arranged against him, powers that insisted he maintained a planned path, a safe route.

Teresa had always known that their paths would diverge, that her ambition would take precedence. Harry admired her focus, lamented his curious ability to obscure the truth, to confuse ambition with dedication, convenience for love, fact from deceit.

He sat quietly, the noise of the road, the marauding traffic, filtering through the thick stone walls.

Six months.

Then what?

A truck rumbled past the house, the vibration passing vaguely through saturated sands, the foundations of Dhaka, the quicksand of a city. Harry looked into the endless chasm, the rift in the fabric of the earth's crust as the continent collided, twisted, tearing deep patterns in the world, filled with the refuse of the Himalayas, the great mountain's outpouring, the eroded litter that was Bangladesh. He saw the abyss, the desired emersion in its depths, the oblivion it could provide. He didn't understand the emotion and the resurgent, futile hope that Andy was mistaken.

Harry stood, walked to the front door, a threshold to the chaos that was Dhaka, and called for his driver, his car, the months he needed to plot a course, some sort of path out of this mess, the muddle of his life – a sign, an epiphany, a miracle.

He laughed. *Like winning the lotto*, he thought. *Damn near impossible!*

He opened the door, stepped onto the broad verandah, smelt the aroma of two million trucks and buses, five million rickshaws, twenty million people, thought of Anika, her dark, fathomless eyes, the bubbly laugh, the disarming smile, the intensity of her commitment, and the hours spent in quiet conversation. Maybe, just maybe, he could resurrect some meaning in his life.

He joined the endless stream of humanity, hurrying through the roundabout at Gulshan, along the crowded Kemel Atatürk Boulevard. They crawled through impatient traffic over the bridge along Airport Avenue, past the bastion at the military airport, to his six-month test, his thoughts haunted with visions of ambition, desire, infidelity, love lost, and love betrayed.

9

Late Winter 1915

The valley, the river, lay like a map below, cleared paddocks spreading like a sore across the low ground, the forest fringes growing a healing margin.

Jimmy looked down, shirt saturated with sweat, breathing hard from the climb. Cara was close behind, and he had to admit the lad was handling these conditions better than he expected, probably better than himself. They were cutting through the hills, a straight line to where he hoped he would find Gurley, the mob, the horse and their shadow.

He followed a faint trail covered by jagged boulders, thick undergrowth, woody trunks, branches bursting from fissures in the rocks, a murder of glossy crows flying head-height through the fractured terrain.

'Gotta keep mov'n, Cara,' said Jimmy. 'Reckon they'll almost be 'round the hill by now.'

The boy was silent, looking to where Jimmy pointed. Jimmy could feel as well as hear the muffled beat of wings, the faint wheezing of birds as they appeared to float around the trunks of the stunted trees.

Jimmy felt a pressure in his guts, a stubborn resolve to reach Gurley, a determination to prevent the inevitable shattering of his family. Bracing his legs, feet, shoulders, against the uneven ground, he pushed forward, hoping for the strength to make the distance, to triumph even when the last of his energy dissolved.

The birds had wheeled in a wide arc, returning to the gnarled trees about them. Jimmy glanced up as the jarring, plaintive carrion call echoed through the boulders, across the hillside. At least a dozen birds peered down, like a Greek chorus watching a tragedy unfold, witness to the futility of his effort, declaring an end to his trial.

Jimmy ran.

He took a weaving path through the broken land. Time seemed to stretch, elongate, slacken to the measured beat of a metronome – the one he remembered Doreen using when practising piano in her drawing room – a beat in time with his heart, the sweep of his feet across the rocky ground, the movement of his arms to maintain balance along the steep path.

The crows were wrong!

He would succeed, prevail, triumph.

When he finally topped the rise, he could see the river far below, its reflection like a silver ribbon wrapped about the base of the moun-tain, a light breeze forming deep pockmarks at the water surface. He started down the steep path, almost falling, digging his heels into loose gravel, teetering on edge, desperately regaining balance.

Concentrate! Disaster might be only a heartbeat away!

He saw them as he lifted his eyes from his feet. A small group, a dozen or more people hurrying along the riverbank, a horse ambling at the rear, a lone figure slightly separated from the mob, striding forward at the front. They were specks still, but free.

His heart lifted. He knew it was Gurley; he could almost taste victory!

He thought he caught a movement to the left, amongst the gums that crowded the riverbank, behind Gurley's group. As he strained to see, he almost fell again.

Balance!

Strength!

He constantly repeated the mantra as he ran: *Balance. Strength.* He looked up again, to the place where he had imagined movement – there was none. He felt a release, a calm despite his headlong descent from the mountain.

More dissected rocks rose before him, boulders with jagged edges, teeth to cut shins to ribbons. Jimmy glanced back as he negotiated a smooth patch. Cara had fallen behind, but still bravely struggled on.

Jimmy stopped at the top of a particularly steep incline, bent forward at the waist, arms like struts, hands pressing hard against his thighs. He sucked in a deep breath, sweat cascading from his forehead. He loved her, loved her hair, her irreverence, independence, liveliness, her connection to their past, loved everything about her. How could anyone ever best her? And yet, here she was, pursued by a seemingly irresistible authority. Loathing surged briefly, disgust at what those powers had done, sadness at their mess, a dream that moved from the ugliness of the result to divine celebration. The instability of his life swamped him. He closed his eyes, feeling the rasping breath of his boy at his back.

'Looks like they're clear of that whitefella,' he said, pointing to the river.

A light breeze brushed Jimmy's face, rising along the ridgeline, gaining momentum until it burst free from the restriction of the cliff. He squinted into the westering sun, looked again towards the thin, silver ribbon, felt the urge to wave, shout at the moving dots, to reassure them that he was near. The full futility of their lives threatened to overwhelm him again.

'No, they're not!' said Cara.

He swept his gaze, urgently to the left.

A quiet, focused moment. He could see nothing wrong.

Then he saw it.

A horse and rider were moving stealthily through the trees!

Appalled, he realised that the rear of Gurley's desperate company was now within the enemy's grasp.

Jimmy launched himself forward, over the sharp line of the ridge, no further thought for safety. He *had* to reach Gurley, *had* to right the wrong, *had* to stem the tide of destruction and decay, appease the souls of those abandoned to extinction.

He ran for his life and the survival of those he loved.

*

The thin, tortured scrub gave way to taller trees, the ground levelling a bit, stones and rocks mostly buried now beneath thin scree. He accelerated, thighs beginning to ache, breath beginning to rasp, face stinging from the whip of low branches.

Desperation ate at him, his family at the apex of his fear. His uncle had told him to deflect the spear, to remain calm even in the face of terrible odds. There would always be a gap, an opening to slip through, however small. *Mistakes,* his uncle said, *were the trademark of the confident,* but Jimmy knew that if he couldn't get to Gurley, then the mistakes wouldn't matter – he wouldn't be able to make it right, defy the inevitable, pass the test, reach Gurley and deflect the spike.

Jimmy thought, I'll just be another poor bloody blackfella, face down in the dirt, no future, not trusting anyone, anything, jobless, no family, kicked around, just wanting it all to end.

He found that prospect strangely comforting; he reckoned that once you got used to it – the nothingness of such an existence – life would pass like a dream, a biblical paradise without any real cares, where the list of worries did not contain the concerns of others.

A paradise perhaps, but one with nothing, devoid of feeling.

Jimmy looked at nothing as he ran, Gurley and Cara, the company of people ahead in his mind. The destruction of dreams frightened him, the scent of imminent corruption, of a judgement undeserved; it was destruction he could not allow.

Jimmy pushed forward, dug deeper, drew on the last of his reserves.

The trees were thinning now; he could see the rust-red patches of the river gums outlining the water's edge.

A trail!

He stopped, looked behind for the first time since the scarp. He could not see Cara.

Best, he thought, for what he now had to do.

He swivelled his head to the track; thought he saw faint movement beyond a line of trees.

He trotted forward, cautious now, hoping his rasping breath would not expose him.

A horse!

Saddled.

No rider!

Jimmy edged forward, ducking tree to tree, listening, finally the acrid odour of stale sweat.

A shout!

Jimmy ran again, driving his feet deep into the loose river soil, charging headlong into the back of a monster, a massive man, arm outstretched, fingers hooked about a stock whip, ready to strike. The man lurched forward with the shock, almost fell, knees bent, Jimmy clawing at his back, shoulders, head, face. They collapsed under Jimmy's weight, to the dust.

Jimmy felt the shudder as they hit the ground, was dimly aware of time once again dilating, stretching beyond his reach, a creeping void where he observed his actions, foresaw reactions, could time his responses. Reality, it seemed, was suspended, yet he did not feel divorced from its consequences.

The man struggled free from Jimmy's grasp, staggered back, blood streaming from a deep gash across his face, eye to chin.

'Fuck!'

Jimmy climbed to his feet, braced for another charge, stopped, straightened his back and laughed, a cutting laugh through clenched teeth.

'What are you do'n here, Strepford?'

*

They stood, silent for a moment, bound together by an invisible cord. This was as close as Jimmy wanted to be with malice, to the discharge of vitriol radiating from the bloodied, distorted face. He realised there was no easy way to end this standoff. Someone would need to back off, and soon.

'Why are y'here, Strepford?' Jimmy needed to stay on the front foot.

'My woman ...' Strepford blustered the words across the gap, saliva and blood spraying a wide arc before him. 'I want Mirri back!' Hysteria mounting?

Silence.

Jimmy glanced to the side, met Gurley's frightened eyes, spotted the fading form of the young woman, just a girl, behind the cowering mob, and thought for a moment: *He could give her to him. He would go away. They'd be rid of this menace.* He had to admit, it was an enticing idea.

'She's mine!' Strepford bent forward; Jimmy believed he was about to charge.

Jimmy flicked his eyes to the river, noted the line of smooth boulders, back to the huge brute, couldn't afford to lose his focus just in case the fool decided to rush forward. Strepford stank of shit; dishevelled, greasy hair; and small, red eyes, mad eyes. Jimmy abhorred shit, was repulsed by red, and recognised fathomless cruelty in Strepford's eyes. The first time Strepford had approached him with his red eyes, Jimmy knew he was treacherous, treachery demonstrated more than once, the girl the butt of his anger, deceit and violence. One of Gurley's cousins; she was an unfortunate who had thought that attachment to Strepford would mean a shield against want, need, a cruel world. Looks didn't deceive with Strepford. Violence always accompanied him.

'She doesn't want you!' It was the best thing Jimmy could think to say. It was a shout of defiance against the unbalanced; an ultimatum. He remembered the Sunday quotation: *A soft answer turneth away wrath, but grievous words stir up anger*; but couldn't think how any *soft* words would penetrate this wall of loathing. Words were worthless here.

Jimmy saw the movement, a slight lifting of the shoulders, neck cords vibrating.

Jimmy ran forward.

He ran directly at Strepford, shoulder low, head braced for the impact.

He struck an iron wall, felt the compression in his spine, registered the lightness of the fall.

A yell, they hit the ground, a grunt, silence. Strepford lay prone beneath him, unmoving; arms spread wide. Jimmy lay atop the stinking heap, an involuntary spasm rippling through his nose.

Jimmy climbed to his feet. The rocks had done their job; the man was unconscious, not quite lifeless, but for the time being, he would take no further part in any discussion, wrathful or soft.

'Well, that was easier than I reckoned it would be,' he said, shaking dust and reek from his limbs. The rocks had bent Strepford's back into an awkward arch, his head oozing red liquid across the smooth rock carapace.

'Is he dead?' asked Gurley, a hint of panic in her voice.

Jimmy peered closely at Strepford. 'He'll wake up soon ... won't be want'n to carry on with this blather though,' said Jimmy, exhaling softly, relieved it was over.

He turned to Gurley, cast his eyes across a stunned, immobile mob. They needed to get moving, along the trail, as far from this place as possible.

'Y'need to get go'n,' he said above the wail, the echoing sobs of a panicking Mirri. 'Clear out!' A shake in his voice. It seemed he couldn't entirely shake off the fear that had brought him here, the brutality of his arrival.

They all turned abruptly as Gurley hustled the mob towards the edge of the clearing, pushing Mirri forward. The clearing gradually emptied of people, the horse a reluctant passenger. Gurley stood for a moment, the last to exit, wordless, her arm tightly enfolding Cara. She looked over her shoulder, a smile, wan, passed across her broad face. Silent, she nodded and returned to duty as a rear-guard of the mob.

She knows what I must do, he thought.

But what must he do now? He wasn't sure how far he should go.

Jimmy tasted bile, a sour taste in his mouth, mixed with dust and decayed leaf litter from the saturated ground by the river. The place he realised was gloomy now in the failing light, the shine from the river dimming, the reflection fading as the sun dipped below the horizon, birds coming and going, perching, squabbling, some abandoning the roosts altogether, moving to alternate climes in the forlorn hope that a change of view, less congestion, would brighten their night. He squatted close to the ground before Strepford's prone form, watching as the colour drained back into the pale face. The birds seemed to sense the terrible decision that had to be made, their insistent chortle waning with the declining light, quiet, expectant, critical. Once he had ended a critically injured dog's life, gored by a bull, a favoured worker with them all; that was in the early days at Kempton.

The dog's name was Dinga. It meant 'to wander without a home', the old Boer war veteran had told him. Jimmy heard now the echo of that character, the terrible decision, the termination of life.

He squatted before Strepford, perhaps for an hour, patiently waiting for signs of consciousness. Eventually, the body stirred, eyes opening.

'I reckon I know what y'think'n Strepford?' he said, not waiting for a response. 'What's my way outta this shit?'

Strepford remained prone, eyes, fully open now, drilling through the gloom, orienting, looking for a chance, any chance to survive.

Jimmy, tiredness almost overwhelming him now. 'I reckon there's no way, seeing you're such a shit.'

Strepford tried to lift his head, attempted to raise his chest, failed, slumped back to the ground.

'Could y'stop me beat'n the life outta ya right now?' A sinister tone in Jimmy's voice.

Silence.

Jimmy screwed his mouth into a cruel gash. 'Y'think'n I'll get back on that horse and ride away, I won't look back, I'll forget all this.'

Jimmy stood, sighed, walked towards Strepford, a visible recoil from the prone form. He stopped, towering over the broken man.

'Girl's gone, we're gone, you're gone.' The finality in Jimmy's voice was brutal.

Silence.

Jimmy turned, walked slowly to the clearing edge, looked back once before disappearing into the gloom of the encroaching night. He knew Strepford would harbour deep, violent resentment against this travesty; would continue as a threat whenever, wherever they crossed paths. The alternative to the warning was death. Jimmy knew he couldn't take that step.

He ducked through the dense forest undergrowth in pursuit of Gurley, considering the lost opportunity and the possible consequences of not despatching a dog — a mad, rabid dog.

10

WARRUMBUNGLES – NORTHERN NEW SOUTH WALES

Early Spring 1915

They camped close to the stream that fell from the cliffs about the cauldron; a bowl hollowed from the land, encircled by jagged peaks, knife-edged slivers that seemed to burst from deep within the earth. Jimmy walked beneath a cloudless sky, the fresh winds from the east pacified by the heights, the light gusts carrying a smoky taste of campfires, people, humanity. He sweated despite the cool, a weariness descending upon him. He just wanted to sleep, renew, forget, move on to better moods, delay the inevitable dark reality.

He saw a clutch of pilgrims by the river, clustered about the edges of the circles, a thin wisp of smoke rising from smouldering leaves held aloft, fanned by a large woman with a battered hat and a long, tattered skirt. His link with the past was too disjointed; he didn't understand most of the things that passed here as rituals; felt that the concentration on the past meant, somehow, abandonment of their future. It was so hard to reconcile a desire for self with the other bloody obvious needs: safety, shelter, sanctuary.

Walking on past the grove by the quiet billabong, he felt before he saw Gurley amongst the small group of people. Jimmy said, 'The Wiriyaraay mob are gett'n ready for the *bora*.'

'We're join'n 'em tonight.' Gurley seemed distracted. 'You'll need to take Cara along early.'

Jimmy thought about how unprepared Cara was. He, himself, hadn't ever been through rites like this, the jump into the realm of men, the revered scheme. He had learned the truths, the realities of their past by listening, observing and building on his mistakes. He didn't resent the cost of lost status, didn't dwell on ceremony, or covet the honour of men.

Continuance. Survival. The survivors wrote the story.

'Yeah, reckon they'll be ready soon,' he said.

'Jimmy,' said Gurley. 'Cara should be with his uncle, now.'

'Where is the boy?'

'Do'n the songs and stuff his uncle taught him. Down at the river. He's hav'n trouble remember'n.' She laughed.

'Can't help him,' said Jimmy. He thought he sensed a reproach from Gurley. She laughed though, a warm smile, caring, loving.

'Uncle's done it,' she said. 'Cara just can't remember all the bits.'

'Won't be able to watch either.' Jimmy, unversed in the ways, resented only his exclusion from the initiation, the lost opportunity to watch his boy's passage.

'We can watch him go down the path from the big circle.' Jimmy heard pride in her voice.

'Can't be with him,' he said.

'Jimmy, you saved us!' Gurley moved to him, long fingers lightly touching his cheek. 'Without you, we wouldn't be here. Cara's safe, we're all safe!'

Jimmy shook his head. 'Strepford knew the girl was with you.'

'Just luck.' She was grasping at straws.

'Nah, he knew.'

'He's gone!' she said. 'Won't come back after you put the frighteners on him.'

Jimmy shook his head again, more vigorously this time. 'He won't give up, Gurley.'

'He's gone!' she said again.

He thought for a moment about Strepford. Crazy buggers like that never gave up unless they were bloated, stinking corpses, with no possibility of a miraculous resurrection, departed to some hellish netherworld, the sort that the Sunday priest promised to anyone who refused the sacrament.

'Yeah.' He left it at that, resolving to find a way to protect his family from Strepford's extremes, and the worst of the whitefella's excesses.

He went in search of his boy.

*

Jimmy looked across the valley, a fine smoke haze, a delicate curtain against the blue of the hills; men, women, children, late risers after a long night's celebration. He turned from the camp, walked to the cleared flat ground, the fertile point bar nestled between the arms of the river's meander. The horse glanced up from its grazing, assessed Jimmy as he approached and decided to return to the sweet grass – who knew when such rich pickings would be presented again.

Down the short slope to the river, a diminutive man coughed and cleared his throat, failed and tried again, a raw sound that cut across the crisp air, his head bowed with the effort, expelling a wad of something into the swift-flowing river.

'Times past,' said Gurley's Uncle Henry without raising his head, 'we'd have weeks here.'

Jimmy stood, silent, waiting.

'Lotsa water, plenty kangaroos.' He finally levelled his eyes with Jimmy. 'No reason to move … 'til some dill made up his mind to get upset and leave.'

'Still can. Stay,' said Jimmy.

'No! Whitefellas don't want us hang'n 'round these days. Gotta move soon, or they'll come, round us all up and take the kids.'

Jimmy saw his own worry in Henry's eyes.

'Gurley's decided to stay on for a while with you and the mob,' said Jimmy.

'Yeah.'

'I gotta be back … promised Eiric.'

'Yeah? What for?'

Jimmy thought it sounded like a reproof, maybe the start of one of Henry's lectures; though he had to admit, it was a reasonable question.

'You not stay'n here then?' said Jimmy.

'Nah. We'll head to the Black Hills for a few days, then the caves for a while.'

The caves, it seemed, were the heart of it all.

'Cara. He's keen to show he's a man now.'

'He's still got heaps to learn. I'll look after them, Jimmy.'

Jimmy thought, *Would the caves help him cope with the whitefellas' world?*

'Gurley reckons the caves have the answers,' Jimmy said.

'The souls are in her, Jimmy, she needs to be there for a while.'

'It's not far from Kempton ... and I made a promise.' Jimmy felt it necessary to explain, justify.

'Maybe you're not think'n enough about your family,' said Henry. Was this another rebuke? Henry could be very disapproving, particularly where Jimmy was concerned.

'They can't stay at the caves forever. Need somewhere safe from them government men and mad bastards like Strepford.'

'And you reckon the old man is reliable? He kicked you, us, off the place!'

'Strepford almost got'ya.' He had to try to convince him, the memory of his desperation stabbing at him.

'Yeah, 'cause you lost us.' There it was, the reprimand.

'Don't want him hav'n another go at ya.'

Henry was silent, then looked abruptly over Jimmy's shoulder, towards the camp.

'Dunno about the old man ...' Jimmy had to admit it. 'Worth a try, though.'

Henry shook his head. 'You might be right, Jimmy. You off then? When?'

'Tomorra, take the horse, pick up the wagon where you lot left it.'

'Y'could stay.' Jimmy felt the temptation. He heard the swish of footsteps behind him, through the grass, across the flat ground. He turned to Gurley's broad, beautiful face, the glow of the night's celebration still lingering about her dark eyes. He looked into those eyes.

'We missed you,' said Gurley. 'You didn't stick around for breakfast.'

'Talk'n with Uncle,' Jimmy said. Gurley's eyes met his, glancing briefly across to Henry.

'About leav'n?'

'Yeah, tomorra maybe.'

'The old man can't be trusted, Jimmy.'

Jimmy started a turn towards Henry – he figured he needed support – and caught a glimpse of Henry walking silently away along the riverbank.

'Uncle will help you get to the caves,' he said, watching the small, muscular man stroll away along the water's edge.

'Yeah. Maybe. Another week here, then we'll head home,' Gurley said.

'Henry reckons the whitefellas will move us all on.'

'We'll all be outta here before then.'

'Don't take a chance, Gurley. Come with me now.'

'No, Cara needs time with all the rellies.' She moved closer. Jimmy could feel the heat of her body radiating through the chill air. 'Are you sure you want to leave?'

'Gotta,' he said. 'Made a promise to Eiric, you heard.'

'What about your promise to me?' Gurley pulled his arms about her, wrapping hers loosely around his back, tightening slowly as she drew them together, head resting lightly on his chest. 'You said we'd always make love, have lots of kids, live at the caves forever.'

Jimmy pulled her close, they sank to the ground, into the deep, lush grass above the riverbank. It was the first of spring, the sweet smell of blossom, seeds, the hum of insects. How was he supposed to make everything right, safe, secure when there were mad bastards like Strepford on the prowl? Nothing could prepare you for it: the madness, the rage, the thirst for vengeance.

He caressed her firm, supple backside, marvelled at her power. Perhaps he could make good on the first of her desires?

'On the way back, stick to the bush will ya?' he said. 'I'll leave the horse and wagon near the caves; get to you when I've sorted things at Kempton.'

Gurley just nodded, fixed her ample mouth against his, guiding his hand to the source of her desires.

Maybe it wasn't time to leave just yet.

11

Kempton Homestead
– Northern New South Wales

Winter 1916

The old man was waiting for Jimmy in the stables. Sweat and dust drenched everything; tired cattle, horses and men.

'They've done it, Jimmy,' said Angus. 'Like a bloody den of thieves.'

'What's that, Boss?' said Jimmy.

'The boys ... ungrateful twerps!'

'They work hard, Boss.' Caution ahead of the explosion to come.

'The boys, Jimmy!' The old man was repeating himself, starting to froth at the mouth, spit floating free from thin, stretched lips becoming unhinged. Jimmy thought it best to stand his ground, say nothing. 'Buxton confirmed it. The lot of them lined up at the recruitment centre, tried to enlist.'

'When?' said Jimmy.

'Stopped two of 'em. Couldn't stop Ted.' Angus gestured with his hand, waving it in the air like an expunging broom.

'They come'n home?'

'Ted is over the consent age. Couldn't stop it.' Jimmy thought he saw the pain in the old man's eyes. 'Thought this might happen ... sent a letter to Buxton a while back.'

'They're short of good fellas, the Light Horse.'

'Well, they'll be short of a couple more for a while.' He took out a folded piece of paper from his coat pocket, held it up to Jimmy, evidence of his handiwork. 'Buxton promised to talk to me if they turned up, sent this note before he went through with the paperwork.'

Jimmy knew that joining the Light Horse was on the boys' minds, joining the adventure in Palestine. Despite the horror of Gallipoli and the virtual extinction of the 10th Light Horse at The Neck, the papers had been full of the heroics and glory of it all. They didn't want to miss their chance at the grandeur of battle, each explaining to him the reason for their proposed enlistment. He still didn't understand the whitefellas' need for such a fight when neither food, family or women were at stake. Ted, the most determined of the three, caressed the strongest desire to be amongst the action.

He remained silent and wondered why the old man was trying to involve him.

'Need to tie them down here.' Was that irritation or desperation in the old man's voice?

'Eiric and Joe come'n home then?' said Jimmy.

'Get 'em off to run the other property. Away from here.' Yes, it was desperation. Jimmy knew Angus had proprietorial regard for his boys, same as everything in his life: stock, land, house, wife, mistress. But fondness? Enough respect to want to protect them? He decided to keep quiet, see what developed.

'Can't stop'em forever,' said Angus. He seemed to be conducting a debate with himself. As always, Jimmy felt he was there only while he continued to be useful.

What use was he here, now?

When Eiric had confided in him, Jimmy really couldn't understand what was at stake, what this war was about, why so many people, young men, boys really, were anxious to be involved; and the old men, mothers, cheered them on. A fervour even infected quiet, reserved Eiric, imbued him with a jingoistic pride. He had never seen any of the boys so keen to fight. Ted saw it as a duty, Eiric could only see it as an opportunity to see foreign places, Joe just followed his brothers. All had a patriotic gleam in the eye.

Jimmy planted his feet firmly on the stable floor, nodded as Angus continued his tirade. The old man's large, dimpled nose had turned deep purple, more so than its usual alcoholic hue. Cheeks flushed red, he appeared to be talking to an invisible audience, oblivious now, Jimmy thought, of his presence.

'They're want'n to get amongst it, Boss,' said Jimmy, immediately regretting interference in the old man's rant. Angus stopped talking, startled at the intrusion.

'Eh?' said Angus. 'What?'

Jimmy hoped he hadn't divulged evidence of his counsel to the boys.

He decided, once again, to remain silent.

'What do you mean?'

Silence. *Shit!* Jimmy thought. *Here it comes.*

Angus spat, deep yellow phlegm that hit the straw-covered stable floor, cleared his throat, and swung his eyes from the distance to rest on Jimmy.

'Can't stop'em forever,' repeated Angus. 'But this war's turning ugly.'

Jimmy thought, *Aren't they all?* He'd seen spearing, blood, death when there was a quarrel between the Kamilaroi and the Wiradjuri from south of the Namoi. The way Eiric had described it though, this stoush was much worse.

'Pity they're real healthy, Boss,' Jimmy said. 'They never fall off horses or nothing.'

A pause.

'Could organise a spearing.'

Jimmy frowned. Had he gone too far?

The old man seemed to consider this course.

Jimmy felt a sudden lurch in his stomach – he wasn't seriously suggesting a spearing!

'No,' said Angus. 'I've got a better idea.'

'Boss?'

'Can't stop'em forever.' He looked squarely at Jimmy.

Another lengthy pause, Angus shuffling his feet, reaffirming his grip on the ground.

'You've been with them now most of their lives.'

'Boss.'

'You've always watched after them.'

Silence.

'They are naïve and headstrong.' Angus had a curious softness in his voice, the anger dissipated.

Jimmy could only hear their breathing, time lingering. He wondered how the world chose the moment, the instant of delay when he could identify all the components of an event, could almost perceive a future. Angus, shoulders slightly rounded now, tiredness beneath his eyes, mouth released from its rigidity, arms, hands, slack to the side, the smell of horse dung, straw and oiled leather. He felt time like the brush of a faint breeze, familiar, memorable because it brought with it the pale aura of recollection *and* prediction, the feeling that the real story was a circle, that there was nothing new under the sun.

Jimmy saw the outcome of this day written in the play of shadows and light about the straw bales and stalls.

*

Jimmy could feel only light pressure as Angus, his immense bulk swaying slightly forward, had a large hand resting on his shoulder. It could have been intimidating, an attempt by the big man to force the world into submission once again. The touch was fleeting, an aberrant surrender to emotion, disquiet apparent in such close contact.

'I want you to go with them to Palestine.'

'Boss?'

'Can't make you.'

'No, Boss.'

'Your family,' said Angus. 'They'll be looked after here, at Kempton.'

'Not my fight, Boss.' Jimmy felt the tug at his chest, desertion, his abandonment of trust. He regretted the words, but couldn't see any sense in this war.

'We've been together for ... for how long?'

'A while, Boss'

'More than fifteen years?' Angus looked reflectively about the stables. 'We've done a lot in that time.'

Jimmy was silent; he had to let this play to the end.

'I've always supported you and your family.'

'You told me to fuck off, Boss.'

Angus visibly drew back from the rebuke.

'Yeah, but only for a while ... the boys needed time to stand on their own feet.'

'They've been all right for ages. They know how to take care of themselves.' Jimmy couldn't see the old man's logic.

'This is different.' Angus shifted his gaze to the ground, reshuffling his feet. Jimmy thought the old man was struggling with his case.

'Ted's already gone,' said Jimmy. The old man grimaced.

'They need to keep their heads down,' Angus said. 'And they need someone ... *you*, to make sure they do.'

'Not my fight,' Jimmy said again. He felt the conflict in the old man, in himself. He couldn't see how the abandonment of his family would benefit anyone.

Angus frowned, valleys from forehead to chin, an antediluvian face, ears with sunburnt crests, prominent at the sides of a close-cropped head. He had his hands resting on hips, legs extended to the side, braced against some force, eyes still averted, pensive, absorbed it seemed in the state of his shoes. Jimmy knew the old man considered him dependable but artless, useful still, particularly in a tight corner. With resurgent superiority, Angus raised his eyes to Jimmy and said, 'What were you fixing on doing for the next year or so?'

'Time on a horse, here, Boss,' Jimmy said. 'Time with Gurley, she's stay'n with her folks near Coonabarabran right now.'

'We need to focus on the long term, Jimmy.'

'I'll be dead, Boss.'

'I mean, over the next few years!' Angus paused, ground his teeth, exaggerating his projection of patience with a loud sigh as if he found an explanation of higher-order thinking impossible. 'This place is going to keep growing, lots of work, security for your family.'

'Good thing, Boss.' Jimmy wasn't going to make it easy for the old man.

Silence. Angus held up his hands, a resignation.

'Well, I'll leave you to think it over. The recruiting station has been alerted to you possibly showing up.'

Jimmy remained silent. It was just the sort of thing Angus would do. The old man assumed everyone would submit to his wishes, everyone, even the recruiters.

Angus turned slowly, to the stable door, towards a freedom Jimmy wished for himself. Jimmy thought about the trap laid for him: attachments – the bond with Angus' boys, a life connection to Gurley, Cara, the rifts of the past, the ruin of his people. How much independent choice did he have, could he ever have? *He could run*, he thought, *get out of here, go bush, back to the caves, go somewhere, anywhere!*

'The silly buggers are killing each other for noth'n,' he said to Angus' back as the old man reached for the door.

Angus stopped, hand resting on the latch.

'God ...' he said, half turning, 'and glory. Those bastards can't expect to stab us in the arse and get away with it.'

The reasoning escaped Jimmy. War against those you didn't know, so far away? He understood the earth, sacred ground – time at the caves had renewed that foundation – the need for an accord between people.

War for pride?

He silently watched as Angus left the stables. A flash of light from the waning day bellowed at him, cut short by a slammed door.

He turned towards the stable stalls. 'All right, Horse, hear all that? We need to talk.'

12

BANGLADESH – DHAKA

The Present Day

Anika leaned towards the woman opposite, they laughed, stepping backwards amidst the jest. *Enjoying the moment*, Harry thought, *oblivious of any audience*. The club stalwarts ignored the laughter, either stolidly fixed on alcohol consumption or semi-comatose, in the cloying humidity.

'Must have been funny,' he said.

She turned to the sound, disconcerted by a voice, so close, yet unnoticed. Her dark, curly hair swung wide, then settled, bobbing slightly in the aftermath, her lips slightly parting, showing even white teeth. Gone were the tennis sweats, replaced with a loose, knee-length skirt, a lightly patterned blouse, high open collar accenting her high cheekbones and eyes that curved upward slightly, in a Eurasian way.

'Oh, hello Harry,' she said, with a slight American lilt. 'Heidi … have you met Harry? Heidi was just telling me about a rickshaw incident. So funny.'

Anika laughed again.

Harry waited, trying to look expectant.

'Heidi was walking home from the club yesterday. The rickshaw *wallahs* can be very insistent, particularly with us expat women. Didn't want to take *no* for an answer.' Anika stopped to laugh again. 'When Heidi insisted she needed to walk for the exercise, the *wallah* said ...'

Heidi, a short, plump lady, smiled, assuming control of the story amongst further laughter, '... and said, "Yes, you are rather fat!" Well, that was it, wasn't it? He wouldn't ever get my business!'

Harry watched the two women enjoy the story once again, his eyes drawn to Anika, her abandonment of pretence, guiltless enjoyment of the moment.

The lighthearted moment subsided, Harry, filling the sudden silence. 'Would you ladies like a drink?'

'Not for me,' Heidi said. 'I'm wanted elsewhere: children, husband, the full catastrophe.' She laughed as she scurried away.

'What about you, Anika?'

She paused, seemed to be weighing up the advisability of such a move, looking intently at Harry. He had a feeling that he was being assessed, for what, he couldn't decide – his purpose, his ultimate goal? *Women*, he thought, *could be suspicious.*

'Yes,' she said, eventually. 'A drink would be good.' Harry was held for a moment longer by her dark eyes.

He followed her across the lawn, feet sinking slightly into the thick, broad-leafed tropical grass. The bar squatted close to the pool, a cool relief from the sun.

'Haven't seen you here all week,' he said when they were seated.

'I've been down south, sorting out relief funding for communities of the Sundarbans.'

'The Sundarbans?'

'Biggest mangrove swamp in the world,' she said with a short laugh, but Harry reckoned it wasn't humour.

'People live in it?'

'No, around the edges. It's an international heritage area. Fishermen go in there, sail up the tidal channels, get their catch, come home, hopefully with enough to feed their people.'

'Sounds idyllic.'

'Not!' Anika exclaimed. Harry saw the first severity, a sign of passion. 'Cyclone season is a visit into hell for those people. And they're eating away at the boundaries of the national park.'

'Guess that's happening all over this country,' said Harry, the teeming hordes of Dhaka fresh in his mind.

'No, this is different. They're pushing into tiger country.' She looked at him – he saw the pain in her eyes. 'Women, kids get taken, eaten by Bengal tigers! Then villagers hunt them.'

'What? The tigers?'

'Yes, then more people get killed. The people get angry there aren't many tigers left. A cyclone then drives more tigers to the edges – people are easy prey. It's a vicious cycle.'

'They need a buffer zone.'

'Easy to say, too many people, just subsistence living.'

'What's the solution then?'

'We're trying to fund some sort of industry, community-based stuff, jute carpets, weaving, that sort of thing, but it's hard.'

'The government?'

'Do nothing; nothing useful.' The regret overflowed. 'These people have nothing. If they have land, it's likely gone in the next flood – washed away by the next change in the river course.'

'I wonder ...' said Harry, pausing, carefully selecting his next words. '... if there might be something I could do to help?'

'Like what?' *Had she*, thought Harry, *heard such offers before, and considered them worthless?*

'I don't know ... yet. We *are* a large international company with resources.'

Harry was silent. He felt Anika's passion, the lure, the hold it could have on him, his desire to plunge into its depths.

She raised her full face to Harry, her eyes and her mouth holding the hunger of her words, seemed to consider, to weigh her next words, 'Perhaps you could come with me next time, visit the place, see for yourself?'

'Yes.' A quick response, *perhaps*, Harry thought, *too quick*?

Harry considered the commitment. He looked unwavering into Anika's eyes; thought he saw an eagerness there – perhaps he was mistaken. More likely, it was just the opportunity to secure funding for her work, to boost aid for distressed people, a chance to transform lives, make history, secure her part in it. And yet.

He asked Anika a loaded question, didn't want her to raise her defences. 'And is Mr Anika involved in all this work as well?'

She regarded him quietly for a moment. 'There's no Mr Anika, Harry.' Was that wariness?

Harry nodded inwardly. Women, beautiful women like Anika, had every right to be suspicious.

*

Anika and Harry went through security, such as it was, into the relatively calm airport realm. The pushing and shoving at the grubby portal continued behind them. As they walked, she said, 'Internal flights over here.' She pointed. 'Only a forty-minute flight, but they never leave on time. Sometimes hours late.' She hefted a small bag further onto her shoulder.

'Always glad of some quiet time in this mad city,' said Harry. 'Nice cup of tea, a bun, some lively conversation.'

'No first class here,' said Anika. 'Just lots of body odour, bottled water and the occasional livestock.' She smiled.

Harry felt a calmness descend as they entered the waiting area, the bustle of the airport hall replaced with a quiet expectancy. He glanced about the waiting passengers, noted a resignation, a familiarity with habitual delay, with information drought.

In the aircraft, a twin-engine, high-winged job, crammed together, Anika's shoulders, arms, hips pressed close, Harry felt for the first time, the fragility of his existence.

'It's a short flight,' said Anika.

His eyes were drawn to the imprint of an old oil spray on the engine cowling, buffeting from ground thermals punctuated by brief smooth flight interludes. Through clenched teeth, jaw aching, Harry said, 'Only short?' He glanced again at the offending engine cover. 'A pilot once told me, *It's far better to be down here wishing you were up there than up there wishing you were down here!*'

Laughter. Anika placed a warm hand over his, looked into his eyes. 'Believe me. This is far safer and quicker than attempting a road trip.'

Harry said, 'We could always rent armoured cars.'

'Thousands die every year on the roads here.' She was silent a moment through a particularly violent bang. 'It's the buses. The drivers race each other between stops. It's a competition to get there first for passengers.'

'Armoured trucks, then, maybe even ...'

He paused, the engine sound changing, a lower tone.

'Told you it was a short flight. We'll be in Khulna soon.'

Harry's eyes met Anika's. She smiled, a brief beam of sunshine, then quickly withdrew her hand. He felt the loss, the fleeting intimacy, noticeable, desired. He wondered where that would take them.

Take them? Wasn't he getting ahead of himself? Wasn't this a likely excursion into reproach, bitter antipathy, self-loathing, the release of hostility in those he cruelly ignored?

'The roads are quiet down here,' she said, 'mainly bicycles, light traffic. None of that murderous crush in Dhaka and to the north.'

'Murderous is an understatement,' he said, then thought such negativity needed to be offset. He smiled. 'A few days of quiet. A blessing.'

'Monzur will meet us with a car. We shouldn't drive ourselves.'

Harry felt a slight jump in his heart, despite his self-recrimination. 'Your team?'

'Yes, we'll be with them going south from Khulna.'

Harry said nothing, looked through the window at the rapidly encroaching earth, felt the jolt as the wheels slammed into the ground; reckoned he needed to get a grip on himself. *The last thing I want*, he thought, *was a further complication, added twists to my life, the creation of angst in myself as well as others. Treat this as a reconnaissance, a humanitarian expedition, a chance to learn, an opportunity to further the interests of the company.* He could feel the pressure of Anika's mood, passion, her ability to switch from benign to severe, maybe even hurtful? It was a quality he wished for himself, that he saw in Teresa, found difficult to accept, yet curiously dominated his affections, his affairs. Silence was a refuge, he realised, a chance to deconstruct his failures, to discern the missteps, recover from mistakes – silence and his ability to run; and he could undoubtedly sprint with the best of them.

The aircraft shuddered to a stop. Khulna, the Sundarbans, lay ahead – a chance for redemption, proof he could control his destiny.

*

Day one, they travelled south from the Khulna port – thankfully only a brief taste of road chaos, the small boat waiting amongst large multistorey barges. Harry felt the weight of the Bangladesh hordes lift, the rhythmic vibration of the old diesel, the wake of the boat impressing soft patterns on the stagnant, muddy brown water.

'You told me the roads were better here,' he said. 'Thought we would be stuck in that traffic forever.'

The clattering sound of a truck reached them from the near bank of the river.

Anika regarded him for a moment, smiled. 'Yesterday would have been better. Fridays always keep people at home or at the mosque.'

'It's warfare out there.'

'Saturday's their day of release, time to get away, ever so briefly, from the struggle, have some fun with their families.'

'Do they need to all charge out at the same time?'

Anika laughed again. Harry tried to ignore her vitality, the way the moment seemed to take control of her, the enjoyment flooding from her face to her whole body. It was contagious; an animation that was difficult to resist.

Harry stood back from the upper deck rail, looking towards the riverbank, the mass of cultivated land looking benign, idyllic under the slightly hazy light. Anika turned to face him.

'Looks perfect,' he said, pointing to the well-tended, green fields.

'Fertile, yes,' she said. 'High productivity ground, but most of these people are tenant farmers. The land's owned by the wealthy, many living in Dhaka or abroad. A good part of the crop goes to the landlord.'

'And you're trying to change that?'

'No, we're trying to set up community industry and lines of distribution, so these people can be free.'

'Revolution,' said Harry, then regretted the taunt as he saw her draw back, ready, he guessed, to fight for her cause.

Anika pushed away from the rail, a new edginess; fight, not flight. 'Harry, something has to happen!' Arms, hands animated now. 'These people are victims of circumstance. Every year they get hammered by the elements, cyclones, floods, flattened crops, starvation.'

Harry thought, *Keep your mouth shut.*

'Big circumstances. Only going to get worse with global warming, sea-level rise, intensifying weather,' he said, not able, it seemed, to accept good advice.

'We're just trying to give them viable alternatives.'

'Any response from the landlords, the powers?'

'Plenty of resistance.'

Harry looked once more at the slowly passing fields, at the reality of brief lives and shifting land, and recalled his grandfather's journey. *Wasn't it*, he thought, *only a short time ago, that my family had the same tenuous hold on existence, misfortune drawing the baying dogs to our heels, wrong steps bringing calamity?*

'Reckon things are stacked against you,' he said.

'Like Bosnia? The Arab Spring? Liberté, Egalité? Got to try.' Harry felt the intensity of Anika's stare.

'More like Mother Teresa,' he smiled, 'though, perhaps not so pious.'

Anika stood for a moment, solemn, quietly regarding Harry, then erupted with a laugh.

'Like that song, *We Can't be Beaten*,' she said, laughing still. 'There's a lot of hope in the song, in the lyrics.'

More like Pleasure and Pain, he thought, wondering how the other Teresa would take the Mother Teresa reference.

Harry remained silent, Anika departing to prepare for their first landfall. The cultivated lands persisted until, abruptly, beyond the Mongla port, thick mangrove forests closed in about the riverbanks. Slick mud banks, steep in places, confirmed the large tidal range, frequent channels disappearing into overgrown, tangled, shaded jungle. He had almost accepted the disappearance of humanity when a small clearing, some timber and reed huts emerged, crude stockyards made from crudely cut branches, several children rushing to the top of the bank to wave. He waved back. They continued south, deeper into the wilderness, into the darkness that seemed to envelop everything, deep, entwined, twisted, the clawing maze, the occasional thinning of the vegetation revealing small, fearful spotted deer. He saw it then, the smooth tributaries that fell down the mud banks, widening at their base amongst the mangrove roots that burst through the mud – grey, horned, sinister crocodiles, mouths gaping, waiting patiently amongst the sticky, sucking mud for luckless, inattentive beasts.

Harry wondered again at the brevity of life, at the role of luck in providing, in such fleeting existence, opportunity or disaster, wealth or poverty, the fulfilment or abandonment of dreams. He felt the jaws, the teeth close about him, sinking into his flesh, dragging him down, consigning him to extinction. Was this his last gasp, his last chance, the last opportunity to set himself upon the road, to make a difference, take charge of his life?

The crocodile moved, the speed terrifying, the whip of the tail, the thrashing of its short, spiked legs, into the water, gone, never a ripple, as if it had never existed.

Harry exhaled – he had been holding his breath – and felt his body relax. It was as if a barrier had been lifted, that time was once again moving, carrying him forward, to clarity.

He turned to the stairs leading to the lower deck, their rooms and the future.

13

GLEN INNES
– NORTHERN NEW SOUTH WALES

Winter to Early Summer 1916

'I'm not say'n yer can't ride,' he said. 'But ...'

'But y'reckon 'cause I'm black, I'm not fit to fight for me country?'

'No. You blackfellas can ride and shoot with the best of us.'

Jimmy was astride a saddle perched on a wooden vaulting horse, pulling at a set of reins attached to a flimsy, wooden crossbar. He spat a thick wad of green, dusty phlegm to the ground, a precision shot that splattered across a hapless rock.

He swivelled in the saddle, to look directly at his detractor, uniformed, cadaverously thin, long mournful face.

'So, why don't we cut this crap, Major,' he said. 'And get out a real horse?'

The man hesitated for a moment, looked sideways at his two silent, but amused associates, returning his attention to Jimmy.

'Well, y'see Jimmy,' said the Major. 'We reckon you're too old.'

The Major paused.

'Too old to ... erh ... to keep up ... to handle the pressure of a campaign, of the severities of Palestine.'

'Eh?' Jimmy recognised flimsy excuses when he heard them. 'I sit in a saddle ten hours a day, most days,' he said. 'Ride you fuckers inta the ground.'

'It's a young man's game, Jimmy.'

The Major and his cohorts were preparing to walk away.

'Reckon you should read this then,' said Jimmy as he climbed down from the fake mount, pulling a crumpled envelope from his vest.

Jimmy knew the essence of the letter, knew from the old man, that corruption came from influence, the power to manipulate the weak, the feeble-hearted, the ambitious. He was familiar with the susceptibility of people like these to the moods of tyrants. He always expected reversals, excuses, lies, sudden demonstrations of thorough agreement with a contrary opinion. He saw the signs – hesitation, reflective stroking of the long, pointed chin, a muted exchange between the cronies, the slight drop of the shoulders as the Major finally turned to face his opponent. He knew what was coming, knew the die was cast, that his fortune was now firmly in the hands of others.

'Friends in high places, eh,' said the Major, as they walked back to the interview room.

'Just want t'join up,' said Jimmy.

'Seems you've a wealth of experience.'

Jimmy thought it best to listen.

'Somewhat of a horseman as well.'

Jimmy was fascinated as his resume expanded.

'And your stock management, reconnaissance, hunting and survival skills are exemplary.'

'Told ya I could ride … and shoot.' He smiled, a broad, friendly acceptance of the accolades.

'Well, Jimmy, welcome to the Light Horse,' the Major said. 'I think we can dispense with the practical riding test … and the medical.'

The Major leant forward, offered a long arm, shook Jimmy's calloused hand. 'My associates and I will complete the enlistment forms. Just sign here, we'll finish the rest.'

Jimmy grasped the proffered pen, scrawled an elaborate looping signature, returned the quill to the desk.

'And you can write!' The Major's eyebrows shot heavenward.

Ignorance and stupidity, it seemed, were not the exclusive preserve of the unqualified.

'Induction will be here in three weeks. You will attend basic military training, then travel to Sydney via Orange, then Melbourne.'

'I've got me own 'orse,' said Jimmy, expecting further push-back, but they had already turned to go, amused now with other matters.

Going down the hallway from the interview, Jimmy's attention was drawn to the gallery of photographs, portraits of rigid, starch-collared luminaries, groups of people posing at picnics, women in broad hats, long white dresses, children clustered tentatively about skirts, trouser legs, picnic baskets, men holding the reins of large horses.

At the heavy, timber entrance doors, he paused, top of the worn steps to the road, blinked into the glare of the day. Gurley hadn't returned from the caves; he hadn't had the opportunity to tell her, to explain that this was the best way, the only way to safety for them all. On the second day, the old man had confronted him, end of the day, alone, in the yards. Angus wanted to know, to be sure, to plan for the inevitable, to be in control even when a devastating blood lust consumed the world.

Jimmy stood at the door, regretting the lost chance to share his thoughts, the sense, the correctness of his decision, with Gurley. What choice did he have? The old man had repeated his words, a veiled ultimatum dressed up as a commitment: 'Your family will be safe with me while you watch my boys through this bloody war.'

Angus had looked a lot older, less than a week since the first exchange at the stables, slightly stooped, a resigned, hollow quality in his eyes. Jimmy was inclined to say *no*, that he would take his chances at the caves, go south to Gurley's relatives, or west near Walgett, wherever he could minimise contact with the government men. He felt an echo of his condition in the old man's barely curbed anger. 'You've got to make up your fucking mind or else ...'

'Yeah, Boss.'

'I know you had some strife heading south,' said Angus.

'Yeah, didn't bother us again.'

'Your folk will be safe here. The government men won't come on to Kempton.'

'Yeah, know that, Boss.' Angry, arrogant, narrow-minded he might be, but Angus wasn't a fraud; to the contrary, though he often over-stressed a point, he never dissembled, always held fast to an opinion, to a commitment. Jimmy could feel the weight, the logic of the old man's position and believed in the honesty of the offer.

On Friday, the day of his commitment, Jimmy woke early, saddled Horse as the magpies wound up their morning chorus. It was a crisp, clear day, a good one for riding a distance. He led Horse towards the road, on the path that passed the homestead. The old man stood on the verandah, a steaming cup of tea firmly held in a large hand, silently watching Jimmy as he approached the bougain-villea-draped fence.

'You off to Glen Innes, then?' said Angus.

'Yeah.'

'Decision made then, is it?'

'Yeah.'

'Back tonight?'

'Yeah, got a long ride.'

'Right.'

The beginnings of a slight smile. Angus rarely even attempted a smile. Everyone would have cut and run if he had succeeded. Jimmy felt embarrassed, witnessing the attempt. Passing the gate, Jimmy said, 'Got the letter you gave me.'

'Don't forget to give it to them, Jimmy,' Angus said, ever the thoughtful adviser.

'Yeah. Right here,' said Jimmy, patting his vest pocket.

'Better be off then. Days are short still. They won't be open Saturday.'

'Have a beer for me when I get back?'

'Don't push your luck, Sunshine.' *And that*, Jimmy thought, *about summed it up. The old man had got what he wanted. Time to move on.*

Jimmy hopped down the recruitment hall steps. It was time to embrace the decision he had made, sit with his family, make sure they all understood. He knew they wouldn't fully understand what he was getting into. He couldn't imagine it himself. He believed, though, that Angus would hold to the bargain, that their survival depended on the fate of the brothers.

As Jimmy neared the stables, it struck him that he had failed in his duty, in his obligation to a friend, a confidant.

He thought, *What the hell am I going to tell Horse?*

*

Joe said, 'All these dimwits hanging about. They reckon they can ride 'n' shoot.' Jimmy had ceased acknowledging Joe's mockery of the assembled recruits.

'They're just like us, Joe.' Eiric could never leave a comment unanswered.

'Yeah, maybe. And maybe they won't be able to hack basic.'

Jimmy looked across the hall at the excited crowd, wandered away, towards the main doors. He had to spend some quiet, considered time with Horse. His view of the world was suddenly cockeyed amongst all these young, naïve boys, adolescents bent on adventure. Maybe Horse would have a better perspective. Reaction to his arrival here was varied: pompous, distant recruitment officers; back slaps and cheer from all the young lads. He saw the relief on Eiric's face when he realised Jimmy was part of the adventure. The burden of military service worried him though, the ease he felt at the caves, his time at the *bora,* gone; and an old nemesis had once again resurfaced.

On the walk to the stables, he thought of Gurley. She hadn't returned before he left Kempton! He imagined her face, head tilted, questioning eyes thinking, *Why are you doing this, and why didn't you at least wait 'til I returned?* Determined, stubborn, although she knew her part in it all, it was in her nature to always defy the inevitable.

'Where you heading off to?' The familiar voice came from behind. Eiric didn't want to be left alone right now, isolated amongst the clamour and clang of excited, newly-inducted soldiers.

'Head'n off for a natter with Horse,' said Jimmy. 'He needs a bit of encouragement now that we're here with this mob of galahs.'

'They're just excited,' said Eiric.

'Move'n on tomorra as well. Off to the big smoke.' Jimmy hadn't been further south than the Warrumbungles, further east than the rough country of the Dividing Range. 'Have to warn Horse. They'll shove him in a truck.'

'He can ride with Tuppence.' A ghost of a smile from Eiric. 'They seem to get on pretty well.'

Jimmy stopped before the stable door, turned, reached out a hand, firmly held Eiric's upper arm. Eiric withdrew slightly at the touch, eyebrows raised, setting his attention on Jimmy.

'Need a few moments alone with Horse,' said Jimmy, though in truth, he needed time to consider his abandonment of Gurley, the plunge he had taken into the unknown, the precarious position of Horse, the welfare of Angus' boys – so many people affected by this one decision, so many lives diverted. The risks seemed to be mounting, threats beyond his control.

Eiric watched him, an innocence, a naïveté that amazed Jimmy.

'Give us a few minutes.'

Eiric nodded his head. 'Righty-o,' he said and turned, calling, 'I'll get Joe. See you back here in thirty,' as he strode across the yard to the hall.

Jimmy, silent, looked at the tall, youthful boy, a man now in a fresh uniform, with little to justify, redress or explain. Maybe he should saddle Horse now, ride south, join Gurley. It would be a release, evaporation, a merging with the bush, back to the dreamtime of his people. He could join Uncle Henry, survive on his knowledge of the land, go west into the flat, dry country, roam from waterhole to wetland and hallowed ground with Gurley.

Those places need protection too. It was a responsibility he couldn't ignore.

Jimmy swung open the stable door, stepped inside, inhaled the warm, humid smells: hay, horses, dry timber, a foundation for the senses, the sweep of a broom across life's distortions. At the rear, amongst the stalls, he took up a brush and bucket, unlatched Horse's gate, stepped inside, gently running hands across his friend's withers, over the shoulder, ribs and flank. He stood for a moment watching the light trembling of the skin and felt Horse's eyes upon him.

'We're away tomorra,' he said. A slight shuffle of legs and hooves from Horse at the sound of Jimmy's voice.

'Head'n south to Sydney, Melbourne ... you gotta go by truck.' Horse bent his neck around to look directly at Jimmy, knowing eyes.

'Y'know already?'

Jimmy looked up at his friend, nodded.

'Might 'a known ... y'been talk'n to Tuppence over there.' Jimmy laughed. 'Reckon y'know then we're off to Palestine.'

Silence, except for the shuffle of other horses.

'Might be better to head off bush, instead ... consider'n the danger we might be in.'

Horse continued his stare at Jimmy.

As Jimmy contemplated Horse's response, the stable door, the sound of rusty hinges, crept into the stables; covert, stealthy, light footfall. Jimmy could sense big; guessed a man. Jimmy signalled for Horse to remain quiet, stepped close to the stall door.

Silence.

Then, a breath, exhaled in frustration, and a familiar odour.

'Know yer in here!'

Jimmy remained silent, looked at Horse, held a finger to his mouth. *Quiet*!

Chances were that Strepford would give up, maybe think that Jimmy had only been here briefly, be interrupted by Eiric and Joe as they arrived. It was not the time for a fight. He'd be beaten to a pulp by that giant.

Steps closer now.

From across the hall, Jimmy had seen them, two men talking: the officer, a short, plump grazier, soft, well-fed; and Strepford, a sergeant, tall, solid as a tree, with greasy, black, thinning hair; the image of a cruel bastard, the wound on his face now a livid red scar and which reminded Jimmy of how lucky he had been.

'Y'know I'll get ya!'

Would he work his way to him, stall by stall?

As footsteps approached, Jimmy heard once again the shriek of the door hinges, the cheerful chatter of men, the slam of the stable door, hesitant shuffle of feet, finally footsteps receding, the slam of the door once again. Jimmy emerged from his sanctuary.

Eiric and Joe radiated excitement.

'Off, tomorra!' said Joe. 'We'll be in Palestine before you know it, in amongst it!' He hurried away to his mount.

Jimmy looked at Eiric, at the eagerness; and read only innocent courage.

'Better look after y'horse if we're move'n,' he said.

Eiric looked at Joe intent upon his task, a horse peering eagerly over the stall gate. It seemed that Eiric wanted to talk, perhaps to bolster his nerve, the grit he instinctively sought. Jimmy stood, mute, really just wanting to return to his conversation with Horse.

'Already brushed Tuppence twice today,' said Eiric.

'Well, there's your gear. That needs oil'n.'

'Yeah, done that as ...'

The shriek of hinges.

A shout.

A huge mass careered through the door, staggering like a deformed crab, disjointed arms, legs seeking purchase against the door, walls, the ground.

'You toe rags get your arses off to parade,' said Strepford, bared teeth, face red. Jimmy could smell the sour breath, a mixture of beer, spirits, and corroding teeth.

Startled, Eiric backed up, almost tripped over Jimmy, steadied.

Jimmy stepped forward. *Where was this going to take them?*

'Yes, Sergeant.' Jimmy wasn't sure who said that.

''Cept for the black cunt.'

Jimmy knew his time was short, what was in the balance, how things would play out now with this thug, a brutal bully, just an opportunist who knew the best way to curry favour, how to secure a link to power, how to ensure survival while minimising risk to himself. Strepford regarded this as the best place to even the score.

Without looking at Strepford, Jimmy attempted to step further forward, felt an elbow against his chest, strident but muffled words, a push in the back; and he was through the doors, flanked by Eiric and Joe, hurrying away from the slam of the timber barrier.

'Jimmy!' Eiric's voice filtered through the fog.

Jimmy thought of the people he had saved from this animal. The poor girl who had suffered from Strepford's beatings, Uncle Henry, Cara and Gurley, all vulnerable to pitiless whims. Did he have the right to expose them to such destructive powers? Did his abandonment of them make things worse? Would his enlistment save them from the worst? Should he elect a servile path and submit to the notions of the army and this whitefella war?

'What in God's name was that about?' said Eiric.

'Another life,' said Jimmy.

Another life, Jimmy thought. *Another way to save them all, another purpose, acceptance of another path to a destiny he could not sense.*

The army, he resolved, would be his home, for now; the boys his responsibility.

14

Melbourne

Summer, Early 1917

Jimmy took the duffle from Joe, looked at the crowd on the wharf as he turned: woollen uniforms; men, rifles slung about shoulders; a sprinkling of women, long, white dresses, large lacy hats; excitement; laughter. *Hysterical,* he thought, *maudlin demonstrations of self-pity, the dread of impending loss.* It towered above them: a pulsating steel cliff, balustrade set at its summit, teeming with a horde of khaki-clad soldiers; *HMAS Commonwealth* paraded in huge letters at the bow; the bay, sparkling water, all wreathed in acrid smoke from the ship's funnel.

'Need to get the horses through this mob,' he said, a shout above the din of the crowd.

'No, they're taking them to the rear loading. Away from the crowd,' said Eiric.

Jimmy felt a flush of concern, pushed it aside. Experienced handlers, safe, and yet …

'Yeah, let's get onta this thing.' He was in a hurry now. Horse needed support despite all their reassuring natters. He looked to the edge of the crowded dock, at the dockside hands preparing to cast off the myriad lines tethering the ship to the quay. 'Never been on a boat before.'

'Me neither,' said Joe. 'Least, not one this size.'

'How do y'get up there?' Jimmy said, pointing skyward, to the gallery bursting with noisy men, some waving, others singing.

'Don't know whether I want to.' Joe winked at Jimmy, his attention now fixed on a young woman, long flowing dress, elegant, white hat ruffled by a gentle sea breeze, excited, cheeks aflame with the fervour of the farewell. Jimmy followed Joe's gaze, an ogle really, saw instead the approach of an officer accompanied by a stocky Sergeant.

'You lot follow me,' said the Lieutenant. 'And be quick about it. You're late, and the boat's ready to cast off.'

'What about me 'orse?' Jimmy wouldn't be comfortable until Horse was located.

'Your mounts are already loaded, just you lot now.'

As they skirted the multitude of well-wishers, laden with their gear, Jimmy saw a mixture of elation, hope, and distress in the upturned faces. He saw well-dressed men, he imagined, from the ranks of Melbourne's influential, clustered together in earnest conversation; sombre, elderly matrons looking distractedly into the distance as if they had seen all this before; plump wives, mothers blinking away their concern, distress, fear of the unknown, children running riot amongst the legs of the crowd, fuelled by the excitement of the farewell. Close to the gangway, a solemn group of aboriginal people stood together, watching, silent. As Jimmy passed them, one of the women locked eyes with him, acknowledged him with a slight smile, fleeting, passed by in the rush to the ship's passageway.

From the top of the ramp, Jimmy glanced back to the wharf, saw armed soldiers pressing the small clutch of people away, forcing them back from the crowded platform, the woman almost falling under the weight of the crush. Jimmy felt alarm strike through his chest, down into his guts. Those people were his people, black, lost in a whitefellas' realm. *Were Gurley and his family now suffering similar handling*, he thought. The events on the dock were abruptly obscured by the throng of onboard soldiers. He reluctantly turned to follow Joe and Eiric and the sturdy Sergeant.

Joe got to the hatch first, stepped carefully through, head immediately disappearing downward, into the bowels of the throbbing steel monster. Jimmy felt fear, genuine, mind-blanking fear, for the first time in his life. He was not afraid of imminent war, the chance he might be maimed, or the possibility of death; he feared the stretching of his ties, the breaking of the bonds that held him to his land, the land of his people. Would the souls that had accompanied him for so long, had given him support, nourished him through the Kamilaroi lands, find him in Palestine? Was he now alone, irreversibly separated from every important person, place, his lifeblood?

Eiric turned to Jimmy as they descended the narrow stairway, his face clouding with concern. He tried some encouragement; Jimmy almost didn't hear him.

'More than three weeks to Suez in this old bucket,' said Eiric, smiling. 'Plenty of time to lounge about, enjoy the fine sea air.'

Jimmy, mute, looked skeptically at Eiric. He had never seen the sea before, far less been on it. Jimmy sucked air through his teeth, shook his head. He couldn't utter any words just yet.

Jimmy looked at Eiric, at Joe, he wet dry lips with his tongue; they were dry, really dry. He was more nervous than he had realised; the scene on the wharf had shaken his balance. Finally, he said, 'Where the horses at, then?'

Eiric laughed, a gentle chuckle. 'Down in the hold, most stable part of the boat.'

'Let's go, then.'

'Turn left,' said the Sergeant from the rear.

'Reckon we should stow this gear first,' said Eiric, hefting the weight that pressed into his shoulders. 'Our horses'll have to wait.'

The beautiful horses they had brought with them would have to wait; hardworking Walers, sturdy, determined, perceptive to their needs, keen to please, yet unwilling to take any shit.

Who was watching over Horse? Certainly, no one who understood him, no one who would settle him properly in these surrounds. Horse hadn't been to sea, either. What had Horse said? *He couldn't see anything, the future veiled in a thick haze, nothing to predict, no discernible end.*

'Turn left, again,' said the Sergeant, louder this time. They immediately entered a long room crowded with double bunks and a rowdy mob of soldiers. 'To the end, the last three are yours.' Jimmy turned to thank the Sergeant – he was already gone.

'We're near the shithouse,' said Joe. 'Not far to go when this army tucker gets hold of y'arse.'

'Yeah, but we get the smell of all the shit as well.' Eiric was unimpressed.

'I'm off t'see Horse,' Jimmy said as he dumped his load of gear onto the bed, turned and walked towards the nearest doorway.

'You don't know where he is!' Eiric said.

'Can't be far ... probably down from here?' He strode away, stooped through the nearest low entrance, found a ladder running down to the entrails of the ship: dark, the smell of oil, grease, heat, cloying heat that drew the air from your lungs, the source of the giant that shook the hull closer now, the clank, rattle and clang ringing from the steel walls. *What sort of hell*, Jimmy thought, *had he brought Horse to? He remembered again, the Sunday sermons that promised hellfire, wondered if he had reached that objective: A place with no return, of eternal torment.*

Jimmy stopped at a closed hatch; no other available avenues, only forward or back. He felt Eiric behind, close, laboured breath in the thick air. Jimmy glanced at him.

'Tuppence ...' said Eiric. There was no need for explanation.

'Don't know where we are,' said Jimmy, smiling. 'Might be hell behind this door.'

'Only one way to find out.' Eiric tried to reach around Jimmy, fingers stretching for the lever that bound the door to the wall.

Jimmy quickly moved forward, swung his weight onto the latch, applied all of his strength to hauling the heavy steel door towards them; hinges groaned, a deathly shriek, the door swung, a blast of cool air threatened to push them backwards. They stepped over the threshold.

'Shut the fucking door!' Two men at the end of a long hall glanced up, the third stepping towards them, irritation turning to anger as he grabbed the door, slamming it shut. 'Let that shit in here, and the horses'll get sick.'

Without looking at the man, Jimmy hurried forward to the

hay-strewn stalls that held the myriad horses, desperately searching for his friend.

They had reached the mother lode, the residence of their companions, light, clear air filtering unabated into the clean, cheerful space.

*

Jimmy knew what side land lay despite its withdrawal below the horizon, what route they were taking from the eastern shores of the continent, through the Bight to Albany in the west, how many men were packed onto this shaking, swaying, sleepless, iron vessel, a torture to the senses day and night, a prison for body and mind, a blind against the ties he felt stretched, strained to breaking, thin, frail, waning with each day on the ocean, tempered only by the love of his friend and his obligation to the boys.

Horse was not happy, never quite able to secure his balance against the writhing, twisting swell, forever closeted in the bowels of the steel monster. Jimmy felt a pang of guilt, a shame that he had led his friend to this place, so far from familiar pastures. It occupied his thoughts, consumed him in the quiet moments between drills and the care of kit and weapons. Horse once again showed his discontent.

'Yeah, I know,' said Jimmy. 'What can I do?'

Horse watched him silently.

'They won't let me take you up on deck!'

A long pause; Jimmy shook his head.

'Y'wouldn't like it up there anyway.' Jimmy once again raised the brush to Horse's back – the coat surely sparkled. 'Just water, as far as y'can see ... and masses of bloody gulls.'

Horse was not convinced. *How could he be*, Jimmy thought, *without seeing it for himself?'*

Jimmy thought of the people he'd left behind. Gurley's arrival at Kempton, had she been appropriately treated by the old man? Did she, Cara and the rest have the protection that was promised? Was his bargain with Angus, honoured? Was there a government man, right now, pulling his family apart?

'Time for a turn on deck,' said Eiric, head appearing over the stall wall. 'Sea air, sunshine, like a holiday, eh?'

Jimmy looked curiously at Eiric. 'Holiday? Yeah, heard about them ... never had one.'

'Well, here's y'chance.'

Jolly, cheerful music greeted them as they stepped through the aft hatch into the bright sunshine, a stiff breeze buffeting them from the south, the dank smell from the hull instantly displaced by a strong, salty bouquet carried on a fine spray. The ship plunged and rolled across a slight swell, the strains of the band carried aft with the breeze.

'That's a good song,' Eiric said, shouting above the music and the wind. '*Over There*, great tune!'

Jimmy turned his attention to the horizon. On the port side, another larger ship was dipping through the small swell, sending sheets of spray back from the bow; it seemed to be wallowing in the conditions.

'Reckon I'll find me a cuppa,' Jimmy said.

The music soared, the new tune a strident, brass band version of *Take Me Back to Dear Old Blighty*. Eiric seemed pleased at the selection.

'Of course, we could be stuck in Albany for a while,' Eiric said.

'Why, y'reckon they won't need us in Palestine, yet?'

'Nah ...' Eiric lifted an arm, pointing to the south-west.

Jimmy followed his signal.

'Weather front coming in.'

'Shit! What does that mean?' said Jimmy.

'Some rough sailing, I reckon. Maybe a chunder or two.'

The band, fighting against a stiffening breeze that carried away the sound, had switched to a jauntier tune.

'Ah, *Smiles and Chuckles*,' said Eiric as he bobbed with the music.

'The horses?' Jimmy looked towards the hatchway.

'Plenty of time to see to them.' Eiric was bent on enjoying the weather and the music. 'Hours, I reckon, before the front gets here.'

Jimmy felt anxious, such nonchalance wouldn't help an already struggling Horse. He needed to deliver a warning, secure his friend, ensure the safety of them all. He turned to Eiric, raised eyebrows in question. 'Time for a cuppa?'

Eiric smiled, nodded. 'Yeah.'

'A quick one, then.'

The first of the weather change preceded the actual front. While Jimmy enjoyed a drink, the pitch and roll of the accompanying boat grew, spray sheeting over its bow. He looked forward, realised they were also beating into a stiffening breeze, the ship dipping sharply in a shortening, intensifying swell.

Then the band were packing away their instruments, the decks suddenly thinning of the basking men, the air with a sudden chill;

still, the sun shone brightly, the bank, a wall of clouds to the south, only a distant menace.

Jimmy stood, looked south to the horizon, felt uneasy. He couldn't define any immediate threat but wished he were on familiar ground, any ground rather than this ever-moving, seething mass of water. He couldn't suppress a deep distrust of this metal contraption they were bound to, constantly fearing for the life he had committed to this strange power.

The noise of the wind rushed about his ears. It was a wind now, not just a breeze.

'Makes y'wonder, doesn't it?' Jimmy said, low voice, almost to himself, as he gazed at the horizon.

'What's that, Jimmy?' Eiric raised his eyes, turning towards the source of Jimmy's worry.

'Demons ...'

'What?'

'The demons in those clouds.' Jimmy, musing, pinched his nose absently, between fingers and thumb.

'What?' Eiric looked directly at Jimmy.

'Do y'reckon they've got it in fer us?'

'It's just a weather change, Jimmy.' Eiric frowned, a cloud of concern passing over his face. 'We'll probably be in the harbour before it gets here.'

Both men stood for a moment, eyes fixed to the horizon. A flash, forked, ephemeral, brilliant, passed across the distant cloud bank. Jimmy turned on his heel, headed directly to the ladder that led into the ship's guts.

'Y'come'n?' he said. 'They need us.'

*

The first shuddering crash pushed them sidelong into the bulkhead. It came as the ship slewed against the deepening swell, a giant wave that attempted to breach the flimsy barricade, watery fingers feeling for the entrails of their fragile haven. In the ghostly light of the hold, Jimmy saw the panic of the horses, felt his own despair mirrored in the eyes of his friend.

A crash!

Another.

It was bone-jarring.

The boat swerved again, into the path of another giant water wall.

The bangs, thundering now through the hull, were almost continuous, every minute filled with echoing aftershocks. The lights almost extinguished with one mind-numbing boom; an explosion that left him disoriented. Jimmy wondered how the horses could survive in this sound-saturated hell.

They had done what they could to secure the horses, every minute until the storm hit, reducing the stall widths and lengths, pressing the animals tightly to prevent panicked movement, broken bones, destruction. Horse had complained, wanted out of the place, any account Jimmy gave of their predicament falling on deaf ears. Horse just wanted out of there!

He hadn't been a decent friend to Horse.

He hadn't done the right thing by his family either. He'd neglected to appreciate the path they were to follow, the distress that his action would invent. He wasn't ready for the upheaval, much less this discord. He made decisions, committed those he loved, went to war. Gurley had little choice, did the mother thing, worried about the kid, family. He had left, vague acknowledgement of Gurley, set off, ridden away, concerned more with Angus, Kempton, the boys. How could he have done that?

Midnight, the storm unabated, and another unbelievable roll of the ship. Jimmy thought the horses would tip from their stalls; the pitch of the deck was so steep. Tied to the ladder rail, he thought he was still going to fall to the roof. When would this stop?

Jimmy glanced upward, to the closed cargo hatch, the open deck above. A waterfall leapt from the allegedly sealed edges, huge volumes cascading onto the deck, dousing some of the horses, and Eiric, strapped tightly to one of the stall's supports, hit by a wad of foaming fluid.

Shit!

They were sinking!

'Demons! I told y'so,' shouted Jimmy.

'Gotta end soon,' said Eiric. 'It's been going for hours.'

'Not 'til they've had their fun with us.'

Larry, one of the horse handlers, a skinny little bloke, strapper from the Randwick racecourse in Sydney, poked his head around Eiric's left shoulder. 'Done this trip b'fore,' he said. 'Seldom lasts more than twelve hours.'

'Shit, how much more then!'

More water drenched Eiric and the strapper. Eiric shook the water from his hair and coughed.

'Couple hours maybe.' The strapper smiled.

'What about all this water?' Jimmy could taste the salt from the ocean as it swilled about the deck, carrying drifts of loose straw from one side of the boat to the other. Jimmy felt queasy.

'Waves break'n over the deck,' said Larry.

'Yeah ... but are we sink'n?'

Another crash. Was there less power in that strike?

The boat shuddered under the impact of a following wave. Perhaps not.

More water.

'The pumps'll keep the water from gett'n too high.'

Jimmy was about to say he hoped the bloody pumps were reliable when he felt a swoosh of air to the side, turned to see, the world evaporated, and black enveloped him.

*

A faint breeze wafted across his face. One eye open, then the other, bright light. He closed his eyes again. Sounds, not the crash of the waves against the hull, firm land, it had all been a dream? He opened his eyes, sunshine, the light salt aroma of the ocean. He was still aboard the ship? An officer, medical, bent over him, casting a shadow across his face.

'You've got a hard head.'

Jimmy attempted to sit up, fell back onto the stretcher. 'Uncle always said I did.'

'Slight laceration, stitched, bandaged, for now, should heal pretty quickly.' The officer peered at Jimmy. 'We'll get it seen to again when we dock.'

Jimmy carefully swung his legs over the side of the bed, saw a sunny deck crowded with soldiers, a jostling mass peering over the starboard rail.

'We're almost ready to dock,' said Joe.

'How's Horse?'

'Fine,' said Joe. 'Eiric says he's a bit grumpy, though.'

'Where were you in that storm? Didn't see hide nor hair of ya.'

Joe smiled. 'Wasn't fool'n around with the horses.'

'Y'should 'a been help'n.' Jimmy raised his hand to the dressing on the side of his head.

'And get hit with flying shit, like you were?' Joe's grin broadened. 'I strapped myself to the bunk. Safest place.'

A bump, a cheer from soldiers at the rail, a slight slewing of the ship as it sidled to a stop at the Albany wharf.

Jimmy raised his head, watched as Joe joined the men at the handrail: *Maybe the boys would be better without him.*

Sitting back, light headed, a tightening in his guts, he realised in the deepest part of himself that, regardless of his doubts, there was no escape, no turning back, the die had been cast, their fates were now irreversibly entangled in the fortunes of a foreign war.

He stood, a slight tremor in his legs, joining Joe at the rail, his first sight of a new land, the country of the Noongar, the Minang, the Koreng, the Pibelmen.

15

ALBANY

Summary, Early 1917

The line of buildings, a sparsely wooded hill, and smooth, pink, granite orbs bursting into the sunlight. The regimented line of soldiers, complete with uniform, packs, rifles, slouch hats, marched along the broad avenue that skirted King George Sound, bystanders crowding against the granite-lined curb. The town had paused to gawp.

Joe, the soldier now, parading, trudging, boots hurting, talking obliquely to Jimmy, 'Reckon we'll get some time off in town after this parade?'

The metallic airs of the band, forced now into ordered servitude within the ranks, reverberated against the tall buildings, soldiers' voices rising above the cacophony:

We're horsemen from Australia of the good old British breed,
We rallied to the colours when we heard the Empire's need.

'The Major said *no*.' Jimmy had answered this question at least three times already.

The metronomic thump of the bass drum.

'We're back to the boat after this, packed off, heading out when the weather is right.' Eiric to his left, indulgence in his voice.

Joe looked to the side, beyond the soldier's ranks. 'Crikey! Would you look at that!'

Jimmy followed Joe's stare: a long, flowing, white dress, tight about the waist, a glimpse of ankle, the promise of shapely, inviting legs.

The music rose with a gust of wind, voices in concert.

For though we got it in the NEK, we'll fight with might and main,
To square our mates who took the count before us.

'Cute nose,' Joe said. 'And look at that chest.'

'Calm down, Joe.' Jimmy grinned, thought of Gurley, recalling their last hours at the *bora*, her agile frame, legs that rose forever, inviting his touch, demanding his caress, tribute to the last of their freedom and the first of his bondage.

The voices rose almost to a shout.

We are, we are …

The band was awkward now as it attempted to keep pace with the chorus.

We face the odds with ne'er a man afraid,
We lost our gallant comrades and there's many a score unpaid,
Undaunted still we're out for what's before us.

Joe continued to wallow in carnal desire.

'Yeah, but look at that!' Jimmy thought Joe was almost ready to break ranks. 'We could have some of that.'

As Jimmy prepared to break step, grab Joe's arm, hold him in the line, to save Joe from his ardour, a large hand reached from behind. The massive calloused paw fastened firmly over Joe's shoulder. 'Mind y'business, O'Sullivan, eyes front, we're head'n to Egypt, not the local brothel.'

Joe's eyes spun to the front, the Sergeant released his grip, Jimmy noting a slight smile on the mademoiselle's full, red lips.

Send the news to Kitchener, tell Birdwood with a snap,

Say that we Australian boys are busting for a scrap.

We want to tackle Germany and wipe her off the map,

Then toast our mates who took the count before us.

'Good thing we left that prick, Strepford, behind in Glen Innes with recruiting,' Eiric said from the side of his mouth. 'Reckon he would have beaten the shit out of you for even looking at that girl.'

They continued to march through the circle that would lead them back to the pier.

'Still, don't know why we can't have at least one night on the town.' Joe clearly wouldn't be convinced.

''Cause lame brains like you wouldn't turn up the next day, y'tosser.' Jimmy felt then, the enormity of the task: the restraint of Joe, the protection of the brothers, the safe reunion with Ted, responsibility for the preservation of lives other than his own amidst the bombs and bullets, among the promised carnal lures.

Joe said hopefully, 'They reckon Cairo is a great place to get y'end in.'

They continued the march around the loop that returned to their fate.

'Leave off, Joe. We've gotta get there yet.' Jimmy needed to quell this silliness. 'You saw how that bloody ocean tried to stop us get'n here.' He thought of the demons, their murderous intent, the warning they had set upon the ship.

'Nasty,' Eiric still wore the proof, a bruised shoulder; Jimmy a swollen forehead.

The column turned abruptly right; the brass band silent for a moment.

Jimmy realised the day was turning curiously dim, not just the afternoon lowering of the sun. Clouds were crowding against the tall, granite hills behind the town, another weather change, the promise of rain, even as summer approached. The weather seemed in constant flux in this place; warm, cloudless sky surrendering to cold, driving rain, it seemed, in an instant. He wondered how one could cope with such sudden change, then figured he wasn't one to talk; his life had hardly been constant.

He laughed.

'What?' Eiric looked at him sideways, smiling in response.

'Just think'n 'bout Cairo,' Jimmy said.

'What about?'

'How we're gunna keep *him* collared.' Jimmy inclined his head towards Joe.

'Yeah, like a barrel of monkeys.'

They both laughed, glanced at Joe who was leering at another attractive maiden, swung right again into a long, straight avenue, to the wharf, the transport, the bay, the ocean, to the genii awaiting release.

The band, the chorus – they swept away their wants, their fears, the monsters that shadowed them all – lifted their voices in a union.

We are, we are, the Light Horse Brigade.
We face the odds with ne'er a man afraid,
We lost our gallant comrades and there's many a score unpaid,
Undaunted still we're out for what's before us.

*

Jimmy watched from the stern as the land receded, inch by inch, below the horizon. He felt the tie that had been stretched to gossamer delicacy across the Bight reach its limit. In the days before leaving Albany, the weather had churned the ocean beyond the vast harbour to a seething, lumpy foam. Jimmy had tried to prepare Horse for the next part of the journey. Cramped, dark, close, Horse longed for open spaces, was promised release at journey's end. It was all Jimmy could do, an assurance he had no right to give, no idea where the odyssey would end, little understanding of the nascent trials.

In the gloom of the hold, Eiric said, 'He's got Tuppence.' Jimmy knew he was only trying to help. The remark amused him. Horse could hardly get close and personal in this place.

Horse glanced back at Jimmy, a clear invitation to talk. 'Someth'n up?' Jimmy said. 'Not happy?'

Jimmy looked to the stalls, the line of horses, most in a sort of stupor he recognised as misery. Not quite despair yet, but he feared losses before they reached Egypt. Only a few hours at sea and already stuff to put right!

'I'm coming with you,' Eiric said. 'If Tuppence isn't right ...' He let the words drift away, trailing behind as Jimmy headed towards his trapped friend.

'We'll see.' Deliberately abrupt, Jimmy wanted to concentrate on what Horse could tell him.

He leant over the stall barricade, Eiric's breath close to his ear.

Jimmy listened.

Silent.

He drew a deep breath, sniffed the close air about the sombre beasts, felt the squalid airs clustering about the stalls, heard the sad shuffle of hooves, the low bow of the head, the grumble, the protests unheard, unnoticed by the extant world. Fifteen days to Moascar! He was almost despondent himself.

'Horse says some aren't gunna make it.'

'Who?' asked Eiric; alarm, not yet panic. 'Who's not going to make it?'

Jimmy breathed in again, deeper this time, holding the scent within his lungs, closing his eyes, searching his memory for the message it held, for the conviction he needed. He saw clear skies, brilliant sunshine reflected from dry walls of sand, horses lying still against the parched ground, dark, sluggish rivers attended by swarms of tiny, black insects flowing from beneath the prostrate forms, a deep cloud, black, putrid, drifting slowly overhead.

'Tuppence …' said Jimmy. 'Horse.'

The images shimmered and died.

His eyes seemed to burn, an arcane wound that coiled about the back of his eyes, spread its tendrils into his head, tightening until they hurt.

Eyes open.

'They're all right … for now.'

Jimmy didn't know about the rest of them, not really, not so he could tell Eiric the details. He felt their misery, understood the knife-edge of their temper, guessed the rest.

He turned to Eiric. 'Some of the others. They're just gunna give up.'

'Before Moascar?' Eiric looked at Jimmy, questions in his eyes.

'Yeah.' What more could Jimmy say? He couldn't declare that he had seen a glimpse of their future, their own despair in an alien landscape, the ending. He wasn't sure.

'Horse says, leave it to him, he'll try and get 'em through; keep 'em go'n.'

Jimmy stood mute for a moment, trying to disengage from the vision.

'I'm gunna go, have a cuppa on deck,' he said, turning abruptly, walking away towards the main hatch to the hold.

They went the short way. An officer, shirtless in the muggy heat, waved at them, doubtless wanting help with some task. They ignored him, climbing eventually through a narrow door in the bulkhead, onto a calm, flat deck, the heat of the steel plate burning, despite their thick army boots. A gathering of men beneath an improvised canvas shelter pointed the way forward to the midpoint of the deck, to the heady, tangy, slightly acrid smell of brewing tea. Beside the boiling pot of water, Joe stood. Beyond the tight group, the ocean stretched, oily, flat, limp, almost steaming under the baking sun, all the way to the horizon; not a breath of wind, the ship cutting a neat opening through the flaccid water.

The ship was a tiny, throbbing, steel island.

Joe gave Jimmy a tin mug full of black liquid, another to Eiric. He was sipping at the edge of the hot drink when Joe leaned sideways from the cluster of men who were stripped to the waist against the baking heat. 'Shooting practice this arvo,' Joe said.

'Shoot'n?' Jimmy said. 'At what?'

'Target.' Joe straightened, smiled, pointed. 'Off the back of the boat.'

'What at?' Jimmy couldn't see the sense of it. 'At fish?'

'No! Dragging a target,' Joe said. Jimmy and Eiric examined him intensely. 'Major says because the sea is so calm, it's a good time.'

Jimmy shook his head. A hold full of ailing horses and they wanted to take pot-shots at a target in the middle of the ocean.

'Major says, the first six to hit the bullseye are first up for leave when we get to Moascar.' Joe grinned. 'That's going to be me, into Cairo.' The grin broadened.

'Can't do it. Gotta see to the horses.' Jimmy couldn't see the sense of it, but most of what the whitefella did fell outside sense.

'No exceptions, Jimmy,' said Joe. 'Major says everyone.'

A yell from the sterncastle turned every head. 'Get y'hats on.' A Sergeant strode across the deck hefting a cartridge box on the shoulder. 'We're hav'n some shoot'n practice.'

Jimmy reckoned he would have to submit to more whitefella lunacy.

They all crowded to the stern rail where a large target buoy, tethered to the ship with a stout steel cable, rode calmly between twin wakes.

'Bloody hell,' said Joe. 'That's hardly a challenge.'

'What? A hundred yards off the ship!' said a thin, gangling trooper, scrawny chest exposed above khaki trousers. 'We'll never hit the bloody thing.'

'Just aim and shoot, Slapper.' Joe oozed confidence.

'Bang, bang, shoot, shoot.' Slapper was all smiles.

'Might go first,' said Joe. 'Get it over and done with.'

Joe started to move forward towards the rail. A hand checked him. He looked to the side, Jimmy shook his head slowly, pulled him back, whispering in his ear. 'Wait.'

A squat sergeant pushed through the milling mob, the cartridge box, two rifles now held aloft by an eager corporal as he swept in behind.

Eiric said, 'Looks like we don't get to choose weapons.'

Jimmy stood, mute for a moment until he nodded his head.

'Reckon there's someth'n fishy 'bout this,' said Jimmy, almost under his breath.

'What?' said Joe. 'What do you mean, 'fishy'?'

'Dunno ...' His eyes never left his inspection of the proceedings. 'Yet ...'

'Right! Who's tak'n the first shot?' There was a clamour of eager shouts, arms, waving hands. Everyone wanted to be the first to the fabled delights of Cairo.

A big soldier, ruddy-faced, curly, sandy hair used his bulk to push forward, grab the gun from the corporal's grip, point the weapon at the target, pull the trigger.

Nothing.

'All right, Sunshine, not loaded yet,' said the Sergeant with a gloating smile. 'That's your turn.'

The crowd erupted in protest. No one saw that outcome as fair.

'All right! All right!' The Sergeant had to bellow to be heard. 'Each one of ya gets one round ... that's all. And the first six to hit the bullseye gets on the list, first to Cairo when we dock.'

The noise from the crowd continued unabated. The stakes were confirmed.

The Sergeant continued to shout. 'That's all. Them's the rules. Take it or leave it. And the corporal here will confirm your shot with the spyglass he's got.'

The beefy oaf held his hand out for his one chance.

'Now, form a queue. Now!'

Jimmy moved swiftly, staking his claim to fourth in line, pulling Joe and Eiric with him. 'Right,' he said, again discretely so only Eiric and Joe could hear him over the uproar. 'Watch the first three, where their shots go. I reckon they've doctored the sights on the gun.'

The line behind them snaked about the deck, men pushing, shoving, laughing.

'Make sure you hit the fucking bullseye. I don't want to go to Cairo by myself.' Jimmy smiled. Eiric and Joe were crack shots, though Joe could be impulsive, overconfident. 'Take y'time. There's no wind, just the buggered-up sights.'

Jimmy watched the first shot closely. The crack, the recoil, the exclamation.

'Shit!'

Silence. Every man waited silently for the verdict.

'Did y'see that?' whispered Jimmy.

'Yeah,' said Joe. 'To the right about five yards and down, into the water.'

'No wind,' said Jimmy absently.

'And Coops is a good shot too.'

'That's what he reckoned too.' Jimmy reinforced the lesson. 'Take y'time.'

'Missed the target completely,' the corporal said. The Sergeant grinned.

The second shooter stepped forward, more caution this time.

'Murph's a good shot too,' said Joe. 'He won't be fooled.'

Silence in the crowd.

Murph slowly aimed the rifle, stood still for a moment, legs braced, fired.

The noise of the multitude abruptly returned.

'Lower left of the target, outer ring!' The corporal shouted above the noise. Murph left the spotlight, shaking his head, clearly disappointed.

The third man was unknown to Jimmy or the boys; he hurried the shot; it went far wide of the target.

Jimmy closed his fingers about the forestock of the 303. He hefted the rifle several times to familiarise his fingers, hands, arms, to gauge its weight distribution. Every gun differed in subtle ways, a stock longer, the heel wider, the forestock smoother or rougher than others.

Hand out, bullet delivered, Jimmy carefully placed the long cartridge into the ejection port, rammed the bolt home, nestled the stock against the union of his shoulder and arm, exhaled.

He preferred lighter arms; the Martini single shot his favoured weapon, quick to load, accurate, deadly. Though his days at Kempton rarely required its use, he accepted his shooter's craft, was acknowledged as skilled, was counted upon to deliver the cut, expected to do it clinically and clean.

He exhaled.

'Get on with it, mate.' The Sergeant wanted to move on to the next hapless shooter.

Jimmy heard nothing, aiming high, calculating the error in the weapon, finger squeezing lightly on the trigger.

The butt slammed back into Jimmy's shoulder; he smelled the bitter odour, the gritty taste of the gunpowder. Jimmy became dimly aware of someone yelling at him, glanced to the side as he lowered the rifle. The Sergeant.

'Move back! Next!'

Jimmy wondered at the error – how could he have missed the target? It dawned on him that he was perhaps mistaken, that his confidence was his undoing.

Silence. The crowd, almost to a man, were focused on the result.

A moment passed as the corporal fixed his attention to the binocular. Jimmy turned to go. He would have to be content with time at their Moascar camp. The boys would enjoy Cairo without him.

'A bloody bullseye!' The corporal's shout revealed his disbelief, the Sergeant scowled.

'Right'yo, right'yo, you bastards!' said the Sergeant. Jimmy retreated amidst a deluge of back slaps and envious comments.

He passed Joe and whispered, 'Aim for eleven.' Joe nodded, bent close to Eiric.

He heard the Sergeant, restored to his martial spirit, say, 'Next! Youse won't all be that lucky.' He knew though, that luck had not determined the result, looked across the flat ocean to the south, decided that not all the powers following him were malevolent.

As Jimmy strolled back to the tea urn, he heard the crack of another shot, the cheer of the crowd, then another discharge, followed by thinner praise, the mob now realising that their chances of liberation were shortening.

He filled his cup with strong, black, bitter tea. He heard Eiric and Joe behind him, and hoped they would not be deserted by the attending benevolent spirits.

16

The Present Day

A dark-skinned woman, middle years, bright *salwar kameez*, walked with them from the boat, across the minimalist bamboo jetty onto the muddy bank, along a dusty pathway, raised above the boggy remnant of the last tide. She waved her arms, left, right, forward, talking hurriedly, earnestly, to Anika – Harry forgotten flotsam in the wake of important matters.

Scanty structures, Harry guessed a village, lay beyond the tall, thin-stemmed palms, the ground littered with fallen trees, a tangle of vegetation, a small group of people lounging listlessly about a partly-collapsed building, the gable almost touching the ground at one end.

A man stood as they approached – adjusting his *lungi*, he walked forward tentatively to greet the women.

Harry stopped short of the conference, turning a circle to get a full view of this place. The strong, muddy smell at the water's edge was faint now, the area clean, neat despite the piles of tangled timber, mounds that formed a high wall, a barricade against the world perhaps, halfway to the village.

A noise diverted his attention to the edge of the clearing – like laughing, no … giggling, maybe children playing games just beyond sight, within the abruptly dense forest that formed a wall about its landward edge. *Funny*, he thought while looking about, *no children to be seen anywhere?*

Harry peered, fixed his gaze at the green cordon, straining to hear the noise.

There it was again! High-pitched – it had to be children?

'They're in the forest.' Anika's voice. Harry turned.

'What?' Why were the children in the forest?

'They pick off the rats that turn up looking for food after a storm.' Anika smiled. 'The villagers encourage them.'

Kids? Harry thought. *What sort of people would get their kids to go rat hunting?*

'Seems a bit like forced labour, doesn't it,' said Harry, 'getting your kids to hunt rats in the jungle?'

Anika stood silent for a moment, looking directly into Harry's eyes. Harry felt the intensity of her intellect. Suddenly she moved forward, touched his chest with the palm of her hand, laughing, a full, unabashed laugh that turned the villagers' eyes towards them.

Harry felt drawn to Anika's unashamed response, the captivating laugh. He smiled. 'What?'

'Not children, Harry.' She fought to control the laughter. 'It's the mongoose. Little grey things.'

'What?' Harry was hardly impressed by his own intellectual alacrity.

'Mongoose,' she said, emphasising the *mon*. 'Cute little furry animals that live in the jungle.'

'But I heard children giggling.'

'There aren't any children here, Harry. They were taken to relatives further up the river after the last cyclone.'

'So, the giggling was …'

'The mongoose, Harry. It's the breeding season now, in the dry. That's the sound they make.'

'No children, then?'

'No, you can see the devastation of the last cyclone. They haven't yet recovered.' Anika looked about her. 'And they probably won't, ever, unless we can get them the resources they need.'

'They should move away,' said Harry. 'Upriver, away from these exposed spots.'

'They've nowhere to go. No jobs, no room.' Harry could see the helplessness flood her eyes. 'And, anyway, this is *their* place. They have a right, a right to live in their traditional land.'

Harry stood silent. *Same as home*, he thought. *The first solution has always been to uproot, evict, relocate. Makes the problem go away, for a while, until the generations of dispossessed multiply, until the grief, the sorrow, the confusion overwhelms everyone.*

'So, what's the solution?'

'Give them a right, the ability to determine their own future.'

'Money?' Harry could feel the rise of scepticism.

'No!' Anika's legs were sturdy structures, feet firmly fastened to the ground. 'No, we help them get the education they need, the skills, the ability to make their own way in this ephemeral world. The next cyclone could mean they have no land.'

Harry could see the sense of Anika's argument, but he had seen how temporary land was in the delta, how inevitable sea-level rise would jeopardise any small gains Anika's NGO could facilitate.

'Here today, gone tomorrow, Anika.'

'What?' It was Anika's turn for erudition.

'They're living on borrowed time here.' He didn't want to invoke the dreaded global warming. 'Every year is going to be worse than the last.'

'Yes, I know, but doesn't that make it even more important that we give them enough independence to ride out inevitable change?'

Harry was silent. He couldn't deny Anika's passion had a firm footing in logic.

'Come and meet the head man,' she said, taking hold of his arm, gently tugging it towards the gathered crowd.

Harry felt uneasiness, the flush of anxiety that flooded through him whenever he was pulled from a familiar path. 'You don't need me in your deliberations.'

'They've asked to meet you.' She smiled again, that disarmingly slight tremor of her lips, the glimpse of regular, white teeth. 'And anyway, it would be rude to come to their village and not say *hello*.'

What's she been saying to them? he thought. *Likely trying to lock me into something with these people.*

The head man advanced from the gathering to meet Harry, bowing politely, words in Bangla. Anika stood still beside him, silent, hands clasped tightly before her. Harry had the feeling he had been introduced as someone important, a benefactor, a saviour perhaps. The man threw a hand in the direction of the fallen building, swung it in a wide arc to the tangled pile of vegetation, around to the rickety wharf, talking in the fluid tones of the Bengali language, finally turning to face Harry.

'You are asked to witness the destruction of their homes, their lives, their families. Taslim asks that you consider assisting their community with rebuilding their village,' Anika looked squarely at him, 'so they may have their children with them once again.'

The head man offered his hand. Harry took it. Then he shook hands with all the men in the small group. An awkward silence, he turned with Anika, walking uncomfortably towards the boat.

'You set me up,' he said, feeling the eyes of the head man drilling holes into his back.

'Yes, well, they need help,' she said. 'And you've got the resources to help.'

'Hung out to dry.'

'You need to make a commitment, Harry, one way or the other.'

Commitment! He had spent his life running.

'You mean, for us or against us.'

'Yes, pretty much.'

'You're single-minded, aren't you?'

'You knew that before you sailed down the river, Harry. What outcome did you expect with me?'

Outcome! Yes, what outcome did he expect? He wasn't short on self-deception, on delusion, on mistakes that lead him to expect, hope for more than was real.

The previous evening had been part of that illusion. Down the stairs – he saw it now as a pursuit, a hopeful step towards something new, a revival of a chance at renewal. She took him quietly, a fluid passion that he hadn't expected, a softness that belied a sharp mind, her blatant determination to achieve, create, disentangle the mess of an imperilled world, a softness that enveloped him, drew him into her, surrounded him, kept him so close, so close he resisted any removal. Maybe that was her secret? A moment stolen, an instant that couldn't be restored, revisited, repaid, a moment of respite from the intensity of her existence.

Harry saw it now, the parallel, the repetition, the circle that ensnared him, the pull of the same façades, the same motivations, the sadness that led him to seek the same solutions to his own shortcomings.

A short walk. They stepped aboard the boat.

'Shall I give you the details of what they need?' said Anika.

Harry, silent, walked to the bow of the boat. To deny her, would it be egregious, spiteful?

'How much?'

'A few million. I'll lay the plan out when we get back to Dhaka.'

Harry thought for a moment.

'I'll want control over the deployment and much of the organisation.'

'Much of it will be education, the kids; some the rebuilding.'

'What's the point of rebuilding?' asked Harry. A cynical note.

'Yes, I know, the next cyclone is likely to wipe it all out again, but we have to try.'

'There's technology,' Harry said. 'Cyclone-resistant material. We can get that stuff deployed.'

'So, you're in?'

A pause.

'Yeah, we're in, but I want control.'

Harry watched Anika's shoulders relax as the relief washed over her. A smile.

'Thought you might be pissed off,' she said. 'My little game over there.'

'Already decided.' His turn to smile. 'Before we even stepped ashore.'

'You're not saying I bribed you with my body, are you?'

'No. It's your passion for what's right. Your determination to do what's right, your sense of justice.'

'Magnetic, hey!' There was that laugh.

'Yeah, magnetic is not giving it justice.'

'So, a bit of dinner, then bed?'

Harry felt inclined to resist.

'What if I'd said no?'

'To dinner or me?'

'Neither, Anika.' He had to say it. 'To helping with these unfortunate people.'

'Shunned you would be,' she said, stepping forward, smiling again. 'Now, let's get to know each other better.'

Harry took hold of her, wrapped his arms about her shoulders, against the chill wind generated by the boat's progress. He doubted the sense in this. Was it a replay of past errors, another dead end, a commitment to the dissolution of his life?

Dhaka and his next move, he resolved, would be the pivotal point in solving the mystery of his life, his recurrent errors, the sadness that seemed to pervade everything.

17

Late Winter, Early 1917

They crossed the narrow street near a café – tables spilling out onto the street, men in long, white robes lounging languidly on cast-iron chairs, sipping thick, black liquid from surprisingly delicate glasses, eyeing the soldiers with suspicion.

Jimmy stood for a moment, within a recess, away from the rattle of carts, braying donkeys, and bickering language of the crowd that filled the narrow lane. He watched the collection of soldiers converge on a red, curtained entrance below a sign, in Arabic, a sketched wine glass, a reclining female form.

Joe leading, Jimmy walked cautiously at the rear, stopping outside the entrance, surveying the alleyway. He noted a cluster of idle men at the building's end.

Jimmy pushed through the dense, ruby-red curtain.

The racket of the carts and street sellers faded. Two lamps near the door projected a soft light across the carpeted quiet, with small, round tables sprinkled amongst lounges and ferns, Jimmy's eyes gradually adjusting after the glare from the road, perhaps a half dozen women, scantily clad, several moving languidly towards the newly arrived pack of men.

This was the place. The advice was accurate.

Jimmy walked towards the bar. His mouth was dry from the heat of the Cairo streets. 'Need a beer, Eiric,' he said from the back of the mob. 'A big one.'

A large mug emerged from the mob that crowded the counter, passed hand to hand overhead, small spills landing on shoulder and head. Jimmy grasped the beer, turned back to the dimly lit room, colliding with one of the scantily clad women. She recoiled, shoved backwards in Jimmy's haste to be clear of the crowd.

'Sorry, madam.' Jimmy didn't know what to say, or if he would be understood.

The woman examined Jimmy, eyes rimmed with a shadowed line, long lashes, wide, dark eyes set in a flawless, brown face, and a fine, pointed nose. Jimmy had never seen a woman quite like this one. *Woman?* he thought. *Couldn't be more than sixteen or seventeen.*

'Come with me,' she said, folding her arm about his waist. 'Comfortable seat over here.' A seductive delay on each word, curved mouth revealing ample red lips, excitement, willingness, desire. Arms shepherded Jimmy towards the lounge.

'Didn't take him long!' A jovial laugh from behind.

He chanced a quick glance behind, saw Joe and Eiric both grinning at him, two women reaching for them, intense focus upon their targets. Jimmy smiled, fate sealed, he reckoned he had the pick of the bunch.

Jimmy was pushed down onto the soft divan, his beer slopping as he suddenly dropped; there hadn't been a chance for more than a brief sip of the cool brew. His minder arrived with a light descent into the folds of the cushions, perching one leg above his knee, her shoulder forced beneath his arm. His fingers, almost losing their grip, recovered, brought the jug to his mouth. He wouldn't waste any more of the elusive draught.

Joe and Eiric appeared with consorts, falling into the opposing lounge.

'This is the right place, then,' said Joe, submitting to the entwining limbs of a tiny woman. 'Reckon we could spend the war here?'

'Y'might run out of the ready?' Eiric said, shifting his beer away from an energetic female.

'Mine's already told me how much,' said Joe.

'Jeezus, Joe.' Eiric, as always, seemed shocked by blunt revelations. 'You want to watch out.'

'Why?' Joe's attention was now on his escort.

''Cause they told us y'can catch some nasty things in Cairo.'

'Nah, these girls look good.'

'Y'gotta use the kit they gave us.'

'Yeah, yeah.' Joe's attention was now entirely on his damsel.

Jimmy drained the last of the beer, looked across at Joe, now fully absorbed, hands moving slowly over the body that seemed almost attached to him. Eiric looked uncomfortable.

'Time for another beer,' he said, starting to rise, was held back, the girl raising her arm. Beers promptly arrived. Jimmy felt time drifting away amidst the enticing comfort, the irresistible invitation, the captivating promise, a design to rival Gurley's allure.

Another beer materialised. Jimmy grasped the offered prize, sensed the soft body pressed against his side.

And lost count.

*

Jimmy became aware of a change in the mood of the room.

Joe's voice sounded urgent, insistent, complaining, distant. *Strange*, he thought, *Joe was so cheerful, full of anticipation, shameless, abandoned.*

He felt a slight waft of hot air onto his neck; a faint musty odour following the stream of air.

Eyes open now, he turned his head to the side, inhaling, testing, analysing the aroma.

A tiny figure lay sprawled, naked on the mattress beside him, sleeping. Or was she dead?

No!

She breathed.

More noise. Shouting this time.

Jimmy rose, grabbing his discarded garments and pulling on his boots, he drew back the loose curtain at the small room entrance, vaguely recalling in his thickened memory, his passage to this place, the beer, the invitation, the seduction.

A shadowy figure resolved as Jimmy's eyes adjusted to the gloom of the hallway. A big, loosely dressed man, ballooning trousers, silhouetted against a windowed door, hand aloft holding something.

Jimmy couldn't quite see.

A figure flew from the room to the right, a yell, taking the man at the hips, both men hurtling into the wall, arms, legs flailing. Jimmy saw, felt the shake of the walls, heard the strike of fists, feet, knees.

Jimmy started down the corridor. He heard Joe grunt as a fist connected with his gut. Two strides, Jimmy reached the fracas, hauled with all his strength at a collar, managed to move the hefty assailant's bulk, stamped brutally on the prone body.

More shouting now. Jimmy turned to see Eiric running towards him, one hand grasping at the top of loose trousers; behind him a crowd of determined men, the idle men, no longer shiftless, clearly intent on more purposeful business.

Jimmy bellowed, 'Run! Through the door behind yer!'

Joe levered himself from the floor, charged for the exit, keeping his head low, battering through the locked door with his shoulder. He collapsed, arms flailing, body tumbling, onto a rocky pavement, into a dingy, foul-smelling alleyway.

Jimmy followed closely – driving his thighs, legs burning like fire – took hold of Joe's shirt as he passed, hauling him towards the street, a busy thoroughfare, a sanctuary of sorts, where they could dilute any pursuit amid the bustling crowds.

Eiric came into his mind. No time to check. They had to move!

Donkeys, horses, carts, hawkers and bints, crammed the street, the relative calm of their arrival that afternoon overtaken by a lively nightlife.

He stopped. Where had the day gone?

Heavy breathing behind.

He turned.

Eiric, sprinting now, yelling, a high-pitched wail.

What was he saying? No time to consider. He hauled at Joe's collar. 'Get up!' He raced to the centre of the road, dodging barrows, ambling people; a horse shying as he stumbled past.

He stopped again and turned to face the pursuers. Eiric and Joe turned with him.

A stout, wooden pole in the ruffian's right hand swung as a threat. A short, determined swing; one, two, three; the dull thud of the weapon against the edge of the building. *What did these men want … money, sport, revenge?* Jimmy turned again; they needed to be clear of this place.

Four more men behind them, moving cautiously, stealthily, agile for big men. Jimmy tried to think of a way out. The men were slowly advancing, making guttural, animal sounds, encircling.

A knife – long, thin – a butcher's paring blade. They must be confident. No need to hide it.

Bloody Joe, thought Jimmy, *knives, batons, these bastards want to kill us.*

A smile slowly awakened the lips of the biggest of the hunters.

To Eiric and Joe, Jimmy said, 'Don't move, we might be safe in this crowd.'

He raised his arms, turned a full circle, registered the distribution of the assailants. Surveying the tightening circle, he opened his mouth wide, drawing in a deep breath.

And yelled.

He screamed until his lungs and throat hurt, yelled obscenities, roared out the battalion's marching song chorus, the name of every town he could remember, bawled *God Save the King*.

Madness. The crowded street paused; this was a lunatic from Allah knew where?

The tightening circle lingered.

Jimmy continued his tirade. The men looked quizzically at each other, the crowd about Jimmy thinned.

It seemed to Jimmy that his bid for a delay had failed. People along the thoroughfare flowed away from the three soldiers, now an island in a stream, isolated, vulnerable, an unobstructed target. The hunters gathered themselves, visibly shook off the uncertainty caused by Jimmy's screaming, bracing themselves for a final assault.

Jimmy remembered the cruel taunts, the beatings, the blind alleys of his childhood, nowhere to run, nowhere to hide, alone, exposed to elemental bigotries. Any similarities here though were unconcerned with shade, tint or hue. He could see they were purely financial, their obsession filthy lucre, their purpose its accumulation. The men surrounding them weren't bent upon teaching an inferior a lesson, or protecting a fraudulently acquired estate. They just wanted his money.

Simple, really, aided by the avenue's traffic as it thinned to almost nothing. Jimmy turned on the spot, a full circle, as he yelled. A crowd had built up at the circle's perimeter, eager faces anticipating a grisly show, Christians to the lions, gladiators at the Colosseum.

The largest of the men, the one Joe had tackled in the hallway, swung the stout pole, slapped it several times into his hand, took a step forward, a grim sneer exposing broken, discoloured teeth. The circle squeezed, Jimmy stopped his banshee howl, bracing his legs, arms, body for the onslaught, the beating, the knives, felt the shoulders of Eiric and Joe tense against his back.

Was this it, the end of his days?

Jimmy focused entirely upon the huge brute at the lead. Maybe there was a chance if he could flatten that bastard, and do it quickly, it would sap the resolve of the others; perhaps the only way to clear a way out of this cordon. They were close enough now.

He had to go on the offensive!

'Attack!' he said to his back.

He moved quickly, thrusting forward, baring his teeth, screaming so it seemed his tongue, throat, lungs, would beat him to his enemy; hands, fingers spread like claws. He noted an expression of surprise flooding the thug's face.

Maybe they still had a chance?

He ploughed wildly into the big one, his weight carrying that mass and several other bodies backwards, in an awkward, tumbling mess. The ominous pole made a clattering sound against the pavement as it landed, free from its malicious owner. Instinctively Jimmy beat away hands, arms that searched for him, that grasped at his face, encircled his legs. If they could pin him down, he knew it was lost.

He screamed again, renewed, increasing the violence of his kick, the tearing, clawing of his fingers. He balled his fists, smashing into soft flesh, hard bone, and felt something snap.

Release.

The pressure of the hands, the beating of the fist was suddenly still.

Jimmy rolled onto his back, quickly got to his feet, fists ready for a new, more determined onslaught.

He turned towards a familiar sound. It was a deep-throated, vibrating rumble, a chant, a mantra he recognised, a refrain from another conflict.

At a point, a tear had appeared in the solid ring of spectators. A mushrooming torrent of soldiers, recognisable despite their degrees of undress, flooded the circle's killing ground. They met the remainder of the brutish alliance, pushing, grappling, punching, kicking bodies as they fell, stamping on exposed limbs, finishing the murderous aspirations of Jimmy's assailants.

Jimmy stood, watching the end of their trial.

A thin, gangling trooper strolled over to him. 'Get y'self into a spot of bother, did yer?'

Jimmy took a deep breath. 'Slapper! Didn't think you would make it.'

Smile.

'Well, you made enough of a racket.' Another smile, a broad grin this time.

'Evil bastards chased us outta the bar,' said Jimmy.

'Yeah, heard the noise in the hallway. Interrupted me. Just go'n for the vinegar stroke.'

What could Jimmy say?

'Yeah, left a real cute one myself. Didn't have time for another go.'

'What happened, then?' said Slapper. 'I mean, why was they chas'n yer?'

Jimmy remembered then. He turned, scanned the street, prone bodies, blood running into the gutter from one prostrate form, searching, hoping that the boys were unharmed, unscathed after the brawl.

'Bloody Joe,' Jimmy said absently as he searched the street.

It took several sweeps to locate Eiric. Jimmy watched as he straightened from an examination of the prone, bent body of a thug, a worried expression as he walked quickly towards Jimmy, apparently unscathed.

Now, where was Joe?

Eiric arrived. 'Shit, Jimmy! That was close.'

'Where's Joe?'

Eiric pointed.

Bloody hell, Jimmy thought, *caused a bloody riot, now he's off picking up another fucking bint.*

18

CAIRO – EGYPT

Late Winter, Early 1917

Eyes feeling like buckets of gravel, Jimmy rolled onto his side. The stony orbs swilled pitilessly to the side, grinding mercilessly into the edge of his head.

What was the reason for this cruelty?

He forced his cemented eyelids open a fraction. Light streamed in. He slammed them shut.

Shit!

Jimmy lay still for a moment, struggling to remember.

A noise, close, the groaning of door hinges, metallic, echoing. A reverberating thud, the jangle of keys, shouting, obscenities, another thud, dull this time, followed by a grunt, the scraping of something dragged – like a sack of wheat.

Jimmy forced his eyes open, suffering the pain, its tendrils coursing through temples, into the brain, passing unopposed through the back of his head. He could see a wall, cancerous concrete, deep rust-red staining mingled with wet at the edges, eukaryotic green, slimy, musty, stinking.

He risked moving his head again. A stab of pain lanced through his neck.

The ceiling was the same – pitted, crumbling, foul water dripping from one dilapidated corner – a door, iron, small lattice window halfway up its length, a large, keyed latch.

Another clang, closer this time.

Jimmy rose on the narrow cot to sit, looked briefly at the bare, discoloured mattress, both hands clasping the sides of his head. He covered his eyes for a moment as he sought to orient himself, up versus down, the source of the light, the time of day, alive or dead, his very existence.

Survival would come next.

A moment more as he regained some focus, and he remembered …

Joe was determined to pursue his carnal desires. The local crowd was agitated still in the aftermath of the riot, though braver now with the departure of most of the soldiers. They watched skeptically as Joe blatantly fondled the merchandise.

'Haven't y'done enough damage, Joe?' said Jimmy.

'That bastard, he stopped me in mid-stroke,' Joe said, petulant.

'So? What was he do'n there anyway?'

'Stole my wallet …' Joe continued his examination. The woman – most of them were just girls – looked hesitantly at the dishevelled soldier. 'My strides. Left them near the door.'

'Bloody stupid!' Eiric had to comment.

'Yeah, well, I didn't want to wait.' Joe persisted with his inspection.

'Got y'wallet, then?' Jimmy's hand was now holding Joe's shoulder.

'Nah, we had to run,' said Joe. 'Can you lend me a few quid?

This one looks like she'll do.'

Jimmy looked at Joe, shook his head, exhaled loudly. 'No way.'

'Eiric? Pay you back at camp.' Eiric gave an exasperated huff.

Jimmy looked beyond Joe, over the diminutive girl, noticed a slight disturbance of the watching crowd, a shuffling sideways, a parting of the waters to make way for an irresistible force. The disruption of the spectator wall grew until there was a headlong rush to vacate ground.

'Nah, time to go,' said Jimmy.

'Why? She looks like a real goer.' Joe had not lost his focus.

'Cause, more trouble's here.' Jimmy now held Joe's shoulder in a tight grip, swung him around, shoved him headlong through the surrounding congregation. 'Com'n through the crowd now!'

'Fuck! Not now!' Joe tried to resist.

'Run!'

I'm making a habit of this, Jimmy thought.

Joe stumbled ahead, propelled by repeated shoves from Jimmy. Eiric would be close behind. They left the street, ducking desperately into a side alley. Jimmy stole a quick look at the riot scene where an enormous beast broke free from the crowd, arms, legs, thick as tree trunks – no doubt the minder, protector of the cashflow, overseer of the seduction-pit profits.

They ran recklessly, first left, then right, turning randomly, until the street din faded, the clatter of traffic muffled by dense, stone walls, the cobbled road narrowing to a gloomy, unlit alleyway.

'Where the hell are we?' Eiric's protest was almost stolen, muffled by the ancient brick.

Joe held to his protest. 'We could've waited!'

Jimmy stopped, pulled in a deep draft of air, almost choking on the stink. 'Did you see that huge bastard?'

'No, you were shoving me too hard.' Resentment.

'Well, he was gunna rip y'head off,' Jimmy said, 'seeing you already had y'hands in the store.'

Joe grinned. 'Can't blame me, interrupted like I was.'

'Your fault.' Jimmy wasn't going to be a panderer.

Joe started to protest again. 'That bastard ...'

'Where the hell are we?' Eiric said again, looking, as always, for Jimmy's guidance.

Jimmy couldn't see much. Grey brick walls seeped from the gloom, ill-defined in the dark, cut by thin shafts of feeble light that lanced downward to the path from shuttered windows high above. Clouds of tiny, black insects swarmed into the beams, the occasional, fluttering moth wandering through the light's lifeblood.

'How do we get back to camp from here?' Eiric was insistent.

'Be quiet!' said Jimmy.

Jimmy listened.

The scrabble of rats, the hum of the insect clouds, someone shouting, high above, a family argument perhaps – he could hear a woman's voice raised in protest – and the distant hum of traffic along the boulevard.

'I need a piss,' said Joe.

'Well, no one's stopping you.' Jimmy just wanted him quiet, occupied for a moment.

He waited, the only sound now the splatter of Joe's urine against the alley wall.

'Ah, that's a relief,' said Joe, 'I really needed a leak.'

'Shut up!' Jimmy needed to listen without background babble.

A waft of clean air brushed past him, a momentary relief from fetid air stagnating in the laneway.

'Rain coming,' he said reflectively. 'Not much, maybe a shower or two.'

More certain this time.

'No one following ...' Jimmy turned about. 'Reckon we'll find the road to camp this way.' He strode away, heading deeper into the labyrinth of lanes, paths and passages.

'Gotta hurry,' he said, though he knew they had missed the last ride back to Moascar. It was going to be a long walk.

They weaved through narrow ways, jumping open, running sewers, wading across foul drains, finally breaking free, beneath a decrepit archway, onto a broad, busy roadway raised high against cultivated fields – the edge of the city.

Jimmy waited, cautious, at the boundary, watching the chaotic flow of traffic. He felt the weight of the boys' expectations, the ache in his arms and legs, the aftermath of the fight.

Which way?

'Look! That bus is going to Moascar,' Eiric said.

Jimmy glanced at the crude sign attached to the bus' window. To or from? Jimmy wasn't sure.

He lingered beneath the crumbling arch; mind sharp despite encroaching fatigue. The road was full, even at this hour, with bustling buses, crude carts, gaunt ponies, crowds, the constant noise of klaxons, pandemonium. *Busier now than when we arrived*, he thought. *Made sense, a lot cooler now.*

'Camp, this way,' he said, pointing to the right.

'How do you know that?' said Joe.

'The sign, 'cross the road.' Jimmy moved forward into the traffic chaos. Once committed to the flow, Jimmy knew he had to maintain an even pace through the stream, that the traffic would miss him only if he didn't falter.

Eiric at his shoulder as he walked. 'That sign is in bloody Arabic.'

'Says Moascar.'

'Just bloody scrawl to me.'

'Says Moascar.' Jimmy was tired of the repetition.

The traffic wove its chaotic path around them. They reached the far bank, clambering over a broken gutter onto a narrow path, set hard against a steep drop to a field, a crop of something Jimmy could not identify, the glimmer of the river, unmistakable in the distance whenever the moon broke clear from the growing mass of clouds.

Jimmy moved along the uneven path, sure of the direction, unsure how they were going to get to the camp before dawn, or how they would explain their absence. 'Better get mov'n,' he said. 'A long walk.'

He lowered his head, walked, buried himself in thought, in his concern for Horse, the chances of their survival. This venture, initially only a brief interlude, was now a marathon hike towards an uncertain dawn.

He raised his head, scanned the path, the road ahead – the mix of wagons, dilapidated vehicles, people, an endless disordered parade, siphoning through a dimly-lit conduit. He knew this would be a dogged march towards the eastern light, so he lowered his head again, set his mind to his stride, to his feet, to the goal.

'What you walking for?'

Jimmy wanted to concentrate.

'Faster this way.'

There was no time for talk!

'Keep walking if you want.'

Jimmy finally looked up.

Joe grinned.

Jimmy stopped.

'This fella's going our way,' said Joe, pointing to a scrawny, old man, ragged, stained *gallibaya*, worn leather sandals. The old man gave a toothless smile. 'We've paid him for the ride.'

'I've paid him,' said Eiric. 'He'll take us to the train.'

'What?' Jimmy shook himself free of his fixation.

'Quicker that way. A train every hour.'

'If you're lucky.' Eiric had a contrary view of their luck. When had they become authorities on Egyptian train timetables?

Jimmy shrugged, hopped lightly onto the rickety cart, settled amongst the buckets and cans, resolved to doze if he could. Wherever this took them, it couldn't be worse than the long trek he had envisaged.

*

Jimmy woke, startled and wondered what had disturbed him. The sound of shuffling feet, distant echoes of activity. He could only guess at their purpose.

Laughter filtered through the iron door, humourless, strident, like the ridicule from those bastards who taunted him as a child.

The heat, radiating from the high, barred window was waning, the light not quite so intense, the putrid smell of a baking, partly dismembered rat in the corner of the room, dissipating with the encroaching evening cool.

Jimmy stood, raised his hand to the side of his head, felt the crusted scab, his fingers coated with the flaking, black remnants of blood when he pulled them away. The wound seemed to sweep from his temple to the jawline below his ear. His fingers found the sweet spot, a sharp stab of pain. He wondered whether it was a broken jaw.

His attention was suddenly diverted to a metallic crash beyond the high window, shouting, a revving motor. The commotion died, but as he subsided once again onto the low, stained cot, he recalled his mistake ...

In the carriage, surely close to camp by now, a slight fading of the black hinted at the first of dawn as it crept into the eastern darkness. People were reclining at awkward angles on the wooden benches; Jimmy straightened, stretching to clear the pain in his joints, rose high enough for a look through the window, no glass, the acrid smell of the coal-burning engine an assault.

He realised the constant rhythm of the wheels and the rails had changed. They were slowing.

He dropped his feet to the floor, throwing his arm to the side, a light punch to Joe's shoulder.

'We're here,' he said, the carriage jolting as the train braked.

He caught Joe's eye, wasn't sure if Joe fully understood, and repeated it, more emphasis this time. 'We're here!'

The only response a grunt.

Jimmy rose, squeezing sideways past Eiric's prone form on the bench, to the carriage doorway with door missing, the refuse of previous passages a blur at the side of the tracks.

'Short walk to the camp, then,' Joe said, pointing to the east.

Jimmy lifted his gaze to the twinkling lights of the camp.

'Trick is,' said Jimmy, 'gett'n inta the camp.'

'Only a short walk,' said Joe.

'Provosts.' Jimmy felt he didn't need to clarify.

Jimmy stood at the doorway, silent as the train slowed amongst the squeal of wheels against rails.

'They're fat bastards,' Joe said. 'Slow, lazy dimwits.'

While agreeing with the 'fat bastard' tag, Jimmy couldn't see them as lazy or dimwitted. Their arrest record was typical of zealots, a fanaticism that translated to misery for those caught, grabbed, held, beaten. It was almost a religion for those sad characters called to its service. Jimmy would need to be quick to evade their attention.

He swung down from the train, stepping lightly across the tracks, a straight line to the camp, lights across the rail yards twinkling in the pre-dawn haze.

'They'll be wait'n,' he said, to no one in particular. 'Those bastards will definitely be there, at the main gate.'

'Sleeping, I reckon,' said Joe.

'Nah. They'll be awake.'

He walked, veered left before they reached the road to the camp, then stopped short of the barricades that defined the camp's limit.

'Horses are there,' said Jimmy, pointing. 'We go through the wire close to the water troughs.'

Still cautious, Jimmy led them in a wide arc. He reckoned a

direct assault on the fence could spook the horses, maybe provide a warning to any provosts skulking in the area.

He stopped close to the objective. Listened.

Nothing.

Jimmy sniffed; thought he detected a familiar scent. It faded.

No. The way was clear.

He stepped through the wire. Strode towards the first line of troughs.

Once, in his youth, Jimmy watched his uncle locate a snake in a thicket at fifty yards, the breeze in his face, no apparent movement in the grass, standing silently, motionless for at least half an hour. When he finally stirred, his uncle moved quickly to a point, plunged his spear into a clump of long, dried stalks, came up with a writhing, black rope skewered on the ugly, serrated barbs. It left Jimmy with a lesson, not only of information gleaned from the air and the need to move quickly but the need for patience.

Amongst the horse troughs now, Jimmy felt a niggling unease, that he had missed something, had not heeded the lesson of his youth. He stepped into the yard beyond the troughs and instantly recognised the error.

Four men stepped from the shadows, each with the red colours of the provosts, each carrying a heavy baton. They moved quickly towards him, Eiric and Joe gathered closely behind.

'Fuck!' said Joe. 'Another bloody fight.'

Jimmy didn't wait.

He ran, yelling, headlong into the waiting ranks. The beating began.

*

They carried short cudgels when they came to the cell. Jimmy stood as the door swung open, squared his feet and legs to meet the attack. They formed a tight arc by the door, just stood there, looking at him. He thought they were playing with him until the ring parted in the middle. A giant pushed through the cordon, face decorated with a livid scar, a sneer through a cruel mouth, foul teeth, foul odour, foul temper.

'Y'free to go, y'black bastard,' said Strepford.

For a moment, Jimmy stood his ground, not sure whether this was a ruse, a cruel joke that would end in another beating.

'Go on, bastard!' said Strepford, yelling now. 'CO needs ya with the horses.'

Jimmy finally stirred, pushed through the line, shoving the reluctant mob aside, could see their hands flexing hopefully on their weapons, expecting a renewed assault from behind, as he headed down the bleak corridor.

Nothing came until he stepped clear of the stout, wooden door at the prison portal. A shout, a crazed snarl echoed from deep within the dingy cavern.

'I'll get you, you bastard!'

Jimmy looked to the sky, saw fleeting clouds edged with the gold of sunset, glanced across the yard, saw two figures waiting in the encroaching dusk, and thanked the spirits for his deliverance.

19

Spring 1917

Eiric was at the end of a row of tents, white canvas, bright against the glare of the midday sun. He raised his hand, shielded his eyes, squinted into the distance, wore a puzzled expression, glancing briefly behind him as Jimmy approached.

'Storm coming,' said Eiric. 'A shitload of dust.'

Jimmy stood silently, peered at the horizon, scanned the sky directly above them. 'Nah.'

'Dust storm!' Eiric held to his view.

'Wrong direction,' said Jimmy.

'What's kicking up the dust then?'

Jimmy sniffed the air, still free of the fine grit, the parched particles drilling furrows into his face. He had taken to wearing a *shemagh* when the breeze became a wind.

A familiar scent.

A reminder of home, the comforting smell of long days on the trail, mixed with the dry, acrid aroma of the bush. This was different though, the distinctive eucalypt replaced with what? He couldn't quite place it.

Eiric raised a hand to his eyes, craned his head forward on a spindly neck, eyes peering into the distance, as if that little bit closer would decide the issue. 'Got to be some sort of wind making all that mess.'

Jimmy said nothing. His eyes squinted against the glare from the bleached ground, radiated heat building towards midday. He just wanted to subside, away from the growing intensity of the day. As he watched, the dust cloud billowed to the side, a budding that swelled up and out from the locus of the storm, along the ground, alive, devouring, engulfing.

'Shit!' said Eiric. 'It's growing. That's a worry. We'll need to nail down the camp.'

Jimmy turned towards Eiric, shook his head. 'It's you I worry about sometimes, Eiric.'

'What?'

'Horses.'

'Horses?' said Eiric.

'Yeah, horses. A shitload.'

Eiric pulled at the brim of his hat, already showing the stain of sweat wicking its way to the crown. He shuffled his feet, dubious. 'How can you tell from this distance?'

Jimmy didn't know how to describe it. He remembered trying, failing, trying again. His uncle lamented, eventually told him, *not everyone's got it*, abandoned the lessons, moved to other, obvious things. It was more than two years later that he sensed a change, a still day. He recalled the shift, sudden, almost subconscious; he felt the coming storm. After a while he didn't even acknowledge the skill, it just came to him. No one could do it better. It was always reliable – horses were approaching. From somewhere, Horse's excitement came to him, an eagerness to get on with things, to move forward, to abandon this dry, baking place. He accepted Horse's sense.

'Yeah, well, we'll know soon enough,' said Jimmy. 'The storm's coming our way.'

He turned, took several steps, stopped, and looked back at Eiric. It had only been a few months since he'd herded the boys aboard the boat, had finally accepted his charges, the days the cord had severed, abruptly separating him from his legacy. He saw the change in Eiric, felt the transformation in himself, noted the impact on Horse – rootless, drifting, homeless, preparing to fight someone else's war, struggling to spot any purpose in the quest.

'Horse knew they were coming,' he said. 'Told me yesterday. Reckons we might have an interesting few days with them horse tamers.'

As they both turned their backs on the encroaching dust cloud, Jimmy breathed in the last of the clean air as they were enveloped by the first of the powdery grit.

*

The sky was beer-bottle brown, dust everywhere, a roiling mass that refused to settle. Jimmy approached the rail. Powdery clouds obscured the view, the yard smelling of piss, shit and sweat.

They walked towards the small mustering enclosure, joined to the main yard by a narrow chute, cautious, unsettled by violent crashes, animals careening into fence rails, the hoots, the whistles, the shouts, careless obscenities floating free from the ruckus.

When Jimmy stopped at the seething, compressed mass of horses, he felt their confusion, the terror of dislocation, the disorienting departure from home. Horse had confided that all the mounts from home, particularly these Walers, found the shift hard.

He looked towards the end of the chute. The mob was near panic.

The last few days, mending after the beatings from Strepford and his helpers, he spent hours with Horse, avoiding reminiscence of home, their focus the newly arrived Walers. Several boatloads of horses, poor condition, some chronically ill from their time at sea. Their urgent need was recovery. It wasn't going to happen soon, the failed jockeys and blunt stockmen of the Remount Service were programmed to bludgeon any creature into submission, to ready the mounts for battle, to shun subtler means.

Today was a day off for Jimmy and the boys, freedom from the constant drills of the past week, banned from the Cairo bars, thinking of home. He needed a diversion. Horse had urged Jimmy to find out what was happening with the men, the horses, their condition, their future. He promised to take a look.

Jimmy leant elbows against the rail, watching the dusty performance. He could see the clumsy treatment of the animals meant poor results. *Ham-fisted handling*, he thought. A horse and rider were weaving drunkenly at the centre of the yard.

The impact came from the side, lifted Jimmy into the air, the world awry, briefly his feet above his head, the ground meeting his arm, something slamming into his shoulder. He grasped at it with his free hand, vaguely noted shouting, screams, a horse? He tried to rise, and realised he was pinned to the ground by a heavy object. He heaved at it with his back, felt it shift, rolled it to the side.

Dust swirled about him, up his nose, in his mouth, grit in his ears. Confusion, disorientation held him to the ground until he focused for a moment on the grasped object – the remains of a rail from the yard fence, rough-hewn, jagged, broken like a toothpick.

A thought struck him: *Were the boys hit as well?*

He stood, unsteady, brushing away the fine dust from his eyes, finally shifting his focus from the ground to glance about as steadying hands closed about his arms.

'Shit!' Eiric's voice. 'That was fucking close!'

The horse he had noted in the confusion lay on its side, panicked groans, legs flailing, trying and failing to rise.

'Broken leg,' someone said.

Jimmy shook his head, stepping quickly towards the horse. The animal's distress sent sympathetic shocks through his body.

'Careful!' said the same voice. 'Those legs and hooves could tear your guts out.'

Jimmy bent over the terrified horse's head, placing a gentle hand close to the rolling eyes, lightly stroking as he carefully knelt. The horse's agitated effort gradually subsided.

'Got a gun?' said Jimmy.

'Yeah, but y'gotta get it slightly above …'

'Yeah, yeah.' Jimmy didn't want instructions. 'Just give me the gun.'

He held out his hand, keeping his attention firmly on the horse. The cold weight of a revolver dropped into his hand.

'This horse got a name?' Jimmy said.

'Nah. Too soon.'

Jimmy shook his head. *Pity*, he thought. *A soul leaving us without a name, love or purpose.* He closed his eyes as he continued to run his hand along the placated head to the soft nose. His fingers felt the warm air struggling from the nostrils.

'Loaded?'

'Yeah, full cylinder.'

Jimmy's uncle always said it was needless to have anything or anyone suffer, that when the time came, to end a life, it should be done for a reason, done cleanly, done quickly, and with thanks for the sacrifice made. Right now, Jimmy could see neither a reason for this nor a reason to be thankful. He suspected their future would be littered with similar inanity, where compassion and reason would have to be abandoned, replaced with anger and expediency, just to survive. He felt the horse relax now, trusting his hands, believing in his purpose, expecting a just outcome.

He lifted the weapon to that point on the forehead, slightly above the intersection of two imaginary lines drawn from the eyes to the opposite ear — and fired.

*

Jimmy returned to the camp, to Horse, friend, a guide to many things, to a judgement of his crime. Horse would no doubt regard it as murder, a needless waste, a spilling of native blood onto foreign soil. He left the boys, they were confused at his silence, headed directly to the makeshift stables, lines of makeshift stalls, canvas covers deflecting the increasingly brutal sun, faced with temporary troughs that provided catchment for food and water.

Right from Jimmy's approach, Horse, suspicious, turned away, avoiding eye contact. *Perhaps he already recognises me as a killer,* Jimmy thought. Horse expected more from Jimmy, more than careless disposal of life, the debasing of respect, something other than the brutality he had shown. Before their removal from the old lands, the answer to such suffering would have been more considered, perhaps one of many choices. It seemed to Jimmy that his link with the ancient truth was fracturing, perverted by circumstance and new desires that followed expediency rather than compassion. Even Horse, he knew, struggled to connect in this alien landscape. His friend maintained a stillness, finally holding him with an appraisal Jimmy could barely fathom. Horse always took his time to consider things, always left Jimmy with the impression that, if the need arose, he could almost bend their reality to his will, could intervene to change their destiny, their purpose, their calling. Horse worked beyond Jimmy's reckoning.

'I had no choice,' Jimmy said.

Silence.

The quiet stretched thin, a ghostly gossamer floating between them, silence that reverberated, roared within his ears.

Finally, he understood the meaning of his friend's stare, the reply: *You've always got choices.*

'Yeah, could've helped with the healing.' However, he did not believe in that solution.

Jimmy dropped his eyes, examined his dusty boots, then cast his eyes briefly upward, stole a glance at Horse.

'Bloody awful way to go,' he said. 'Hang'n in a sling for weeks.'

He could see Horse was unconvinced. The stillness returned,

redolent of hours spent in the bush, alone, silence except for the wind, the occasional brush of a tail switching away a biting fly, the clearing of a nose, the shuffle of hooves, the screech of a passing flock of galahs.

'And we're mov'n from here ... soon, they say, north. Gotta have four legs for that!' He knew he was making a case, feeble as it sounded, a justification for actions taken in haste.

Horse sighed. Jimmy saw his friend was tired of this conversation, half-turned to go, but stopped.

'More of us are gunna die,' Jimmy said, more intensity in his voice than he intended. 'Gotta make hard choices.'

He knew it was a weak defence. Horse silent, stoical.

'They offered me a job,' he said. 'Break'n in them new horses.'

He recalled the approach. A Major, tall, a limp, calm, bearded face.

'You seem pretty upset. Just a bad horse,' the Major said. 'Reckon you can ride these brumbies better?'

'Better? Yeah.'

The Major appraised Jimmy for a moment.

'You a stockman?'

'Yeah.'

'Right ... try that one.' The Major's finger pointed to a panicking horse, young, eyes rolling, lathered in white, foaming sweat.

Jimmy didn't pretend that he possessed magic; he just saw things as they were, divined the truth, saw the soul that resided within. It came to him the same way he perceived changes in the air, in the traces of the lives, despite the circumstance.

'What? Y'want me to ride'im?'

'Yeah. Give it a go.'

Jimmy calmly regarded the agitated horse, stressed, pulling violently at the halter, constantly backing away from the struggling handler. He didn't advance, didn't raise a hand.

'Well, you going to do something?' A wry smile crossed the Major's lips.

'Talking to him,' said Jimmy.

'Can't hear you.'

'He knows; he can hear me.'

'Riiiight.' The Major, unconvinced, glanced about the group of rough-riders, now gathered to watch a spectacle. 'Curly, tie the bugger up to the rail.' The handler obeyed, abandoned his position, joined the spectators.

'Got a stick?' Jimmy said as he turned to scan the growing assembly.

'What?' The Major's moment of confusion. 'Yeah, here. Snowy uses it to poke them, whack them.'

Jimmy took the stout branch, held its length to his thigh, strolled towards the horse. He realised the expectation from the crowd was conventional – threat, the anticipation of a beating, lust for violence.

He stood only yards from the beast. Their eyes met.

'They want me to kick your arse,' said Jimmy.

The horse continued to stamp hooves, distressed.

'Not gunna do it.' He broke the stick across his raised leg, threw the remains to the side, heard the complaint behind him: *That was a bloody good stick*!

Jimmy slowly raised his arm, hand palm down, fingers spread, still fixing his own eyes to the horse's fearful gaze. The stamping gradually reduced; the head dropped slightly.

Jimmy didn't move.

'Yeah, I know,' he said to the horse. 'I've been cut off too. Feel like me guts have been sliced up sometimes; it hurts so much.'

The horse craned its head forward. Jimmy could hear the indrawn breath through its nose. *It's test'n me*, he thought, *try'n to decide if I'm real.*

He thought he could hear crows. Funny, he hadn't seen any since he'd been here, just those bloody brown kites that came by the dozen to circle every fire.

It took another minute or two. The horse finally came forward, to the limit of its tether, Jimmy ambled to meet it, wrapped his arms about the muscular neck. 'Gunna jump up on y'back. All right with you?'

He felt the horse relax a little bit more, went with the moment, swung his leg upward, over the back of the hapless Waler; the horse backed up slightly under Jimmy's weight, settled, stood quietly. 'What's y'name?' he said.

Jimmy sat for a moment, leant forward, released the leash from the rail and turned the horse gently towards the gathered mob.

'He'll be right now,' said Jimmy. 'Just don't whack him.'

The line of spectators parted, the Major stepping to the front. 'Impressive. How'd you do that?'

'Dunno. Just luck, I reckon.'

'No, not luck,' said the Major. 'Like a job? Means sticking around here with the Remount Service, leaving the First.'

Jimmy silently regarded the Major.

'Need to keep me own horse,' Jimmy said. 'And a couple of me mates with me too.'

'No, just you, I'm afraid.'

Jimmy considered the Major, jumped down from the horse, handing the reins to one of the idle handlers, scanning across the line of enthralled faces. His gaze rested on the worried faces of Eiric and Joe.

Silence.

'No, reckon I'll stay with the First.'

'Pity. You could be famous.'

Fame. Jimmy couldn't see a blackfella ever being famous amongst this mob of crazy whitefellas.

'Name's Gubuthuu Yarraaman, the horse, comes from near Tamworth, means Dove, Dove Horse. He's a good'n.'

He walked, flanked by Eiric and Joe, away from the blanket of dust, into a light breeze springing up from the north.

'Maybe you should have taken the offer,' said Joe. 'Safe, good work.'

Jimmy said nothing. They headed for the camp, his intention a quiet moment with his friend.

'Someone else would'av taken you away,' he said to Horse. 'The job didn't include you or anyone else.'

Horse did not offer a response.

He waited, felt the lingering gulf that momentarily separated him from his friend, sensed the growing abyss dividing him from the old land, tearing him from reality, ripping from him his sense of self.

'We're stick'n together until the end of this shit,' he said.

He left, walking back to the rows of tents.

20

The Present Day

Harry sat at his desk, staring absently at the window. The office hummed beyond the door, the occasional ring of a telephone filtering through the glass wall at his back.

'You are booked to fly today.' Harry turned to the voice.

A pretty, slight young woman, hair neatly pulled back from her face, tied behind with a colourful ribbon, dressed in traditional Bangladeshi clothes, stood in the doorway.

'I've been thinking,' he said. 'I'll need a car as well, pickup at the airport, accommodation for at least five days, maybe more.'

The look of disquiet on Rifah's face. 'You are being met, Harry, at the airport,' she said. 'You won't need a car. Arrangements have been made.'

'So, a chaperone then.'

Rifah stood, silent for a moment. 'Your mother rang.'

Well, talking about chaperones, Harry thought. He nodded.

'Right.' He tried to remain impassive. 'Is she still on the line?'

'No, I believe she would like a call from you, Harry.'

Harry sat for a moment, alone in the big office. He turned again to the window, watching the rickshaw pullers straining with their loads amongst the chaotic transport and trade on the avenue far below – lives caught in the stream, the flood of humanity that was Dhaka. The rush of vehicles and people seemed oblivious to the traffic lights at the intersection as they turned red, an unstoppable torrent until a uniformed figure brandishing a large, white-tipped stick stepped bravely, commandingly into the midst of the hurtling transports. Harry heard the distant report of the baton, muffled by distance and the thick glass of the window, as it smacked onto the bonnet of a decrepit yellow taxi.

The mass of vehicles miraculously stopped.

Harry wished for himself, such a command of life, bravery in the face of overwhelming opposition.

His mother!

What was she up to now? What demands would be placed upon him? Where would this phone call take him?

Harry lifted the phone, hesitated, still with an eye on the street chaos below. The traffic was moving again, a torrent going some-where, perhaps nowhere, just going? He sighed, swivelled to face the office door, stood, walked forward, a peculiar weight about his shoulders, and swung the door closed. No need to involve the office in this conversation. The Sydney number took a while to connect – he could hear the clicks on the line. *A chance*, he thought, *to disconnect, get on with his life without his mother's angst, her insistence that everything should move to a formula, her view of the world, her scheme.*

The line buzzed. At that moment, he felt relief. He could move on.

'Hello?'

Harry felt a severe ache in his joints.

'Mum, Harry here. You've been trying to get me?'

'Harry, I've been trying to get you for months,' said Ruth.

Harry sighed again. This was his mother's standard response.

'Yes,' he said. 'I've been busy.' An image of Anika filled his mind.

'Well, there's things needing your attention here too,' she said, the severity of her voice prompting an automatic reaction, the memory of childhood, a cringe that awaited worse to come.

'Frances has been trying to get you, to talk to you about ...'

'Yes.'

'... about the house, the baby. And the dog's gone missing.'

'Yes, I know about that.' Harry recalled the flood of emails from Frances.

'What? About the house, the baby or the dog?'

'All of it.'

'Well? Why haven't you talked to her.'

'Busy, Mum. Flat out dealing with stuff here. And I'm flying out to the Middle East today.'

'It's just a phone call, Harry.'

Just a phone call. Harry felt the weight of that prospect – explanations, argument, inevitable tears.

'So, anything changed? I mean, since last time.'

'Nothing's changed, Harry. Frances needs help with a leaking house. Your father has tried to help, but you know him, halfway there and he gets distracted. Takes forever.'

'It's limited what I can do from here,' Harry said. 'But I can get a tradie around, pay for him from here if that's a problem.'

'And there's the baby,' said Ruth. 'Had a fever, can't pin down what's wrong.'

Harry didn't feel the need to be involved in transient health issues.

'Frances can handle that,' he said.

A moment of silence.

'Just give her a call, Harry. She'd like to hear from you.'

Harry drew in a deep breath. This was a recurring theme in all conversations with his mother – her desire to control his relationship with Frances, govern his responses, clear his path, sweep away the debris that was his life – a mood that triggered a desire to run, a need that seemed to be growing.

'Yes, I'll call her,' he said.

Silence again, until he heard his mother draw breath, a deep breath. *Here it comes*, he thought, *the real reason for the call*.

'There is another thing,' said Ruth.

'Yes, thought there might be.'

'I got our DNA done, you know, by one of those ancestry outfits and ...'

'Yes, I'm familiar with them.' Harry suddenly felt a chill descend his spine.

'Nothing extraordinary about our DNA. Just lots of Irish, a bit of the Viking, you know ...'

'Yeah, I know, Mum. Where's this leading?'

Silence. *A lot of silence from my mother*, Harry thought.

'Well,' she said. 'They've got this connection thing.'

'Connection thing?'

'Yeah, when someone is related. A cousin or something like that,

that's done the test as well, they can ask to connect.'

'How much of a cousin, Mum?'

'Ah, back to your Great Grandfather, old Angus O'Sullivan.'

Harry pictured the old man, tall, rugged, big hands, charming with the women, dismissive of children, in his nineties; Harry, just a nuisance child at the edges of a gathering. The old man loved being the centre of attention.

'The old man was a philanderer, Mum. Not really a surprise.'

'Yes, we all knew that,' she said. 'But ...' The hesitation was unfamiliar – Ruth always strode into any discussion, never indecisive, never faltering.

Harry remained quiet.

'... this person is different, I mean, her background is different.'

'Yeah, well, Mum, not everyone is like us.'

'No, I mean ethnically different, and my Dad, Eiric, and her grandfather were close. She's about your age.'

'So old man Angus screwed close to home then?'

'Don't be crude, Harry.'

'Not crude, just realistic. They didn't get around much in those days, and the old man treated Doreen like shit. We all know that.'

'I've met the young woman,' said Ruth. There was an odd resignation in her voice.

'Right. Well, who is this unsolicited relative?'

'She only knew her grandfather through stories, from her grandmother.'

'Get on with it, Mum.'

'I knew her grandfather,' she said. There was sadness in her voice now. 'Though only as a child.'

Harry could hear an uncharacteristic emotion in his mother's voice.

'He went to the war with your grandad. His name was Jimmy, though I never knew his surname.'

It felt like a slap, fresh, stinging, sharp across his face. Harry raised his hand, stroked his temples with the fingers and thumb of his left hand, his mind trying to piece together the fragments of this knowledge and the history he had gleaned in his short time with Eiric as an old man. He needed to digest.

'Right,' he said. 'So, correct me if I'm wrong. This person's grandfather was Jimmy, the same Jimmy who went through the war in Palestine with grandad, who had the same father as grandad, who was, in fact, his half-brother?'

'I guess so.' Ruth's voice almost broke.

Harry thought for a moment.

'So, what happened to Jimmy?'

'No one knows. He just dropped off the map after dad deserted the farm and family, and then mum lost the farm.'

'What happened to this woman's grandmother?' Harry stopped talking, pondering the implications. 'What's this person's name?'

'Jessica,' she said. 'Jessica Franks. Lovely person, Harry. She just wants to figure it all out.'

'Yeah,' he said. 'Bit of a bombshell, eh.'

'Her grandmother is still alive. Pretty old.'

Harry had to be decisive. 'Give me her details, Mum. I'll give her a call.'

Harry sat for a long while after Ruth ended the call, considering the implications, searching for a decision. His mother's focus on such a minor diversion only served as an irritation. There were more pressing matters that needed his attention. He would need to return home, to deal with the demands of his employers and attend, as well, to the minefield that was his family, to pursue the thread that carried the story of their family, the journal of misdemeanours, miscalculations, and missteps.

First, though, there was his task in Israel to complete – the hidden purpose, the illumination of that part of the story.

He told Rifah to call for his car to the airport, for the journey into hopeful enlightenment, to the severing of the cord that bound him so tightly to this cruel path.

21

The Coast – South of Gaza

Late Spring 1917

A bird called as Jimmy was sitting, almost dozing in the saddle, within a dry wadi that wove its thirsty way towards the distant sand dunes and the sea – cool, reviving, safe.

It was a sunbird.

'Now, there's a bit of life.' Joe was despondent in the heat.

'Black, like me,' Jimmy said, catching a fleeting glimpse of the bird, from the corner of his waking eye.

'Lots of colours,' said Joe. 'More than you've got.'

Big, sleek, upturned talons grasping the thin stalk, beak probing the purple bell of a flower, the bird glanced their way, as if judging the distance to threat, decided there was time, resumed its culinary break.

Jimmy knew them. Sunbirds brought a high-pitched, quick, jingling tune to an otherwise quiet, dry, desolate coastal fringe, nesting in creations that dangled like purses from branches. Someone, Joe, or was it Slapper, reckoned they could make good eating, had taken a pot-shot, missed, the frightened bird breaking into a raucous, alarmed chorus. Then other distant voices had joined the refrain. It was a warning; they didn't see any more for the remainder of the day.

He watched the bird dip its head to another flower, stop, glance once more their way. It suddenly took flight into the desiccated scrub that vowed to survive the encroaching heat of summer, landing several yards from the trail; the line of horses, men, the cloud of fine dust enough to require caution, but not an alarm.

Jimmy, reconciled to their narrow road, followed the bird's path, lifting his eyes towards the horizon, the coast to the west, the shimmering water visible from their slightly elevated way. Resigned.

Joe's horse danced sideways as he dug into its flanks. 'Bored,' he said. 'Dust, flies and we've been sitting in these fucking saddles for hours.'

The inclination was to tell him to shut up, tell Horse to move, ride off. Get away from this inane chatter and dust. He looked towards the head of the column of riders. The air was clear there. The Major waved an arm to the right, finger pointing to the low, baking hills.

A minute went by, Major Tubby Matthews straightened in the saddle, signalled again, turned.

'Could do with a cup of tea,' Joe said.

'Might hafta wait,' said Jimmy. Anticipating the next question, he pointed forward, through the dusty haze.

The leading riders disappeared behind leached, pitted boulders, sucked into obscurity, dust the only remnant.

The Major waited at the turn.

Jimmy felt the pull, felt the exposure of the march that led away from the security of the ocean, its cooling relief, the watery sanctuary discarded. The line of Light Horse seemed to pause, horses and men suddenly crowded, jostling, bickering, bumping forward, stopping again, until the Lieutenant broke free from the crush, rode ahead to the rocks to see what was happening.

The Major still waited by the boulder, at the turn.

Dickie leant forward in the saddle as he reached the Major, nodding his head, briefly glancing beyond the corner, gazing into the unknown. Jimmy felt Horse flinch, felt a shuddering from the ground, the morbid air suddenly alive. Several blackbirds flung themselves upward from their hideaways in the scrub; raucous alarms, gaining height until they flew away to the south. *They're getting the fuck out of here*, he thought.

Then a dull thud met them. It sounded like distant thunder, though Jimmy knew that there was no rain. It flowed over them, a percussion, striking, threatening to break eardrums, fleeing to the west and the ocean, to the great sink.

Horse shuffled to the side. Agitated.

'What the fuck was that?' Joe fought to control his horse amidst a stirring mass of restless mounts.

Jimmy made a chuckling sound, like the distant beat of a hammer against wood, as he calmed Horse. 'Cannon, I'd guess.'

'It's started, then.' Joe's tongue brushed his lips. Nervous. Still struggling with his mount.

Jimmy shook his head. 'Not for us, Joe.' Joe looked up from his struggle.

'Dickie says, we are to stay at Division HQ.' Jimmy had explained this already.

'That might change.' There was hope reflected in Joe's face.

'They fucked up the last go at Gaza,' said Eiric. 'Don't really want to be part of the body count on this one.' Nervous.

Jimmy held his breath, looked at the brothers. Joe stared back, flushed with eager anticipation and nascent fear. 'Just, keep y'heads down,' Jimmy said.

'Yeah, right!' Joe, exasperated, petulant like a schoolboy. He'd heard Jimmy's advice numerous times.

Jimmy leant forward, stroked Horse's biddable neck, looked forward to the turning point. He felt unease, saw eager faces, heard the distant crump of the guns. 'Yeah, well, you just might get to see some of the heavy stuff.' He pointed forward. 'We're turning the corner now.'

Jimmy urged Horse forward, the dry wadi to his right, the ocean, the refreshing oasis behind, beyond the narrow, stony passage, the junction filled with jostling horses. He pushed away his own un-certainty, the persistent fear, straightened in the saddle, closed his eyes as he felt their descent into the wadi, the broad avenue leading towards an intensifying clamour. Eyes still closed, dry-mouthed, he reached for his water bottle.

The thought came to him: *A distant time, stars, the emu in the south, the wheel of stars twisting, spiralling, wandering, delicately guided by the vein, the strain of truth that bound the heavens to the earth.* He recalled the conditions that led him to this place, doubt-ed whether he could satisfy the demands, didn't understand yet, his part, resisted the desire to think of home, to bathe in the memory of familiar smells, to remember familiar faces. The wadi baked in the midday heat, a contrast to their start, before dawn, cold, the dry face of the Negev hidden in the dark. The dazzling orbs of the stars wheeled close, and for a moment, he saw how they linked, understood their coupling with the earth, almost grasped the connection of all things.

The solid crump of the artillery grabbed him, held him, bound him. He opened his eyes, a flash of light, the sky turning red, mayhem; horses dancing wildly, men struggling to remain in the saddle, and a shout.

Horse leapt, desperate.

Jimmy suddenly realised that it was his own voice that yelled above the din.

A brief lull. Then the bombs resumed as a cascade.

*

Jimmy instinctively ducked as coarse sand rained heavily onto his hat and shoulders. He purposefully dulled his senses, seeking diversion in memories of home.

She was naked, lithe, muscular, but not in a mannish way, with well-formed arms and thighs. Fit enough to match him walking, running, anything. Her mouth curled upward at the corners, seemed to smile even when serious. She moved to him, knew him well, wrapped one leg around his body, pulled him down onto the thick mat of she-oak needles, a soft bed, yielding as he pressed down, moving slowly as he entered, gentle. He didn't want to hurt the most precious being in his life, the one, and yet, that seemed the outcome of his life, the end of all things, the only completion he could ever manage. The image of his love faded, morphing into the rise and fall of a horse's rump, the flutter of a long mane.

Jimmy held tight to the reins, pressing inward with his thighs against Horse's flanks, felt the power of his friend's frantic stride, their escape; he only vaguely registered their direction. They passed open-mouthed infantry, soldiers huddled against low rocks, thin vegetation, rifles, fixed bayonets, fear streaked like blood across their faces. He let Horse have his head, couldn't prevent the desperate flight, wouldn't revoke his friend's better judgement.

Horse raced on, head strained forward, Pegasus unleashed.

The wadi gradually narrowed, the walls crowding so close that jagged boulders, rooted within the banks threatened to tear into Horse's flanks. The detonations slowly ebbed, muffled by the steep wadi walls, the crump of the shells, as they burst above, distant now, the rhythmic drive of their escape slowing to a jarring trot.

Horse stopped.

Jimmy half turned in the saddle, gazing back along their path, towards the distant melee. He could see no signs of the battle, wondered if it all had been a mirage, an invention of his mind, an illusion generated by his desire for a fight, a chance for relevance in this senseless conflict.

He shook his head, clearing the dust from blurry eyes, finally swinging down from the saddle, trying to clear his ears, to dispel the panic that threatened to overwhelm him. He bent forward, hoping the change in elevation would clear his vision. He tried to look up, walking slowly, bending low again, so his face pointed to the ground, head clearing, approaching the group of horsemen, all still grappling with distraught mounts; Horse would look after himself. He had never experienced such a calamity. Until you experienced the deafening roar, the detonations, the mind-sapping percussion, you couldn't anticipate how numbed senses led to such confusion. No matter the amount of instruction, you had to learn these things first-hand.

He finally stood upright, watching the remainder of the troop arrive, scanning the numbers. He realised they were all there … except, where was Joe? His eyes locked with Eiric, disorientation waning, bewilderment growing, vacuity yielding to awareness; a shroud of despair finally settling about Eiric's face.

'When did you last see him?' Jimmy needed to know if he should return to the battlefield. The thump of the distant artillery seemed to intensify.

'Don't know,' said Eiric. 'I just put my head down. I let Tuppence do the thinking.' It sounded like an excuse.

Jimmy could relate to that.

'Well, he's not here.' Jimmy squinted into the distance, back along the path. It disappeared around a bend in the wadi.

Jimmy and Eiric stood for a moment, silent.

The troop gathered behind them, on foot now, the racket of their excited talk an irritation. 'Any you fellas seen Joe?' Jimmy had to shout. The noise of the guns was no longer distant.

'We need to move on,' said Dickie. 'Sounds like the bloody artillery's coming this way.'

'Yeah, but where's Joe?'

'Saw him right behind you when you took off.' Dickie was already climbing onboard his mount, fixed on other things. 'Can't go back into that mess.'

Shit!

Jimmy looked back along the path, peering intently, hoping to catch a glimpse of Joe as he rounded the wadi's bend.

A cloud billowed upward from the locus of the artillery storm.

He sighed, and without turning, whistled, a high-pitched tweet, felt a nudge from behind, wheeled about, took the reins in his left hand, swung his right leg high over the saddle, settled for a moment hoping for a sight of the rebellious Joe. 'Can't leave him, Dickie. I'll catch you up.'

He dug heals urgently into Horse's flanks, careering breakneck, back into a thick, dusty cloud. The grinding noise of the artillery was gone, groups of infantry lurched like spectres from the gloom, some bent into curious shapes, broken, deformed, others milling in confused clusters.

He slowed Horse to a sedate trot. How was he going to locate Joe in this mess?

A lone horse appeared, riderless.

Joe's horse.

Jimmy desperately scanned the scene, litter from the infantry advance scattered beneath the wadi walls, soldiers streaming across the dry riverbed, others clambering over the lip of the wall, bayonets fixed, the distant clatter of machine guns, the occasional thud of mortars.

Jimmy thought: *It's like the pastor's hell, no beginning, no end, confusion, torment, and noise, deafening, mind-numbing noise.*

'Where the hell is he?' said Jimmy, twisting in the saddle, glaring over his shoulder. Eiric stood in the stirrups, squinting into the dense haze.

'Thought you were stay'n with Dickie.'

Eiric swivelled to Jimmy, looked him square in the face, straight back. 'Have to stick together.'

Jimmy said, 'Don't need you here.'

The words weren't what he might have planned. He had wanted the mistake to be his, his error in letting Horse loose, not being the last of them to escape the bombs. The risk his, alone.

Eiric held his ground, looked down his nose at Jimmy, stuck out his chin, defiant. He blinked, mouth parted, ran his tongue along the edge of his teeth.

'Here now, not going.'

There was no time to argue about it now. 'Well, there's his horse, where the fuck's Joe?'

Eiric bent forward as Tuppence stepped close to Joe's mount, grabbing the rein. The horse backed away, unsure, suspicious of any interference.

The swarm of soldiers had thinned, just the occasional straggler now, moving towards the wadi wall. Jimmy looked to the embankment; the crest blurred by the dust. A thought came, he rejected it as errant, glanced again along the line of the wadi. He walked Horse slowly down the slope of the watercourse, wondering whether the ocean would once again glitter in clean air if he kept going, whether that could be their salvation, emancipation, freedom from this maelstrom.

He stopped. A feeling, just a glimmer of a mood touched him, amongst the cacophony of the conflict. The thought returned.

He was going the wrong way!

As if reading Jimmy's thoughts, Horse abruptly turned about, moving swiftly back to where they had first encountered the horse, the soldiers. He looked again, to the top of the wadi.

'He's up there,' he said, pointing. An earsplitting blast shook the ground, sand from the wadi's edge showered over them, the horses threatened to bolt.

'Eiric!' he said, shouting above the din, throwing his hat into Eiric's hands. 'Take the horses.'

He threw the reins to Eiric, vaulted from the saddle, sprinted to the wall, scrambling desperately up the rocky slope. He knew now. Joe was amongst the worst of it. The crest was within reach.

Stifling heat slammed into him. It drew the air from his lungs, seared his eyeballs, sucked the water from his body, through his eyes. The ash from the battlefield lodged in his throat, he gasped for breath as he witnessed the emergence of hell on earth.

Jimmy stood for a moment at the portal to an inferno; uniformed men, like mirages against an orange-red sky, bent in a protective crouch, rifles, bayonets thrust forward to an unseen foe, gradually merging with fire and the searing heat, vanishing amongst the billowing dust and sand.

Jimmy ducked as a missile thudded into the ground only yards away, spraying coarse sand over his head. He didn't want to be in this netherworld; it confounded him, it reinforced his disconnection, the severing of the cord that once bound him to the way between earth and the stars, it ended everything.

But where was Joe?

He shook his head, hoping to clear his view, scanned across the battlefield, hopeful of a glimpse of Joe.

Nothing.

Just chaos.

'They're headed for Sausage Ridge.' Jimmy swung to the words.

Jimmy mute.

'Come on. They're almost at the top.' Joe still wore his hat, the emu, its feather still flying, eyes shining, excitement saturating his face.

'What do y'wanna do that for?' Blood rose in Jimmy's face, through the snarl, into his eyes.

Joe half turned, walked a few paces, stopped. 'We're going to win! Have to be there.'

'Can't y'hear the machine guns? It's a bloody massacre out there!' said Jimmy, yelling above the noise.

Joe looked unconvinced.

'We gotta piss off out of this mess, that's what we gotta do.' Jimmy had a bad feeling about this fight.

Joe glanced up the slope towards the ridge, ran his tongue across dry lips, turned again to confront Jimmy. Brief hesitation turned to defiance. He looked to be ready to turn and go. The last of the advancing troop had disappeared into the dusty curtain.

Jimmy tried to hold Joe's eyes.

'Look!' said Jimmy, pointing in the direction of the skirmish.

Joe turned.

Jimmy had sensed a reversal, a change in the mood of the battle, undefined, yet unmistakable.

The first shimmering figures gradually emerged from the festering cloud: ash, dust, the smell of blood, a soldier carrying a body, hobbling. Within seconds a dozen men appeared, some barely able to walk.

Joe stood mesmerised. Jimmy moved to him, seized his arm, shook it lightly. 'Time to go.'

Joe still refused to budge. An injured soldier, a British Yeoman by the look, passed close.

'What's happening?' said Joe, feet firmly planted, leaning towards the man.

'Retreat, mate.'

'What?' Joe said. 'You had them beat.'

'Ordered back to the line.' The man moved on.

'Time to go.' Jimmy was tired of this repetition. He pulled Joe, forcefully this time, Joe complying, still reluctant.

They reached the edge of the wadi, clambered to its base, strode to Eiric and the waiting horses, climbed into the saddle.

'He's confused,' said Jimmy to Eiric. 'Dazed by the bombs.'

'No, I'm not!' said Joe.

'Yeah, you are!' Jimmy was irritated by Joe's stubbornness. 'That's what we'll tell Dickie. And anyone else who asks.'

He dug his heels lightly into Horse's flanks.

As they moved forward, he wondered, *how many more times will I have to rescue Joe from himself?*

22

The Present Day

'Not much of it left,' said Harry. 'A bit like the Rocks in Sydney, all gloss, the past a dim memory, if that.'

Anton Banna nodded his short, solid neck. 'It's a popular place, changed since they started up all those trendy eateries. But for all that, there's still some old-timers in there.'

Harry had arrived early, from the sticky humidity of Dhaka to the shrivelling aridity of Tel Aviv. *Edge of the desert*, he thought, regretting his decision to come all this way, at this time of the year. *Nothing left as evidence.*

Evidence? Too much time had passed. Tel – the Arabs had it right – throw all your refuse into a pile and let it compact until, after a thousand or more years, you had a mountain to build a safe refuge upon. Harry looked along the palm tree-lined boulevard, city high-rise to the left, white sandy beaches swept by the warm Mediterranean on the right. *Not much Tel in Tel Aviv*, he thought.

The flat beach gave way to a sea wall in the distance, a curved edifice holding the ocean at bay, the buildings climbing, like a ragged, multi-layered cliff, to a pinnacle.

'Maybe there's enough refuse, things of the past left in that mound?' Harry said, pointing to Old Jaffa.

'Maybe,' said Anton. 'While you're gone, I'll poke around, with some of the Arab originals, the authentic ones.'

'Can't be many.' Harry's scepticism was running riot. *Why had he come here? Nothing of his grandfather's time would have survived all these years.* He looked across the curve of the bay, at the wandering crowds, the traffic trawling slowly along the strand, ever vigilant for parking, ever hopeful for relief from the pressures of a modern city, diversion from the impressed cares of a nation on edge. They descended steps, closer to the beach, the waves not much more than ripples against flat, featureless sand. *Another two metres and it would be a challenge*, he thought. He laughed to himself. Maybe this pilgrimage, this endless search for something was overlooking, discounting, what he already had. Perhaps it was a pointless obsession with his own deficiencies.

'There are a few left,' said Anton. 'Though the old ones might struggle to remember.'

People drifted between cafés, undecided which coffee and cakes looked the best, which seats gave them the best view of the ripples. They knew there was no real difference; instead, it preserved some façade of choice in a world with diminishing options.

Harry selected a table. 'Everyone looks comfortably numb,' he said, eyeing the crowd.

'Bit of a cliché, that, isn't it?' Anton's eyes followed a young woman in a scanty bathing suit.

'I reckon Pink Floyd had it right. We all try to push away the unpleasant. We fabricate realms where we can pretend things are okay, cheerful, you know, normal.' Harry instantly regretted the comment. Perhaps personal revelations, disclosures like that sort, in a place like this, weren't sensible. He gazed down the strand to the ragged bastion that seemed to be falling into the sea, the remains of Jaffa. He wondered if anything remained of its real tenacity, its story, its sins of the past.

'So …' Anton said, pausing, finally dragging his eyes away from more young, exposed midriffs, 'you'll be gone two or three days?'

Harry wasn't sure. The Negev featured so much in his grandfather's memories; it seemed the place to go.

'How far to Beersheba?' said Harry.

'Just an hour or so,' Anton said, his attention firmly on Harry now.

They were silent as the waiter delivered two coffees, some sticky, syrupy confection and the bill.

'Why do you want to go there?'

'Family history.'

'What? They came from there?'

'No.' Harry debated whether he should go further, reluctantly adding, 'World War I, the Light Horse.'

'Plenty to see,' said Anton. 'Just not at Beersheba though. It's just a place at the edge of the desert. Nothing left of those days. Maybe the Nabataean ruins? To the south.'

Harry felt again the futility of this search – aimless, a pointless digression, a diversion from some path he couldn't yet define. He heard laughter, they both turned their heads towards a group of middle-aged women clustered about an ice-cream stand, the white mounds atop cones melting in the hot sun, mouths frantically catching cascading streams of white liquid, waterfalls in the ravines between their fingers. Harry vowed to make this excursion a short one – he needed stability and realistic resolve in his life.

'Jerusalem,' said Anton. 'Now, that would be more interesting.'

'They were there too.'

'When?'

'Took it from the Ottomans. First to the gates.'

'Then you should go there. Only an hour's drive.'

'Maybe,' Harry said.

Time passed slowly in the heat of the afternoon. The women had left, ambling absently towards the towers of Jaffa, tourists sought comfort from the burning sun under café umbrellas. They moved to a bar open to the beach. Harry drank beer, bowls of greasy fries appeared, deep-fried food that promptly fixed itself about his waist. About him the evening crowd built; he almost missed the change, the gradual encroachment of twilight, the appearance of lights, strings of luminescent pearls strung loosely across the promenade.

Anton left him at some point, reappearing with a lean, young man, white shirt, open at the neck, baggy trousers.

'Salim will take you to your hotel.'

Harry stood, realising that he was less stable than expected. *That's about the sum of it*, he thought. *Stability is an illusion; people, nations, the world, all teetering on edge. Just a little push and we're gone, over the edge, hurtling towards a very unpleasant end.*

'Right, take me home, Salim. And don't spare the horses.'

'What, Boss?'

Harry didn't feel inclined to explain the significance of the link between horses and home. 'Lead on, Macduff.'

Salim hesitated, a momentary pause, a puzzled glance at Anton, finally nodding at a signal, leading the way.

'Take him to the hotel, Salim, and pick him up in the morning.' Harry felt Anton's gaze as he walked away. Take me to the vehicle, take me to the hotel, take me home, the next in a succession of impermanent beds.

*

The fortress frowned at the Negev, a light, warm breeze drifting in the dense heat. Harry watched tired people, small dots against the bleached stone on the Snake Trail, as they clambered up the steep path. *The cable car was the right choice*, he thought, as he felt the radiant heat from the rocks growing, the afternoon beginning to raise curious spouts of shimmering air across the desert below.

In Masada, in the ruins of men, the Dead Sea, like a flat, blue blanket spread at the edge of the horizon, only a half-dozen people wandering through the maze of crumbling stone walls, in the heat of the day. He wondered again why he had come to the Negev. Why this place?

Through the day he had immersed himself in the arid land as it passed by, punctuated by brief flashes of green. The Israelis had been busy. He had thought this place would bring some sort of understanding, a wisp of sympathy for his grandfather's journey, for their destructive passage. But it hadn't. All he saw was the sanitised new model, the commitment to the future – the past carried little weight, particularly the past of others, the unconnected annals, irrelevant diversions for a people bent on survival against crushing hostility.

*Turn around, Salim. I need to get on with my life. Straight to the
airport.*

That's what he should have said, direct, sensible, and made
Salim turn the vehicle about. He didn't know why he continued
with this useless search, the pursuit of an elusive connection with
the past. Why didn't he just go home?

Harry gazed into the distance, saw those bursts of green, sym-
bols of a changing world, signs of a rejection of historical limitations.

He should ring Sydney now. Go home, seek restoration.

No! Not yet.

There were too many questions, too many hidden responses.
This place owed him answers, solutions, keys to greater things.
There was a debt still to be paid, an obligation his mother had always avoided. She had never asked those critical questions, had
never wanted to hear the truth, had avoided the discomfort of the
awful truth. In the end, such discovery might demolish his foundation, ruining his chance for stability.

He had to try.

Harry turned to the exit. There was little value in this place,
Herod's fortress, the grave of an obscure Jewish sect, the brutality
of the Roman Empire – the Light Horse had given it a wide berth.
His only chance lay in half-forgotten memories of Jaffa.

As he turned, an animal moving in the distance caught the
light; white, long legs striding across broken ground, mane swept
back, confident. It stopped and turned to look his way, a fixed stare.
Harry stood for a moment, wondering why a horse should be loose
amongst such arid ground. The clatter of the docking cable car
behind him distracted him, a brief glance away. He immediately

returned his gaze to the distance – the horse was gone.

'Did you see that?' he said to a man standing beside him at the rail.

'See what?' said the man, a thick Eastern European accent.

'The horse, the white horse down there.' Harry pointing.

'No. No, there was no horse.' The man looked puzzled. 'No animals at all, not even a mouse, or a rabbit would live there.'

'I'm sure there was a horse,' Harry said.

'Sometimes the heat on the rocks makes strange mirages seem real,' said the man. 'I have often wondered how that happens.'

Harry was silent for a moment, shaking his head as if to clear his vision.

'Perhaps you are right. I may need some time away from the sun.' He laughed, but he felt no mirth – the memory of his grandfather's troubled revelation filled his mind – remembering the fate of his abandoned friend.

Harry turned to the exit, leaving Masada to its bloody memories. He had stirred something with this pilgrimage. Now, he had to see it to its end.

*

Harry walked along the sea wall in the dimming light, stopped, watched the small boats riding at anchor in the bay, a warm sea breeze brushing against his face, roughing the water. The last of the sun beat against the walls of the old city, ancient, massive, resolute, occasionally punctuated by dark retreats that hinted at discoveries still to be made, inventions of the past, histories that might ensnare him. He saw the man walking towards him, along the stone pier from a row of moored boats, head down, a lithe slightness apparent as he approached.

'Harry, is it?'

'Yes.'

'I have the information you need.' Harry felt the man's green eyes would dismember him. 'Come with me.'

The man turned to go.

Harry had then, a premonition of disaster, but whether it was his or the fate of others, he could not tell. His life squandered trading with the devious, the deceitful, the ambitious, the ruthless, the two-faced, the hostile, the vicious, the deranged, the duplicitous, the treacherous, or simply the unkind, supplied him with an intuition.

Time may have passed, but the legacy of his grandfather lingered here.

He could retreat into abjuration, detachment from reality, escape. Did it matter if he turned and left, didn't challenge the past, made a strategic withdrawal? Everyone would accept the simple explanation: *too much time had passed.* People were engrossed in the immediate, what influence did ancient matters have on modern lives?

Time to go. Just walk away.

Harry stood for a moment, watching the man walk away, the confident amble, purpose, explanation, solution. Was he ready to accept defeat, return to Sydney and the mundane comfort of the daily grind, his mother, Frances, the dog? The white horse stepped into his mind, the memory of Eiric's regrets, lost friends, missed opportunities to do the *right thing*, failure of commitment, the tragedy of abandoned friendships.

Harry brushed his hair back from his forehead, away from his eyes, stepping forward, following the man through an archway darkened with age, onto a steep stone stairway, narrow, footsteps echoing from the high, obdurate walls. He felt a strange abandonment, a release from restraint that seemed to plague his every thought, his every move. Was this a turning point, the fork in his path that he had sought for so long?

Eiric had pointed the way, had opened the door, just a crack, a thin shaft of light, enough to turn him from total destruction, at least in the short-term. The fight, the battle for his soul still consumed him.

The man stopped at a stout wooden door, intricate designs carved lightly into the timber, half turning. *To check*, Harry thought, *that he was still there, still attending, still keen.*

'Wait,' he said. 'Wait here.' A key in the lock, door open, the man disappeared, the door gently closed.

Harry backed against the opposing wall, took a deep, shuddering breath, then the swift climb. *He would need to lay off the beer and fried food.*

Minutes passed, the soft swish of the ocean funnelling along the alley, the subtle salt smell mixed with baking bread. Harry heard the clang of something metallic from further up the stairs, a shout, laughter, a dog barking, high-pitched yapping.

The door swung open.

A head appeared.

The man waved his hand. 'Come.'

Harry pushed away from the wall, head bowed, walking through the portal, the door closing with a faint click behind.

Looking forward along a narrow hallway, his eyes gradually adjusting to the dim light, he saw plain walls, coats hanging in a slight recess, soft glow at the end. The man was a shadowed outline as he led the way.

The hallway abruptly opened into a spacious room: windows, timber-framed glass doors opening onto a roughly paved balcony, the Jaffa port, its myriad boats, masts, moorings visible below. The room was strewn with couches, cushions, carpets, rich textures, a startling contrast to the plain entry.

The man indicated that he should sit.

Harry waited. The distant sound of the port filtered through the open doors, the faint, sweet smell of perfume from the furnishings.

'You have come a long way.' Words from behind.

Harry turned as he rose from the settee.

A woman, old, at least in her nineties, immaculately dressed, stood, supported by an old-fashioned crooked cane.

'Yes,' said Harry. 'Australia.'

'Ah, yes, I have not met an Australian for many years.'

The accent, thought Harry, *not typical Israeli, maybe French?*

'Not too many Australians in this part of the world.' What could Harry say?

'Your name is Harry?' she said. 'You have met my grandson, Emile?' She pointed behind Harry.

Harry turned. Emile smiled.

'I am Francine.' She moved now, deliberately, carefully, her grandson stepping forward to help her sit. Once comfortable, she said, 'Tea? Would you like tea?'

Politeness prevailed. Harry accepted tea, though he would have preferred a beer.

Harry wasn't sure of the protocol, the next step.

Francine looked intently at him. 'You look very much like your grandfather.'

Harry only halfway lifted the cup, replaced it in the delicate saucer. Maybe it was time to be blunt. 'Why do you know that? How could you know?'

Again, Francine quietly examined him. She chuckled, a slight laugh, but still full of joy.

'I never imagined,' she said, 'that I would ever meet one of Eiric's family.'

'You knew him?'

'No, I never met the man, but I do have a unique connection.'

'How could that be, if you have never met him?'

Francine paused and smiled. 'My mother, she, ah, knew your grandfather.'

'How?'

'Intimately. They met in Jaffa during the war in Palestine. My mother ...' She paused again. 'My mother worked in a pleasure house here in Jaffa. They were hard times. She knew many Australian soldiers, but one in particular, your grandfather.'

Francine waved her hand, called for Emile. 'Emile, the photos.'

Emile walked forward with a bundle of old photos, placed them on the table before them.

Harry was quiet as he leafed through the images, many faded and ragged.

'There is your grandfather,' said Francine, pointing. 'With my mother, see.'

Harry looked closely at the stilted pose, the set studio piece with false background, his grandfather, a young, virile soldier in uniform next to a small, pretty, young woman in a long dress, high neck, parasol. Beside his grandfather, two other men, each with females under their arms, one white, the other black, all proud, smiling, rampant.

'They knew each other well, it seems.'

'Yes, Harry.' Francine smiled again. 'You see, your grandfather ...'

Harry's premonition leapt upon him, it rolled itself into a ball, aimed itself, punched him squarely in the guts. He looked up from the photograph, at the face of the old woman as she spoke, saw the similarity, the mouth, the nose, the bearing.

'... was my father.'

Harry saw a ray of light lance across the bay before Jaffa through the clouds gathering for a late afternoon storm. Beyond the port, the dark of the clouds seemed a fitting symbol of his malaise, the maelstrom of his life, the dysfunction of his family. He knew now, like all storms, this one would pass, there would be a clearing, a washing clean, a resolution.

23

EAST OF GAZA

Autumn 1917

The brass had managed to organise some sort of comfort: tents, stretchers to get them off the ground, water – not running, but fresh – enough for at least one wash a day, and a line of troughs for the horses. In a large area at the centre of the tent cluster, a dozen men gathered around a small campfire. It could get cold at night, cloudless sky, shortening days.

Eiric was to the side of the mob, sitting on a cartridge box, legs stretched before him, eyes down, book in hand. One of the soldiers ambled to the fire, threw a thin stick into the feeble flames. A shower of sparks drifted into the cool evening.

Jimmy sat. Watched.

They waited, lingering about the fringes of the Negev, walking the horses out each day, in sight of the Turkish lines, defensive limits alternatively bristling, glowering, slumbering.

Gaza remained inviolate.

'Boring!' said Joe to the mob. 'Just sitting, eating this shit food, walking the horses!'

'Suits me,' said Slapper. 'And the food's not bad. Tasty shit.'

'Yeah, well, you've probably eaten shit all your life ... so you wouldn't know.'

Slapper poked the fire vigorously with a stick, releasing another burst of embers into the air, fireflies dancing upward, *heaven-bound,* Jimmy thought, *until they flicker out, exhausted.*

'Wouldn't mind a nice, cold beer.' Joe gazed longingly into the distance.

'I've given up the drink,' said Slapper.

'What do y'mean, Slapper?' said Freddy, the breaker from Cowra. 'You were the one who drank the bar dry. And that was before Joe's riot ... then y'went back and drank it dry again after we'd beaten the shit outta those Cairo bastards. Y'won't ever give it up.'

'Wasn't my riot.' Joe incensed.

'Yeah, it was.' The assembly turned to look at Eiric – his eyes finally withdrew from the book. 'And we ended up in the clink, the shit beaten out of us by that bastard, Strepford.'

Joe turned his face away. 'Read your book, Eiric,' he said over his shoulder.

'Getting too dark.'

Jimmy looked across the company, the bearing of Crusaders; sacred soldiers immersed in the privations of the Holy Land, a righteous war; young, straight-backed, lean, thin faces, craving the spoils of warfare, even if the only reward was death, the enemy's or their own.

'Dickie says we're headed to Irgeig tomorra,' Jimmy said. Heads turned to him, almost in unison. 'It's over near Beersheba. Shit of a place by all accounts.'

'What's there?' Freddy, always the first to ask a question.

'A railway line, station ... noth'n much else, 'cept Turks.'

'Dug in, no doubt, bloody machine guns pointed straight at us.'

'Might be just take'n a look, a decko, then home for some more of this great grub.' Slapper was smiling, ever the optimist.

Jimmy shook his head. 'Y'know Slapper, if the machine guns don't get ya, the food definitely will.'

'Alls I dream about is this food,' Slapper said, paused, thoughtful. 'It's the only thing I got t'dream about.'

'What?' said Joe. 'You don't dream about that donkey's dick of yours?'

Slapper smiled. 'Yeah, well, sometimes.'

Joe's turn to be wistful. 'What I miss is those girls. You know, the ones with those beautiful rounded derrières ...'

An officer appeared from the growing dark, shirt and suspenders, no hat, no coat. He strode into the firelight, stood for a moment, scanned the collection, scuffed his boots in the dusty ground.

'Tomorrow,' he said. 'You'll get *your* arses up early, real early.' Joe's last comment had not been missed.

'What time, Dickie?' A voice from the crowd.

'Try three in the morning.'

'Then what?' Same voice.

'You saddle up, numbskull.'

Silence.

'In formation, by the troughs, heading east.' *That was final,* Jimmy thought.

'Where we go'n, Dickie?' *Typical,* Jimmy thought, *Freddy hadn't been listening.*

'Irgeig.'

Dickie turned, walked a few steps towards the falling night, stopped, hand, finger pointing skyward, as if recollecting something, then turned to face the troop. 'Sharpen your knives, make sure the bloody bullets don't jam.'

The men fixed their stares on the Lieutenant.

'You'll be needing them.' Dickie trudged into the night.

Jimmy sat quietly, watched the men, the mixture of emotions playing about their faces, the sudden, tense rigidity, the withdrawal. Eiric carefully closed the book, discarded it to the small satchel he carried everywhere – always a book close at hand. Joe looked deeply into the small fire, a nervous tongue washing across his lips, a surge to his feet, impulsive, assertive, impatient. Jimmy understood the miracle that was their escape from the abortive battle to take Gaza half a year ago, a disaster. Such poor execution, so many dead, stupidity. Now, he was sure it was happening again!

'So, what do y'reckon the plan is?' Eiric stood beside him. Jimmy hadn't noticed him move.

'No idea,' said Jimmy. 'Keep y'head down. Survive, I guess.'

'Joe's been wanting this for ages,' said Eiric. 'Been fit to bust for action.'

'Well, we got it now, I reckon.'

Jimmy just hoped that Allenby and Chauvel had got it right this time. *The Generals*, he thought, *always consider fellas like me as disposable.*

'Go sharpen y'tools, Eiric,' Jimmy said, placing his steady, broad hand on Eiric's shoulder. 'If we survive this one, it'll get easier.'

Jimmy considered Eiric as he ambled towards his tent; a straight back, gentle swaying walk. He wondered whether the boy had it in him to kill, to gut an enemy, another human being, questioned whether he, himself, could take another man's life and feel no regret, suffer no recrimination, feel no shift in the fabric of things.

'Still don't know where we're go'n,' said Freddy, one of the last to depart.

'Freddy, you are a bloody numbskull,' Jimmy said. 'We're go'n to Irgeig. It don't matter where it is, just get y'self and y'kill'n gear ready to ride in the morning. This is it. We're ride'n against them Turks.'

The night had descended, the departed sun only a faint memory in the western sky. Jimmy thought of how the sun still shone to the west, across the glittering ocean. He envied the light's freedom, how it wasn't bound by earthly rules or constraints, how it shone so steadily, journeyed from the myriad of stars, held fast to its liberty.

Jimmy bent his neck, eyes upwards, peering into the sky.

Where was the emu? He couldn't locate it, no matter where he cast his eyes.

A feeling of desolation, of foreboding, swept over him.

He walked to his tent. He had knives to sharpen.

*

The hillside was crowded, fifty or more horses and men just below the crest, a few stragglers still walking their horses along the wadi base, a line of prone soldiers at the ridge-top, peering northward into the rapidly fading night. A corpulent figure in an officer's uniform slid backwards from the ridgeline, reached the wadi bed, half bent forward, patting dusty trousers, an audible slap of open hands against his thighs. He was in his forties, shorter than average height, bald pate fringed with neatly cropped hair. *The Major,* thought Jimmy, *pompous git, but a good soldier.*

Jimmy hefted his bayonet, examined the blade. He sensed a change, watching Tubby Matthews closely, in conversation with Dickie and the other Troop Lieutenants, saw the Major shake his head, waving hands left, then right, shaking fingers, as if to solidify some point. Dickie broke from the conference, wove his way towards the troop through the lounging horsemen, cleared his throat.

'You are ...'

'Go'n in first,' said Jimmy. 'Lead'n the charge.'

Dickie lifted his hat, batted away an early morning fly, stood back. 'Wish you wouldn't do that, Jimmy.'

'What?' Jimmy said. 'State the obvious?'

'No, listen in on the conversations of others.'

'Just lip-read'n.' Jimmy smiled.

Dickie stood silent for a moment, grim. 'Means, we'll catch most of the early barrage.'

Jimmy kept his natural smile. 'We betta move fast then,' he said. 'Get under them bloody guns.'

Dickie smiled, a smile he needed to show his self-confidence. 'Yeah, ride like hell,' he said, lifting his eyes to eager faces. 'We go in half an hour.' Hesitation, like there was more to say, then he turned swiftly, strode away towards the horses.

The troop were on their feet, reaching for their weapons, some inspecting mechanisms, checking magazines, expecting bullets to have deserted them, adjusting their jackets nervously, aligning webbing. *Gotta look your best when you stare death in the face,* Jimmy thought. He laughed to himself as he continued to squat, drawing a line with the tip of his bayonet in the wadi sand, recognising the signs in himself, the quiet ridicule of his troop, the smiles, the counterfeit ease. He needed to displace *his* anxiety, bolster *his* own superiority the most convenient way.

Jimmy glanced towards Eiric, absently fiddling with Tuppence's halter, Joe leading his own mount to his brother, with short hesitant steps, nervously batting away the early insects that rose with the growing light.

'Aren't you coming, then?' Joe said, calling across the crowd. 'You need a horse to get there.'

'You'll wear that thing away.' Eiric pointed to Jimmy's shining blade.

'Nah, just polish'n.' Jimmy dug it once more into the ground, ran sand along its edge; it would make a dirty, ragged cut now, something hard to survive.

'Might not need it.' Eiric, now the optimist.

'Yeah.'

Jimmy stood, sheathed his bayonet, whistled, a short, shrill tweet. Horse appeared at his side, head lowered. Touching his friend's nose, Jimmy considered their destination; a war fought in a dry, foreign wasteland, the lack of familiar sounds, the absence of those traces that could quiet the urge to run, to get the hell out of this mess.

'Gotta keep our heads down,' he said, almost beneath his breath. Horse shuffled his feet, a muted response, but recognition just the same.

Jimmy closed his eyes for a moment, took a deep breath, clasped his fingers about the reins, fitted his left foot into the stirrup, swung his right leg over the saddle.

'Right!' he said. 'Let's get at'em.'

Faces turned to him, eager to join with his confidence, grasping at a chance for triumph, searching for a guide. Dickie smiled. A unifying weight was now in the mix.

'We take them head-on,' said Dickie. 'In a line, bayonets drawn, like we practiced.'

'How far do we go?' Freddy had to ask a question.

'All the way,' Dickie said. 'They don't know we're here, won't know 'til we're on top of them, won't have a chance to respond.'

Now, that's hopeful, Jimmy thought.

They moved forward from the slightly elevated position at the banks of the wadi, each man silent in thought, each mastering the fear that could so quickly consume them, could turn victory into flight. Troops to the left and to the right, a line that faded from view in the early morning light, the faint jangle of harness, the occasional clatter of dislodged stones.

The eastern glow was rapidly growing, the sun not yet above the horizon, Irgeig a squat, shambles, dark, lifeless. *Maybe, there's no one home*, Jimmy thought, then dismissed the notion as fanciful.

The line gathered pace, trot to canter, Eiric grim to his left, Joe, eyes gleaming, on the immediate right.

The growing day faded into a memory.

Standing beneath the cliff, fingers of shadow reached out over the enemy camp, the sun low now in the west, dark invading the leached and weathered crevasses between the layers of rock on the south-facing wall, Jimmy sensed the change, a primal shift

221

– nothing would be the same again. Gurley wished, hoped, directed, almost desperate in her desire to deflect change; she wanted *this* life, not the whitefellas' creation, always suspicious of their motives, of the potential for damage to herself and those she loved, the boy, and those she was convinced would follow.

Jimmy thought of the boy, near twelve now, or was it thirteen? A man in the eyes of Gurley's family, already familiar with many things, but with little understanding of life beyond his land. He was ignorant of the veiled thread that bound them all to the past, that carried their fortunes to the future. Here, in this godforsaken place, children Cara's age were aware of all the corrupt practices of man: every sexual thing, beatings, floggings, rape, murder, death. They witnessed daily violence, to themselves, their families, friends, in the villages and towns. Nothing was shocking, there was no joy within their degradation.

The image faded.

Horse flew, like Pegasus, barely connected to the ground, a delicate, quivering ripple passing through his body, into Jimmy, vibrant, thrilling, riveting, the sound of wind.

And the staccato clatter of machine guns!

Shit!

How had they got here?

He glanced, first left, then right. The boys were still with him.

Ahead, close, he saw men, Turks, scurrying along a ragged line of trenches, scrambling to retrieve weapons. He saw their desperate faces, the sound of hooves beating into the dry ground a sudden, hypnotic accord. Then, the appalling noise of screaming horsemen slammed into him, the flash of gleaming bayonets against the rising sun a jarring reminder of their lethal purpose, knives thrust forward, his own hand aiming its lethal point, the wind in his snarling teeth.

Horse leapt, sailing high, a winged god over a troubled ocean.

And they were behind the enemy.

For the first time since his parting from the familiarity of home, Jimmy felt a blossoming awareness, a vitality that sharpened his mind, deepening the keenness of his sight. Fifty or more horsemen fighting to halt their careering mounts, Eiric down from his horse, Joe, still mounted, turning, about to ride into the backs of the hapless Turks, a cloud of grey dust, the product of the charge, enveloping the flat area about the small railway siding.

Jimmy caught a movement to the side. A lone Turk appeared, running towards him, bayoneted rifle thrust forward. Horse stepped neatly to the side avoiding the lunge, Jimmy slashed down with his terrible blade, tearing away a chunk of the man's neck – blood sprayed across Horse's flank, Jimmy's boot turning bright red. The body crumpled to the ground, lifeless.

That was too easy, Jimmy thought.

He looked up from the corpse, squinting into the veil of powder obscuring much of the battle, saw Eiric close to the trench, determination, purpose, murder in his stride, a twisted body left in his wake, Joe, nowhere to be seen. He urged Horse towards Eiric; not sure why, he sheathed the bayonet, pulled the rifle from his shoulder, a bullet in the chamber, ready to go. It felt strangely cold in his hands, a dead weight.

Eiric disappeared into the dusty cloud.

Another Turk suddenly appeared from the gloom, charging

at Jimmy, this time from behind. Horse rotated rapidly, skittered backwards, steadied as if to give Jimmy a stable podium, braced – Jimmy fired.

The soldier's face exploded.

Jimmy immediately turned Horse with his knees, thighs and legs, racing headlong through the pall, to the point he had last seen Eiric, and the hunters, three men with killing in their hearts.

The curtain parted.

He almost ran over Eiric, swerved, turned again, saw the men as they converged on the hopelessly outnumbered, and one additional man to the side, raising a pistol to aim, directly at Eiric's head!

Horse stopped, propped, took in a deep breath.

Jimmy thought, *Is this where I lose one of the boys, in the first fight?*

The rifle was at his shoulder, aimed at Pistolman.

Accuracy!

He filled his lungs, steadied, numb to all sound, feeling, or remorse.

Pistolman grinned.

He hardly noticed the click of the trigger, the recoil, the smell of gunpowder.

It felt like an age, reckoned he could see the flight of the bullet, slow motion, its progress to the enemy.

Pistolman had moved slightly!

Jimmy realised with horror that he would miss the target!

Later, Jimmy would reflect on how luck can so easily change, how fortune could so easy rotate on small things. He desperately injected another shell into the rifle chamber, raised the gun once again, aimed, fired without thought.

The shot went wide.

But it didn't matter.

Pistolman was dead: rivulets of dark fluid flooded from a bullet hole in the chest. The first had struck home, the man swaying, Jimmy guessed, back into the flight of the bullet.

Jimmy breathed out, felt Horse relax.

Then a surge of alarm. Where was Eiric?

He scanned the mayhem, located Eiric. He had one man down, a prostrate body at Eiric's feet, a bloody mass, uniform sliced, torn from its back and shoulders in ragged strips.

Jimmy watched, fascinated, as Eiric stalked forward, then with lightning speed, a headlong rush, a flashing bayonet, the two remaining assailants succumbed to the gleaming blade.

They didn't have a chance! Jimmy thought. *Where the fuck did that come from?*

Eiric stood over the corpses for a moment, laboured breathing, body sagging, knees finally buckling, he fell.

Shit!

Had Pistolman got off a shot?

Jimmy kicked Horse hard, flew to the crumpled heap of bodies, jumped from the saddle, bent, grabbed hold of Eiric's arm, turned his face up, searched desperately for a bullet entry point.

Nothing!

Joe arrived at a run. Kneeling, he lifted, cradled Eiric's head in his hands, lowered his head, an ear to his brother's nose and mouth.

'He's breathing,' Joe said, looking up to Jimmy. 'Saw you nail that one with the revolver.' He smiled.

'No wound,' said Jimmy. 'He'll be right. Reckon he just fainted.'

'Yeah, always was a sensitive fella.'

Eiric stirred, slowly sat upright in the dust. Jimmy watch closely as Eiric looked vacantly at Joe.

'How did we do?' Eiric said, voice thick with dust.

Joe laughed. 'Close call, Sulli, but Jimmy nailed him.'

'Nailed? Who?'

'Nailed the bugger who had you lined up for the grave. Jeez, Sulli, y'gotta do something about your bloody memory.'

Jimmy raised his eyes from the two brothers, gazed about the camp, bodies were strewn in careless form, men, an occasional horse, the fighting all but finished, the airborne miasma clearing now the battle had been won.

Luck, thought Jimmy. *It all turned on chance, the play of the cards, the roll of the dice, the whim of the heavens. How was he to ensure their survival with so much stacked against them?*

He looked back to the boys, heard Eiric's muddled voice still seeking details of the fight.

24

East of Gaza

Late Autumn 1917

Riding south from the camp near Hareira, just the two of them, the light was still low in the east, the scrawny desert scrub held in long shadows. Jimmy kept his eye on Joe, glancing his way every few seconds, checking his mood, hoping for calm, expecting an argument, rancour, bitterness. Jimmy needed to be hard, hardened like the old man, knew Angus didn't see reality like other humans; more like a fish really – cold and slippery. The old man saw everything and everyone, even his family, with dispassion, regarding them as a well of potential profit, for the enlargement of wealth and influence.

Joe seemed to hang in the saddle, no coat despite the early morning chill, shirt sleeves rolled up almost to his armpits, round back, listless.

His thoughts?

Two days of spite, invective pointed in every direction, to whoever would listen; a rage that appeared to have gradually siphoned away all of Joe's energy, leaving a residual deposit of sullen anger. Joe just wanted to kill Turks, forego sleep, exact revenge.

How?

Joe didn't know.

Ted. A life, thrown away, in some minor skirmish as the Ottoman Army retreated northward from Gaza, not even a real fight, shot in the back. Tubby Matthews insisted that responsibility for Ted's death lay with the Turks. Jimmy wondered, *In the back? Whose bullet was it, really? Did it really matter anyway who did it?*

Tubby gave Eiric and Joe the announcement, a scrap of paper, the remains of a life, on Friday, after summoning them to Dickie's tent; a summary, an execution, more like one of the random killings he had witnessed when passing through those squalid villages near Romani. It was brief, detached, typed on thin, slightly yellowed paper.

Station From, No. of Words, and Check

Desert Column HO

ANZAC Mtd Div HO Officially report that Number (ANZAC Mtd Div HO) (3117 Pte TA O'Sullivan) 1st Australian Light Horse previously reported injured is now deceased Kantara, Egypt 17th November 1917.

Col Harris 1 5H

Not for the first time, Jimmy saw Joe's temper flare, usually short and sweet, but this time sustained invective, railing against the world, the army, the Turks. Eiric just stood there, stunned, went into himself, retreating to make-believe, still recovering, he guessed, from the collapse at Irgeig – Eiric had unleashed demons of his own.

Joe had resisted this meeting.

'Why?' Joe asked. 'Reckon it's easy. Just kill the bastards.'

Jimmy took hold of his arm. 'Y'com'n? We're gunna talk it through.'

They rode south to the desert beyond the Wadi el Ghuzze, low, dry scrub, showers of sand, the clatter of stones kicked up by the horses as they turned and swayed between the spiky bushes. The sun thrust its fiery ball above the horizon as the flat country submitted to low, crumbling ramparts, a depression, remnant of an ancient river, of sudden floods that had gouged and snatched away the pillars of the earth. Jimmy knew the place, fissures opening to deep shadow, sensed the violence that had led to its formation, the heaving and buckling of the world, acid waters that burrowed their way to the very centre of existence.

'We're here,' he said, swinging his leg to the ground.

Joe remained in the saddle. 'Where?'

'Wanna show you someth'n. Horse found it a while back. On one of his wander'ns.'

'A shithole?' Joe's face smeared with scorn.

'Someth'n that might change y'mind.' Jimmy walked slowly to the cave entrance, no more than a gash in the ground, ducked his head as he entered, felt the earth swallow as it took him whole, didn't glance behind, let Joe fix his path, stay or go, accept or deny.

Jimmy's eyes gradually adjusted to the gloom, the feeble light from the entrance a guiding lance along a narrow corridor. He walked deeper into the complex of alleys, turning sideways at one point, squeezing past the intruding walls. Further, the light from the entrance now faint, his eyes were straining to determine form.

He felt Joe's warmth behind – he wished now he had brought a coat against the chill of the cave.

'Can't see a thing,' Joe said. 'What's in here?'

Jimmy sighed. You could take the horse to water ...

'Y'don't feel it?' said Jimmy.

'Feel what?'

Jimmy sighed again. He lifted his hand; a match flared, and a vaulted roof briefly illuminated.

Stars?

The match immediately guttered and failed.

Jimmy drew a breath. A match flared again, this time bursting into a flame held aloft, an oil-soaked flame, continuous and bold. He had thought ahead.

You could prepare yourself; you could imagine the effect, the power, the echo from home; the shock sent a wave through the soles of Jimmy's feet.

'Jeeeezus!' It was Joe, head flung back, eyes fixed on the cave's ceiling.

Jimmy silent.

If humankind was bound to the earth, if there was a shared source for all, if the same sun shone on them all, the same winds blew, you could not deny the link, the tie.

'It's the emu,' said Jimmy. Both men fixed their eyes on the intricate inscriptions, paintings, a myriad of finely-painted dots forming an ancient constellation across the vaulted ceiling.

'Yeah,' Joe said, voice distorted as he looked above. 'But how?'

'Dunno.'

'It's not in the sky here. Eiric and I tried to find it.'

'It's old.' Jimmy, as if that explanation was enough.

Silence again, broken only by the faint sound of a growing wind beyond the cave entrance. The popular belief was that everything was separated by the vast seas – plants, animals, people. They would live and die in their own corners of the world, never to meet.

'My people,' said Jimmy. 'They've been 'ere.'

'When?'

'Long time ago.'

'Maybe passing through?'

'Maybe.'

'Yeah, before all this shit, before Jesus maybe.'

'Yeah.' Jimmy chuckled. 'Before 'im.'

Joe tore his eyes away from the ceiling and caught Jimmy's eye. 'Why'd you bring me here?'

'Y'needed to see how small we are, how things 'ave been happening long before us.' Jimmy took a deep breath, 'How those Turk buggers are just like us, try'n t'survive, just like us.'

'Right.' Joe not convinced. 'Like, shooting people in the back!'

'Nah, could'a been anyone done that.'

'Might be the same as us, but we're here to kill them.'

'Yeah, our job,' said Jimmy, nodding. 'But need t'keep our heads straight, noth'n stupid, keep think'n, every time.'

Joe stood silent for a moment and gazed again at the emu.

'How did you find it?'

'One of them camel boys told me there was a cave somewhere nearby. Horse found it.'

'Jesus, is there anything Horse doesn't know?'

'Not much.' Jimmy laughed.

'And how the fuck did the Kamilaroi get here?'

'Might not've been my mob, could've been that bunch of

bastards from over the hill, the Bundjalung, or even worse, the Wiradjuri down south.' Jimmy smiled. 'Don't really matter, Joe, we're all the same, mate, the same people, try'n t'survive.'

Jimmy thought, *This has gotta be when Joe sees sense.*

Joe spoke, a vertical furrow etched deep into his forehead. 'Well, I'm not going to stop hunting those Turk bastards.'

Jimmy sighed. Thought, *Stubborn bastard.*

'Yeah, well, keep y'head down, and keep y'head.'

There was nothing more to say.

If they were to die in this land, then this place would provide a connection, maybe even restore the cord, take his spirit home.

Jimmy turned as the light from the oil-soaked torch started to fade. The brilliant light at the cave entrance promised heat, building to the baking intensity of late morning in the Negev. They had been in the cave longer than planned, Joe more stubborn than anticipated.

Horse stamped at the ground as they approached, anxious to be gone. The breeze from the north, now a wind, flung showers of sand into their faces.

The camp first appeared from the top of the last dune, just to the north of the large wadi, bathed in shimmering heat, enveloped in a pall of dust; the camp was being struck!

Eiric looked bothered, the pall of Irgeig still drifting about his eyes, sitting atop a pile of half-packed gear. Jimmy heard him snap at Joe, demanding an explanation for his absence, lamenting the burden he had to carry.

Jimmy saw the troop gather to leave, caught Joe's goad as he hefted his gear. 'Come on then. No time to wait for you, Eiric, we're on our way.'

'Bloody irritating prick,' was all Jimmy heard as Eiric bent to retrieve his kit.

Jimmy shook his head. Anger, such a destructive emotion, turning opportunity into a struggle, challenge to disaster, lifetime bonds to bitterness.

He felt Horse's presence, looked across the camp, realised his friend needed attention – water, fodder – before they joined the troop.

'Horse says it's time to go,' he said.

Eiric stomped away to retrieve Tuppence, muttering to himself.

*

'You all right?' said Jimmy as he bent forward, rolling the body away from Eiric. The corpse dragged a line of dark, sticky, semi-congealed fluid along the stony ground, leaving a trail, *a pathway to paradise*, Jimmy thought, *a red carpet to the final reckoning*. He wondered what his destiny would provide: if it meant incarceration in some whitefellas' hell, or the freedom of a path to those bright lights, or maybe admission to a virgin-laden wonderland. He laughed, a mirthless chuckle. Meaningless speculation. *What would be, would be.*

Eiric moaned, Jimmy checked for damage. None.

The sound of excited conversation filtered through his thoughts. Joe again, extolling the virtues of death, of Turkish mortality.

Dickie had led them this time – after several days in the saddle pursuing a retreating Ottoman Army – against a pathetically exposed rearguard. Confusion, he was getting used to the mix-ups, the disorientation, the worst of it losing track of the boys in the muddle. *I was pre-occupied*, he thought, *with bayoneting those two men*, fascinated by the way the blade seemed to glide effortlessly into a body until it struck an obstacle, a rib, a bone somewhere. Then you had to get the damn thing out; sometimes it seemed to be glued permanently in place. You had to kick it free!

This one could have been serious, he thought. *He'd lost sight of Eiric in a dust cloud; they were lucky.*

Without a word, Jimmy moved back, squatted gently onto his haunches, pulled a thin cigarette, prepared the day before, from his coat pocket. A wisp of smoke rose from the tip. He didn't inhale much of the smoke, just its presence, the act of lighting the reed calmed him, clarified, confirmed what he must do next.

Jimmy watched.

Eiric eventually climbed to his feet, flecks of blood down the front of his shirt, swaying across the flat ground, wandering, it seemed to Jimmy, looking for something in this blood-stained wilderness. Eiric briefly looked sideways at Horse as he staggered towards the well at the centre of the crumbling village, face blank, mouth slack. Jimmy saw Horse follow his progress, turning to keep him in view; they were both keeping an eye on the hapless Eiric.

Tubby Matthews strode through the village when the men had settled. Without saying so, he intimated that they had done an excellent job in killing every one of the defenders – they didn't have any prisoners to manage. The success of the operation meant, through their efforts, they could now consolidate the capture of Gaza, pursue the Turks, move on towards Jaffa, and push the bastards out of Palestine.

Joe, Slapper, Freddy, the men were pleased. Now, they all had the taste of victory.

Jimmy, still on his haunches, finished the cigarette, flicked away the fag-end, stood. Horse moved to his side, glancing at Jimmy.

'Yeah,' Jimmy said. 'Could'a been bad.'

The men began collecting the dead. The bodies dragged, flung into piles, the shovels appeared.

Horse shuffled backwards, nervous amongst the carnage.

'Gotta get work'n,' he said. Can't let'em rot in the sun.'

Jimmy wondered again, whether he would get used to this, the cruelty, the callousness, life's depreciation. He reached up to Horse, found his shovel.

'Go check on Eiric, will'ya,' he said, 'while I dig a few holes.' He turned to the task, thought he detected relief in Horse as he went searching for Eiric, distancing himself from the product of their pitiless gathering.

Jimmy never spoke to anyone about his misgiving; they wouldn't appreciate its source. His collaborators in these butcheries would think he was soft at best, mad or a coward at worst. He had to press on, that was understood, fulfil the promise, guide as best he could, these two boys, men now, through a growing nightmare, a grotesque depiction of reality. He didn't know where the end lay, its form, its legitimacy, its hold on the truth, but he knew that a fundamental thread secured them all; the caves had revealed some of that bond. Gurley would wait; generations, he knew, were yet to be realised.

'Look'n like y'wanna break,' Freddy said. 'Gotta get'em inta the ground. They're start'n to smell in the sun.'

Jimmy looked up, smiled.

'Where do y'want me t'dig?'

Freddy pointed to the hastily dug, shallow trenches, the defences they had smashed through on their way to this annihilation.

'Those,' he said. 'Dickie says, deeper.'

Jimmy raised his shovel, ran his hand along the shaft, glanced up at the sun, then bent his will to the gruesome task.

25

DHAKA

The Present Day

Harry could never sleep on aircraft – the constant rush of air along the fuselage, the sweaty body crush, the longing for intimacy rather than juxtaposition.

In Dhaka, in the cauldron of the airport, released from the cosy convenience of the aircraft, he lingered in the interminable immigration line, shuffling forward to the clunk of stamps on passports. Harry felt submerged under the weight of the looming city, could already feel the stifling humidity, the city's open sewers sending pungent tendrils that fondled his memory.

Throughout the flight he had thought of the old woman, Francine: tall, beaked nose, she bore little resemblance to her diminutive mother despite the same name. She retained no bitterness, not even residual yearning for what she had missed. Gallic humour clung to her, infused her with pride, a dignity that seemed to elude Harry. Her life was too busy: survival through harsh times, a strong family, businesses to run, some he suspected in the shadows, opaque to the law.

Harry should have asked more, demanded proof, could have

remained sceptical. But he hadn't. What was the point? Francine wanted nothing, her stories were honest, abiding, despite being secondhand from a mother that had survived despite the turmoil of partition, invasion, war – a land usurped. Their lives had separated too many years ago, Eiric in blissful ignorance, oblivious of the consequences of his dalliance.

Did that sum up his grandfather? Plunged into the filth of war, dreams of adventure that turned sour, repercussions flouted, then buried in the aftermath – a runaway train that could only end one way?

Nothing was owing. She had made that clear, her melodious words still echoing.

'Mother thought that Eiric had most certainly died during the attack on Amman,' she said. 'So many soldiers did not return.'

'What did she do?' Harry said.

'What could she do?' Francine smiled, a faint turn-up of the lips. 'She continued to work.'

'But she was ...'

'Yes, pregnant.' The smile abated. 'What choice did she have? A brothel is always assured income in times of war.'

Harry silent. He needed to process the words.

She broke the protracted silence. 'His brothers returned just before the attack across the river. They often gave the men some leisure before sending them against the guns.'

'Who?' Harry felt the approach of the awful truth. 'Eiric only had one brother.'

'No, my mother insisted there were two.'

'Names,' he said. 'Can you remember their names?'

'They are in the photograph,' she said, pointing to the faded image. 'Joe, the white man, Jimmy, the black. My mother liked Jimmy. He gave her money when they returned from Damascus, enough to allow her to escape the brothel.'

Harry sat quietly, the deception, the fraud, the deceit now clear. He thought about the later disintegration of lives, of shredded bonds, families in disarray.

'How did she survive?'

'It started with a small stall, selling fruit, bread, anything really that people might want. Down by the water, not far from here; enough to eventually buy a shop and start importing more impressive goods. She imported many things.'

Importing, thought Harry. *Best not enquire too much on that line.*

'She had other children?'

Francine paused. The quiet extended for so long that Harry thought the interview had come to an end.

'No,' said Francine finally. 'No, she didn't. I am her only child.'

Harry wondered whether he was told the truth, decided that it didn't matter, he had heard enough. An impassable silence gathered about the woman, and she bowed her head. Harry thought for a moment that the old woman had drifted into a deep sleep.

Harry started to rise from the divan, time to go, the meeting at an end. When she raised her head, she fixed him with pale-blue eyes, spoke in a soft voice, 'She loved him, thought he loved her too, thought he was dead.' She paused to draw a deep breath. 'His brothers, it seems, were not truthful, particularly the one called Joe. He said Eiric was dead.'

'He was not the same after the war,' Harry said as if that might mitigate the desertion.

'My mother knew there was little hope for the long term. But she would have loved more time. She described him as a dreamer. Yes, a dreamer, poetic, made her laugh with his jokes and stories.'

'That's Eiric,' said Harry. 'A dreamer, always with a joke.'

Francine smiled, drew a deep breath, raised her eyes to something behind Harry.

'I think it is time to go, Mr Weber. My mother, she needs her rest.'

A driver awaited Harry beyond the chaos of Dhaka customs, the stifling heat seeping into him on the walkthrough to the parking lot. They pushed into the traffic-laden roundabout at the airport entrance, narrowly avoiding a hurtling bus, a return of sorts to familiarity, into predictable turmoil, madness born of shady government, desperation, over-reliance on the will of God.

Harry settled into a lethargy, a torpor required to survive Dhaka traffic, until they stopped at the intersection with Kemal Atatürk Drive – teaming pedestrian hordes streamed about the vehicle. Harry looked to the side, at the wall in the centre of the road. A child, no more than a toddler, stumbled precariously along the top of the divide. He had seen the baby before, had watched it grow, its life at the heart of the road, beggar parents, gleaning scraps from passing motorists. Every year, there were new beggars to replace the old. What happened to the old?

Harry sat mesmerised.

A loud knock on the window!

Harry was pitched from his reverie.

A beggar pushed a hand forward, palm upward in supplication, a wounded, distressed expression.

The lights turned green, the car lurched forward, leaving the beggar in its wake; and Harry's phone rang.

'Hello?'

'Harry, it's Anika.'

*

Harry sat, silent at the edge of the bed.

Anika had diverted him. When he thought the way was clear, when his mother's mass of insistent missives seemed to point to the only solution, Anika had diverted him. *Maybe*, he thought, *there's more of Eiric in me than I realised.*

Beautiful, languid, sensual, femininity that drew him inward, submerged him, forever leaving him in debt.

'I've missed you,' said Anika. 'You've been gone weeks, no messages.' Harry felt the mid-Atlantic roll of the words, the mellifluous tone, a soft echo of an old lady in a Jaffa apartment.

Missed, distracted, detained, the expediency of deceits, the fulfilment of desire, the search for a design; they were interwoven, inseparable it seemed, indivisible.

'You were busy. You're always busy,' he said.

Anika lounged on the bed behind him, rumpled sheets half-covering her naked body.

'Yes, but not too busy to talk to you.' She hoisted herself onto her elbows; the sheet fell away from her breasts.

Harry half-turned to look. *Anika's eyes*, Harry thought, *like deep wells of rich coffee. He could almost feel the swell and swerve of the currents within, the upwellings, the tides carrying the quintessence of her soul to him.*

He thought he saw love; but he had felt similar before, diving hopelessly into absurd fantasies, searching for some external cure for his malaise.

Flawed?

He recalled Eiric's words: regret, neglect, rejection of blame. How close was he to repeating those fundamental errors, embedding those missteps in yet another generation?

'Are you off south again to the Sundarbans?'

'Yes, now that your funding is through, we can get some real stuff done.'

'Ever thought of taking a break?'

'Yes, Singapore occasionally. Why?'

'No, I mean an extended break, weeks, maybe a couple of months ...'

'Harry, there's so much to do here.'

Silence for a moment.

'Come to Australia with me,' he said. Even as he said it, Harry saw the flaw.

Anika rolled her body towards him. He thought for a moment that she was about to leave the bed, leave the room, leave him to his thoughts, his regrets, his self-doubts.

'When?'

'Now.'

'No, not now. The programme. It needs to be managed. That's me.'

'I need to get to Sydney, soon,' he said. 'There's a bunch of things that need me there: the company, family.'

'I could follow you when I've got this project underway.'

Harry felt the resonance, the echo of past promises, saw the repetition of the past. 'Yes, you could do that. That would be good.'

'When will you leave?' she said.

'Tickets booked,' he said. 'I leave in five days, Saturday.'

Anika quiet. Was that desire he saw? A slight flush about the face. She lay down, head submerged in the soft pillow, tossing away the remains of the sheet, kicking her long legs in the air.

'Only five days,' she said, a softness in her voice. 'Only five more days for me to have you.' Her arms spread wide, hands, fingers beckoning him.

Harry subsided, felt the warmth of her body as he lay against her, the heat rising as her legs pinned him close.

'I'll need at least a month to get all the stuff here sorted and working without me,' she said as her lips pressed against his mouth.

Harry wondered again if his penchant for the imaginary was driving him to his grandfather's ruin.

26

AL-AUJA – THE PLAIN OF SHARON

Early Autumn 1918

The soldier, a big man, forties, heavy gait, chin thrust forward, defiant, hard, brutal, was carrying a heavy gun over his shoulder, a machine gun that would have looked more at home in a trench. Jimmy watched, the sun still hours away, foot soldiers swarming beyond the riverbank, labouring against an escalating barrage from the north – the Turks were fighting back at last.

The soldier moved with surprising speed, despite the weight and size of the weapon, dodging holes and remnants of fallen shells. *No wonder,* Jimmy thought, *with all that coming at him, he'd want to hightail it.*

'When do we get off, then?' said Joe.

'Soon as these buggers clear the way,' said Jimmy. He leant forward, stroked Horse's neck, made a soothing sound.

'Was that who I think it was?' Joe said, craning his head forward, peering at the dimly-lit scene.

'Reckon it might be. Not sure though.'

Jimmy *was* sure, couldn't mistake the swaying step, the dip of the brutish shoulders.

'What's he doing out there?'

'Fighting the bloody Turks, I reckon.'

'Yeah, but with the bloody Tommies.'

Jimmy thought about that. While you had to grant it was unusual, what were you going to do with a bum-brusher like that – couldn't lie straight in bed, couldn't shoot, couldn't ride, couldn't be trusted to do the right thing.

'Tubby got him a job as an advisor with the Poms.'

'What?' Joe's scepticism ended in a laugh.

'After he beat the daylights out of us that night ... before we headed for Jerusalem.'

'Not my fault,' said Joe, still sensitive about his part. 'Just needed some relaxation at Madam Bouchard's.'

'Got him away from us, turned him over to the enemy.' Jimmy's turn to laugh.

In the beginning, Strepford's activities were mostly an irritation, minor violence, brief encounters, every contact manageable. At arms-length, life continued, despite his existence. Then one day Gurley changed that. A cousin walloped so hard she couldn't stand, nose broken – they thought she had a busted leg – kicked, bruised, bleeding.

It all changed. Jimmy's disinterest, excuses, the desire *not to be involved*, to walk away and leave them to their lives gave way to outrage at the barbarity of the man.

The girl didn't want to go.

Why?

One of those mysteries – like Strepford's desire to maim anything living, to destroy, to kill.

On the day Gurley convinced her to come with them, Jimmy counted at least half a dozen of the girl's excuses to stay, none mentioned love. She feared his anger; revenge so violent she couldn't imagine freedom. She came to them with nothing other than the clothes she wore, fear on her face, distress in her walk, justified as it turned out. The tendrils of Strepford's violence wrapped around them in the bush west of the Warrumbungles, even catching them in this strange place, Cairo, and the camp at Jaffa when Joe had slipped away whoring – the devil in pursuit of the innocent.

Jimmy glanced at Joe, chuckled to himself – Joe was hardly guiltless!

The last of the infantry slipped into the dark.

He's in the right place now, Jimmy thought, *right in amongst the worst of it, ready to satisfy his murderous soul.*

Joe laughed again. 'Well, he's knee-deep in shit now.'

Jimmy said nothing. Strepford was a thorn, a prick that kept gouging, scraping away at Jimmy, threatening to remove the last vestige of any connection he had with his destiny, with home.

Now he saw the cave, the emu, the cord, threadbare amongst all this torment, yet amazingly, holding still.

Jimmy watched from their slightly elevated position, the line of horses and men stretched across the rise, the shuffling of legs, the gentle jangle of harness, audible despite the deep resonating boom of distant artillery.

'Jesus, what was that?' Slapper to his right stood in the stirrups, starring at the growing conflict.

Machine gun fire, the steady crump of mortars, loud now, not so distant. *All sorts of shit falling on those poor bastards*, Jimmy thought.

'If that shit's falling on that bastard, then he won't be worrying us again.' Joe's face lit up with a malevolent grin.

'They're clear'n the way for us,' Jimmy said.

'Yeah, just hoping he gets it.' Although Jimmy agreed, he just wanted him to survive long enough to create the hole, a puncture in the Turkish defences, the pathway for their charge at the rear of the Turkish Army.

'Strange, not having Eiric here.' *Strange? Yes, and a strangely reflective thing for Joe to say*, Jimmy thought.

Jimmy had never spoken to anyone of the day Eiric botched the test. They wouldn't understand. Madness came in many forms – they already thought his own conversations with Horse were odd – voices, premonitions, beliefs, visions that foretold destiny; he qualified on all counts. He didn't completely understand what happened either. Eiric was stricken with malaria, feverish since the mess on the way to Amman in the spring, at Es Salt. They barely survived in the bloody hills, killing and suffering, only to be pulled away from the increasingly defiant Turks, returned to the Jordon Valley cauldron, only to sweat through the summer, wasting away. Eiric could hardly stand. Horse predicted the outcome, said Eiric wouldn't make it, couldn't stand the privations to come. Jimmy saw it though, the large, white horse moving at the limits of his vision, weaving recklessly through the old orange trees in the orchards above Jaffa. The apparition was reluctant to approach, finally standing, distant, watching Eiric's failure, like some herald of a tragedy that couldn't yet be divined, Eiric vaguely aware, disturbed by the presence.

Eiric almost made it! The doctor walking away, amazed at his recovery, though reluctant, was resigned to re-admitting him to the battle lines, letting him continue the fight. The apparition disappeared the moment Eiric crumpled. *Job done*, Jimmy thought, an influence he could not comprehend.

'Yeah,' Jimmy said. 'Should be in hospital, Kantara, by now.'

Jimmy leant forward, looking along the line of horsemen. At least one of his boys was now out of the firing line. He returned his gaze to the ink-dark ground before them, flashes from the artillery now lighting up the sky, raw power bathing him in wonder, dread, and strangely renewed purpose. They were riding to Damascus, and God help anyone standing in their way.

'Look'n like y'need a shit, Joe.' Jimmy smiled.

Joe maintained his forward stare, lifting himself slightly in the saddle. 'Nah, just a fart.' Another eruption. 'Too many oranges. Bit more water, and it would've been shit.'

Laughter along the line.

'Be glad to get after the bloody Turks again. Been too long.' The malevolent gleam had returned to Joe's eyes.

'Just keep yer ...'

'... head down. Yeah, yeah.' Joe nodded his head vigorously.

Jimmy laughed. He could only laugh and hope.

*

They sat, peering into the dark until the first glimmer of dawn, the false dawn, fought for supremacy over the almost continuous glow of exploding shells and bullets. The infantry tail disappeared from view, rolling their gear, small artillery pieces, eighteen pounders drawn by scrawny ponies, apparitions fading into the grey. The ghostly squeak of the large wheels dwindled, muffled by the tangle of low bushes.

'Why don't they get on with it?' said Joe.

Jimmy bent forward, ear close to Horse's neck. 'They're through,' he said as he rose. 'Almost done.'

'They need to get after it,' said Joe. He was jiggling about in the saddle. 'I'll need a piss soon, need to take my mind off it. And my bum's getting itchy.'

'Worms,' said Freddy. 'Told'y not to eat them oranges.'

'You don't get worms from oranges, you clown.'

'Yeah, y'do!' Freddy was indignant. 'Me mum always boiled'em up t'make jam. Said it was better for us, didn't go off, said noth'n could live in jam.'

'Jeezus, Freddy, but you're thick, thick as your mum's jam.'

The real dawn was now with them, a light breeze bringing a chill from the land, into their faces, the smell of the battle, the acrid scent of exploded ordinance, a fine powdery mist that brushed past their faces. Jimmy took a deep breath, savouring the bouquet, readying himself.

Here it comes, he thought, *the Tommies have cleared the way.*

A bugle!

The line stepped forward, walking at first, rapidly breaking into a trot. Horse took the lead, knew what to do, accelerated, an impetuous rush to the battle, to the inferno that would likely consume them all.

They rushed, five hundred or more horses – Jimmy hadn't counted – men clinging to their backs, a singular purpose: to survive the buffeting of the current as it funnelled northward. They headed for the narrow gap in the Ottoman lines, and once through to sweep back on itself, falling on the Ottoman Army's rear.

The battle surrounded them, the pungent gunpowder smell swirling about. The stragglers, soldiers, bent backs, rifles, bayonets thrust forward skittered to the side as the stream of horses flooded towards the front; two, maybe three horses abreast, hellbent, momentous.

He felt nothing could stop them now!

The acrid cloud thickened and Jimmy lost sight of the way forward. They were amongst the worst of it now, the eddying clouds, the rising battle, the heaving, churning turmoil of detonations, desperation and death. Horse never faulted in his stride, his head straining now, a thin wheeze floating back to Jimmy as the effort of the flight began to tell. The pall of the battle cleared slightly. Jimmy glanced to the side. Men were struggling forward through the haze, twenty or more advancing on a barb-wired trench. He saw a big man emerge from the smoke, separated from the crowd, heavy machine gun supported at his elbow, teeth bared, grim, maligned legs braced against the recoil of the devastating weapon.

The whirling smoke closed, briefly opened again, the man still pouring his murderous barrage at the enemy. Jimmy hugged close to Horse, fearing an irresolute grip, dreading ending up stranded in this part of hell.

Horse dug deeper, hard grit spraying Jimmy's face, the battle raging about them.

The big man stopped firing, raised the barrel of the gun, bent one knee to the ground, hands tearing at the ammunition belts slung across his shoulder, a single fluid motion borne of drill, hours of practice, purpose and resolve. Jimmy watched, amazed that the man had found something other than mindless harassment; he had, at last, a calling for his brutality, violence now for a cause, however bogus the reason.

Horse faltered, a slight lessening of pace, a sudden direction change; they were avoiding some obstacle, almost stopped now, then Horse sprang forward, back legs uncoiled, Jimmy nearly thrown backwards.

More violent direction change.

Weaving runs.

Sudden stops.

Horse finally accelerated, and Jimmy felt familiar stability once again. He glanced behind, saw a mass of horses stepping around distorted balls of wire, through shattered trenches, across a maimed, hellish terrain. He saw the big man, distant now, alone, isolated, suddenly shredded by a burst of fire from his right flank, a hail of bullets cutting him in two, his torso strangely stationary for a moment, before toppling to the sandy ground, the legs still upright, like some sort of battleground sentinel.

Jimmy turned away, knew that the horror was just beginning.

The pace eventually slackened, the air clearing, the thunderous noise of the battlefield receding. Horse, now lathered with sweat, was visibly distressed, taking huge gulps of fresh, untainted air. The Tommies rising had done their job, and they had made it through the Turkish line. Now, they had to ride, ride hard, a wild gallop to wheel about, behind the retreating Ottoman Army, to fall upon their remnants, to embrace an orgy of killing that would stop only when the last of the Sultan's army was crushed.

'Did you see that?' Joe pulled close to Jimmy as they moved once again to a trot.

'Yeah,' Jimmy said. He could guess Joe's thoughts.

'Didn't stand a chance.'

'Yeah.'

The din of the battle ebbing.

'Good to see him bite the dust.'

Gurley.

She reached into his mind once again that day, something he had resisted of late, since their arrival at Moascar. He wondered if *she* felt Strepford's departure. Jimmy wasn't sure whether he felt anything. Part of his degradation in this awful place, in this vile disguise? Most of the troopers didn't care, hardened already to killing, to violent death. He'd seen the carnage on the road to Jerusalem when it seemed they had no choice, when they barely stopped to bury the dead, more concerned with pushing on to the next killing ground, with the score, like the goal tally at a footy match.

There was truth here, though. Jimmy *was* relieved that Strepford was gone, he expected Gurley and her cousin *would* welcome their own release, and he *did* acknowledge his part in the outcome. He wouldn't go back on his wish to be rid of the man. It *was* comforting, and it *did* lighten the load. Evil had been expunged.

The five hundred or more horsemen moved northward, across the Plain of Sharon, along the corridor from Ramla to Megiddo, carrying a lust for blood, with murder in their hearts.

Jimmy settled into the saddle, allowed the tension of the charge to abate and waited for calm thoughts to return. He sensed they were in the final days of this campaign, close to the fulfilment of his bargain.

27

The Present Day

Harry's mother, Ruth, stood amongst the expectant airport mob, an awkward greeting before their silent march to the car. Before they reached the Harbour Tunnel, Harry finally spoke.

'Drop me at the hotel,' he said.

'What?'

'I've got a reservation. They're expecting me.'

Ruth glanced to the side, turning the wheel slightly, veering into the next lane. 'You're expected at home,' she said.

Harry clenched his fingers into fists. 'It's close to work.'

'Everyone's waiting for you.'

'They're waiting for me at the office, too.'

'What can't wait?'

'Andy, lawyers, about fifty people.'

Ruth, with a downturn of the mouth, made another sharp deviation into an adjoining lane. An angry blast from a heavily braking truck was ignored.

'Frances is expecting you there.'

'Tell her I'll see her in a couple of days. When I'm clear of Andy and the Board.'

'She's waiting for you.' Was that desperation in his mother's voice?

'Tell her I'll ring.'

'No!' said Ruth. 'You can tell her yourself! Phone her now!'

Harry took a deep breath. 'I'll do it, Mum. I just need to sort myself out after a long flight. And they want me in the office, right now.'

They drove in silence again, through the Rocks, narrow, crowded streets, the worry of coming confrontations amplified by Ruth's bitter mouth. Ruth swung the car into the loading zone at the hotel entrance. Harry sat motionless for a moment.

He half-turned in the small car's cramped space. 'I first need to clear the decks at work. There's a few things happening.'

'Family comes first, Harry.'

Harry straightened his back, felt the ache from the hours spent in an airline seat, sensed the heat from the crucible of expectations, the demands of family, a breath of guilt amongst half-truths.

Truth?

What was the truth amongst so many deceptions? He suspected his mother knew more than she would reveal.

'You need to talk to her,' Ruth said.

Harry reached for the door. He was anxious to leave. 'What?' he said. 'What do you want me to talk about, Mum?'

Ruth glared at him. 'Don't be awkward, Harry.' Harry felt the flush that used to infuse him as a boy – things never seemed to change. 'Just ring her as soon as possible. And by the way, there is the other thing.'

Harry felt the accumulation of demands. He waited.

'The other woman,' she said.

Harry sat forward, thinking that he would be assailed with re-criminations, the discovery of his impropriety, threats about his dalliances. He tensed his back, prepared his defence, refused to collapse under the weight of his mother's inevitable onslaught – his relationships were no measly flirtations, his vindication would be vigorous.

Tense, through gritted teeth, 'What woman, Mum?'

'The one from the DNA test.'

'Right.' Harry released his shoulders. 'What do you want me to do?'

'Talk to her. She seems like a nice girl.'

'Being a nice girl doesn't mean I have to talk to her.'

'Harry, there's a family connection here.'

Harry drew in a deep breath, paused, considered telling his mother to deal with it herself.

'Right,' he said, resignation in his voice. 'Give me her details.'

Ruth reached behind the driver's seat, pulled a tattered handbag across the divide, withdrew a crumpled piece of paper after rattling the contents for over a minute. She thrust a paper-adorned hand at Harry. 'It's all there.'

Harry nodded, stepped from the car, relieved to be free from his mother's scrutiny. The clammy humidity of a cloudy autumn day in Sydney closed about him as he walked to the hotel. He didn't want to be here. Sydney contained too much that reminded him of failure, his inability to discover the truth of his life, to resolve his doubts, redress his errors, correct his faults. He wished for the calm of Dhaka.

He laughed. What was his life worth if he wished to return to *that* maelstrom?

An image of Anika passed through his mind. Maybe there was a chance? She was strong, passionate, certainly didn't need him – a recurrent theme it seemed with the women in his life. Was this just another ill-fated diversion?

Harry went to the hotel desk. At least this would be a brief respite from the demands of others.

'Mr Weber, welcome back. Your room is ready. There's a message.'

Folded paper slip.

Harry read.

'Can you take my bag, please?' he said. 'I have a meeting.'

*

Andy sat opposite Harry, across a crude, wooden table.

'Shabby chic,' he said, looking across the collection of tables, inhabited by a selection of drab office workers grabbing some lunchtime freedom. 'Not sure if this is an improvement over the good old days.'

'There were no *good old days*, Andy,' said Harry. 'We were so sozzled most of the time we couldn't see the grime, and when we weren't in a daze, we were chasing skirt.'

'You may be right, but I remember being kicked out of here by the Painters and Dockers when they came off shift.' Andy laughed. 'We hightailed it before they could throttle us.'

Harry remembered the drunken Fridays, no return to work, waking up early Monday morning in someone's bed, smelling of alcohol and sex. A return to the office, the job, was an escape, a release from any risk of commitment. He couldn't see what had changed?

'Things are different now.' Harry glanced at two young women at the adjoining table. 'The young dudes get the girls, less money sloshing about, work, career, they're serious.'

Andy looked down, focusing on his beer.

'What's this about, Andy?' Harry had to ask.

'You've done a great job in Bangladesh, Harry.'

'Yes, well, at least we're producing some gas now, some revenue. Everyone seems to be happy.'

'Yeah, well, not everyone, Harry.'

Harry knew what was coming.

'The Board wants to divest,' said Andy. Harry knew it was really Andy's idea; he was the real boss, the one deciding.

'What? Some or all of it?'

'Everything.'

'Timing?'

'Now.'

Harry thought for a moment and sighed.

'Well, I guess I'd better get back there and make it happen.'

Andy looked. 'No, you won't be going back. That's not your forte.'

Harry fixed his stare at Andy. 'Is this the big goodbye then?'

'Harry, haven't I told you before? I'm watching your back.'

'Well then, what's going on?' Harry wasn't sure he wanted to hear the answer.

'North Africa,' Andy said.

'What about North Africa?' Harry felt irritable. Was it a change in his view of things, his life, or was it just tiredness from the flight?

'We need you to consolidate our position in Tunisia, Cyprus, that part of the Med.'

'You've got plenty of people who could do that job, better suited than me.' It was a forlorn hope, but he had to try. An image of Anika drifted into his mind.

'Not for this job. That trip you made to Tel Aviv was just an opener.' Harry thought of the group he'd met in the city before his journey south – hard men, surface-friendly, sharks cruising for a kill. 'You'll be based in Tunis.'

'There's things I need to tie up in Dhaka.' He wasn't surrendering just yet.

'Like what?'

Harry didn't want to unveil his life. 'Like all my stuff, the office, all the people there.'

'Harry, you've got things here you need to get on with before you take off to Tunis, and not just at work.'

Harry sat, quiet for a moment.

'Have you been talking to my mother?'

'No!' A bit too immediate. Harry's glare questioned Andy. Andy capitulated. 'Well, yes. She rang about a week ago. Gave me an earful. Said you were needed back here.'

'Is that why I'm here? This new job is just a fob-off?'

'No, that's real.'

Pause.

'It's real, Harry!' Andy on the defensive now.

He paused again, sighed. *Getting it out in the open*, thought Harry.

'I've heard rumours,' Andy said. 'You've been seen with one of the NGOs in Bangladesh, spending some time with her.'

'My business, Andy.' Harry felt a flush of anger.

His mother!

Controlling, manipulative. Harry had suffered her need for authority all his life. It was time to break the nexus, sever the cord.

'We'll talk through the logistics of the move after I've spent some time sorting the family,' he said finally, fighting to control his resentment. 'Give me a week, should have it sorted by then.'

He didn't know how he would solve the complications that seemed to be growing. He knew at last though that escape would resolve nothing; like rats in the sewer, his problems would proliferate if he ran, finally overwhelming anything and everything decent in his life.

*

They stood at the doorway, the scent of the eucalypts strong in the gentle warmth of a sunny autumn morning.

'You're lucky to catch me at home, Harry,' Frances said. 'I was headed out.'

'I did ring,' said Harry. 'Left a message.'

'Yes, I know.' Frances looked directly at him, an appraisal. 'You look tired.'

'Long flight, into meetings the moment I arrived.'

'Yes, your mother told me.'

Harry glanced over her shoulder into the house he had once shared.

'Have you got time before you go?'

Frances was quiet, seeming to weigh the tolerability of the request.

She stepped aside. Was that a cold expression? 'Yes, a few minutes. Then I have to pick up Sofie. At your Mum's place.'

'The house is the same,' he said as they walked through to the kitchen.

'I haven't got the money to make changes,' she said.

'Mum said you had some leaks.'

'Did. Your Dad made some temporary repairs. They work.'

'I can organise a tradie to ...'

'Harry, I don't need your help.'

'It wouldn't be a problem, just ...'

'Harry. You can't just waltz in here and take over.'

Harry quiet. His imitation of Ruth obvious.

'It's been months, no, at least six months since you last spoke to me.'

'Busy times out there.'

'What sort of excuse is that?'

'Pretty lame.' He had to admit it.

Frances stood, legs braced. 'Harry,' she said. 'I've been doing a lot of thinking since you left. And the thinking has always taken me to the same spot.'

She took a deep breath.

'Your life is a shambles. We don't need to live with your indecision, lack of commitment, avoidance of commitment, *your job always comes first* attitude.'

'I'm here, aren't I?'

'In body, Harry, not in mind. Well, not often in body either.'

Harry looked at her face; she was close to tears – he couldn't deal effectively with tears.

'We don't need you this way,' she said. 'And I can't see you changing.'

She was right. His life was a shambles, a series of shallow experiences, temporary unions, dodging anything other than a veneer of sentiment – in the footsteps of a grandfather who realised his failings only in the final days.

What could he say?

'Sofie,' he said. 'How is she?'

'Nice that you asked,' she said, sourness in her voice.

Harry remained quiet. He didn't want another release of acrimony.

'She's fine, healthy now after some sort of flu.'

'Yes, Mum told me.'

'Happy, most of the time, she grizzles sometimes, but happy, most of the time.'

Harry nodded.

'Harry, we don't need you.'

She paused.

'If you can sort yourself out, there might be a chance, for us.'

The ultimatum. Harry knew it was coming, though he couldn't help feeling that forcing change, change without a basis, change without an understanding of the root cause of his malady, was futile. The glimpse in Israel, of the roots of his muddle, the dim illumination of a path in Bangladesh, seemed only to add to his confusion.

Harry looked inward, examined his susceptibility to delusion. He would need to talk to his mother.

28

Early Autumn 1918

They were walking the horses, down a broad valley, the deep defiles of Mount Carmel behind them, the capture of Haifa, on the coast, someone else's business. Over a day in the saddle already, sunrise to sunset, riding northward into the night, they had skirted the primary battlegrounds.

'Where we headed now, Dickie?' said Jimmy.

He wasn't sure he cared. They had passed a whole Ottoman army caught in a narrow valley to the south, burnt, dismembered bodies a testament to a new sort of fighting, detached, beyond brutal. The buzz of the aircraft as they departed their bloodbath reminded him of bees crowding about a bush hive with the approach of a fire – alarm, suppressed hostility, the promise of violence. He had thought he understood his role in this absurdity. Now, he wasn't sure.

Jimmy seldom thought about the end, the end of everything – witnessing carnage on such a grand scale though, had shaken him. A coat of lethargy wrapped about his rounded shoulders, the barren hills at the rim of the valley gradually giving way to a shadowy void as the night fell. He felt a numbness with no release, a strange, chilly draft from the north fanning his face.

Still, they plodded northward into the night.

Words, muffled against his thoughts, penetrated the silence.

He shook his head.

'What?' he said. 'What was that?'

'I said, Tubby mentioned a place called Samakh.' Dickie arched his back, trying to stretch away some of the weariness. 'On the Sea of Galilee.'

'A holiday by the sea!' Joe spurred his horse forward. 'I'd like a bit of that.'

'Not that sort of sea.'

'We used to go to Manly every year,' said Joe. 'That's by the sea.'

'The railway goes there.' Dickie lowered his eyes to the thin strips of metal, vague ribbons highlighted against the dark background; to Jimmy, they hinted at something formidable, the end of things he could not perceive.

'The railway went to Central near Broadway in the city,' said Joe. 'We had to take a tram to Circular Quay, ferry to Manly across the harbour. Bloody rough some days.'

They rode on, the only sound the squeak of a leather harness, the occasional dislodged stone under hoof, the faint hush of the breeze in Jimmy's ears.

Dickie glanced at his watch. 'It's midnight, lads. A new day.'

'Ted, you know, my brother ...'

'Yeah, heard of him.' Slapper attempting to cut Joe short – they had been subjected to constant reminiscences of Ted.

'Yeah, well, Ted met this girl in Manly, spent hours with her at the beach,' said Joe, not to be deterred.

'Not many of them 'round 'ere.' Slapper sounded regretful.

'Not like those girls in Cairo and Jaffa, though she was pretty well stacked, as I remember.'

Joe paused, *thinking for once*, Jimmy thought.

'Tried all holidays to get into her bloomers.'

'Did he get some?' Slapper and the surrounding troop attentive now at the lustful turn.

Joe smiled as he gathered together the memory.

'Went on the whole summer ...'

'Did he get any?' Freddy, this time more insistent.

'Went the whole summer. First, she let him feel her left tit.'

Joe now had an audience. 'Told him the best way to feel her,' he said.

'How's that? Hard and fast?' said Slapper.

'Not like you, you tosser,' said Joe. 'With you, it's over in five seconds, with the girls screaming with pain and just wanting to run.' Joe paused. 'No, soft and slow, like you've got all the time in the world.'

Jimmy's turn to smile. Joe never had all the time in the world.

'Then, when he got that right, she let him feel her right tit.'

The troop was crowded close now.

'Jesus, get on with it, Joe.' A voice from behind.

'Well, it was just about time for us to head home. Ted couldn't get his mind off it. It was all he could think about, talk about. I told him to put the hard word on her.'

Joe paused again. Jimmy doubted the reality of such advice – at the time, the boy, Joe, was only recently free of a nursing mother, though he wasn't going to spoil a good story.

'Did he?' Another disembodied voice from the crowd.

'No, as it turned out, she invited him in.' Joe smiled again. 'The last week, going for a walk in the park near Fairy Bower, hot day, lying down behind the gazebo, got his hand up her dress, into her bloomers.'

'Jesus, what happened then?'

Jimmy chuckled to himself. He had heard this story before. It became lewder with the retelling.

'Ted tipped her onto the ground, dress up around her head.' The air filled with laughter. The horsemen were enjoying the diversion.

Jimmy noticed something. Breathing deeply, he held his breath, considered the message – a slight humidity, the sort of pungent aroma that comes before a storm. Yet, there was no rain. He lifted his eyes, peered into the forward dark, thought he saw a brief glimmer – reflection from water? The flash of light disappeared.

They plodded onward.

Only minutes later, the ground suddenly dipped, the horses clambering down a steep bank, into shallow water, a rocky river crossing. They had reached the Jordon River.

'Half-past two,' said Dickie. 'We'd better get a move on. Tubby wants us at Samakh by four.'

'What's the hurry, Dickie?' said Jimmy. 'We haven't seen a bloody Turk now for hours.'

'Dunno, Tubby just wants us there, soon as, latest by four.'

'Bloody hell, I need a piss.' *Joe always seems to be full of piss,* thought Jimmy.

'You gunna finish the story, then?' said someone.

'Nothing much more to tell,' said Joe.

'He did the job, did he?'

'Well, not exactly.'

Silence. The audience had been captured once again.

'Well?'

'She was on the ground, legs going everywhere in the air. Ted had his trousers around his knees, bare bum in the air, groping for the bloomers.'

'She changed her mind, then?'

'Nah, she couldn't stop laughing. She was right into it.'

'What then?'

Joe paused. The pace had increased, no longer a slow walk. Jimmy muttered encouragement to Horse. His friend was tired.

'Well …' Joe lifted himself briefly from the saddle, using a hand to rearrange his crotch. *An unconscious preparation*, Jimmy thought, *for the tale's finale.* 'Well, he suddenly felt something cold and wet up his arse, shoving right up his crack.'

'Jesus, what?'

'Ted turned 'round, and a bloody dog went for his balls. He sort-of lost his enthusiasm for the job for a start.'

'A bloody stray?'

'Nah, he tried to beat the dog off with one hand, the other around his dick and balls, fell back on top of the girl …'

Joe could never help laughing at this point.

'Saw her mum coming down the path. She'd been tracking them with the bloody mongrel.'

'Jesus! Reckon I would've run.' Slapper the Brave.

'That's what Ted did,' said Joe. Jimmy always envisaged Ted's bare bum disappearing down the path, hands hauling up his half-mast pants.

The troop laughed.

'We never did see the girl again, Ted, all of us, Eiric and me as well, banned.'

Jimmy laughed with them.

The scent of mouldy earth reached Jimmy once again, this time with the hint of something else; oil, grease, men, fear and Turks.

Ahead, a figure suddenly stepped from the night gloom – a squat, round man, an officer.

Tubby Matthews talked briefly with Dickie and a gathering of the other Lieutenants, turned and disappeared into the night. Dickie returned, deep worry lines engraving his forehead.

'We go at four.'

'Where?' someone said.

'Samakh. And we charge'em head-on.' He looked at the troop, a bleakness in his eyes. 'Before it's light.'

'Christ! We haven't even seen the ground!'

Jimmy stood quietly beside Horse, looking at his friend. 'Yeah, we gotta be careful with this one.' He turned, trudging into the dark. He needed a piss.

*

'How long now?' said Joe.

Jimmy saw the machine gunners move forward, towards the town, a creeping line of soldiers, gradually disappearing into the thick, dark night.

'Not long. That mob will cover us …' said Dickie.

'How can they do that? It's bloody pitch black out there!' Joe's complaint was echoed in the nods of the men.

'They'll fire at the flashes from the Turks' guns.' Dickie clearly wasn't sure. 'They're camped as far on the flanks as they can get. On the rising ground in front of the hills … to the east.'

'What hills? I can't see a fucking thing!'

Joe's just voicing what we're all thinking, Jimmy thought. *Typical, can't keep his bloody mouth shut.*

Jimmy watched Dickie walk away, the slouch, shoulders slightly forward, a drag in his step. They were all tired, so many hours in the saddle, to arrive in this place, this godforsaken patch of night. He shuffled his boots in the soil. *Good dirt*, he thought, *freshly ploughed, ready for a crop of some sort, what nasty surprises awaited them across this ground.*

He strolled forward to the edge of their feeble lamplight – dips in the land, furrows, rows, rocks. Jimmy caressed the span, the flat, open fields, the fissure that could unlock the conflict consuming them. An opportunity, or a sentence? A consignment to some sort of hell?

Jimmy felt a nudge at the shoulder. He maintained a gaze into the blackness as if the dark might suddenly split, like the Red Sea for the Israelites. *Too much time with them priests*, he thought, *and too much time in this cursed land*. He chuckled.

'Yeah, like I told'ya, we gotta be careful.'

Horse strained his head forward, breathing in the damp air as it drained from the sea beyond their reckoning, shook his head, moved backward a few steps.

'We need to do this,' said Jimmy. 'Then it's over, and we can go 'ome.'

A shout.

Dickie's voice.

Jimmy stepped to Horse, a fluid motion that seemed to float him onto his friend's back. One more fight, then Damascus would be theirs; at least that's what Tubby had said, just a stroll north, unopposed, across the Golan Heights.

They moved forward, over five hundred men and horses in lines spread across the plain, lines so long the night seemed to swallow their ends. Jimmy sighed a breath that carried the jaded memory of the lost years, of loneliness, and killing. The line held to a brisk trot at first, into the inky blackness of the unknown, a damp breeze in their faces, the smell of fresh-turned earth in their noses. The lust for killing that had once invigorated them was now a hollow celebration.

The trot moved to a gallop.

Jimmy held a position on the right flank of the charging mob, clear he hoped, of any falling beasts and men. Joe rode to Jimmy's left, preferring the protection of the crowd, always keen to mix vulnerability with the thrill of the fight.

They galloped, and once again they yelled, at what, it was not clear to any of them. Maybe it was at the darkness, at the possibility of home, at the chance of redemption?

They accelerated.

Horse strained, the cords in his neck stretched to breaking, the sound of his breathing, inhalation, exhalation, a steady beat, like a metronome against the rhythm of a tune, the final tune, a song of death.

Jimmy saw a horse and rider go down, a sudden dip of the horse's head, shoulders to the ground, a tumble, rider pitched forward into the air.

Still, they charged into the blackness.

Another horse gone; the following riders caught amongst the flailing legs. Then, it seemed horses and riders were falling everywhere.

This was madness!

Still, they charged.

Jimmy looked to the side at Joe, tight lips, fixed stare into the abyss, grim, obsessed. Joe wanted this, the final reckoning, the slaughter that would make it all right, that would dispense justice for the loss of his brother. Jimmy knew there would be no definitive calculation, no making-it-right, only more blood to be spilt. The Turks were on the run, dismayed, confused, beaten. This was their last stand before the whole thing disintegrated; before their thousand-year empire crumbled to dust.

A point of light flashed ahead!

Were they almost there? He could smell the damp of the sea, but it was subtle, still vague.

Jimmy felt Horse falter, a slight misstep. The ground tilted slightly down now, rocky, treacherous. He tried to ease the pace of the charge, but Horse had his head, wanted this to be over, and like all of them, needed to be finished.

Jimmy saw more flashes ahead, the hiss of the first bullets as they passed close to his head. The Turks had been waiting for them; they were prepared.

The barrage of bullets increased, machine gunners aiming

blindly into the dark, the horse beside Joe hit, a scream, pain, ruin.

Shit! The losses were mounting! Would they enter the town with enough men?

Suddenly a bright line of tracer bullets appeared from the right flank – covering fire was concentrating on the Turk's gun flashed. They now had a chance!

Jimmy crouched low, Horse's fluid motion restored as the ground flattened – Jimmy guessed the outskirts of the town – the furrows and rows of the field replaced by urban roads and paths and new dangers; paths led to walls and structures that could end a charge and a life as quickly as a machine gunner's bullet.

Horse's pace slackened, swerved, stopped, shuffled sideways. Joe careered into Jimmy, straining desperately at his reins, almost unseated by the sudden stop. They had arrived, over five hundred horsemen, crowded now, against a series of short walls that formed the perimeter of the town.

The machine gunners ceased their barrage, an eerie silence enveloping them all, broken only by the wheezing breath of exhausted horses. Jimmy vaulted from the saddle, drew his gleaming bayonet from its scabbard, thrust it forward as if it could serve as a beacon. It was time to search for the enemy, a time for killing, a time to end this madness.

Jimmy turned to Joe. 'Better get after'em, then,' he said.

Joe licked his lips, nervous, agitated, anxious. 'Yeah,' he said. 'Let's start with that building over there.'

Jimmy peered across the open ground – two storeys, railway lines, the dark form of a silent steam engine. He felt a hand close about his shoulder and Dickie's voice. 'Well, that was a wild ride.

Lost a bunch of horses across those bloody fields. Thought the machine gunners would cover us a bit earlier than they did ...' He took a deep, shuddering breath, clearly shaken by the ride, smiled a wan, hollow grin. 'Still, we're all here, all of the troop I mean.'

Jimmy looked past Dickie, to Slapper, Freddy, familiar men that had met the trials from Cairo to Palestine, from Es Salt to Jericho and the Jordan Valley. Fear was always with them, anger a constant, forever suppressed in case it consumed them; Joe was perhaps an exception.

'The railway station,' said Dickie, pointing. 'Tubby wants us to take it.'

They all turned to gaze uncertainly at the edifice, the open ground, the thick, stone walls, the barricaded windows, as the first glimmer of dawn broke above the barren walls of the Golan Heights, forming shimmering reflections across the still waters of the Sea of Galilee.

Jimmy accepted his own fear then, realising that his fate might possibly turn on this moment. He would need to end this quickly.

He moved forward into the open ground, Dickie to the left, closer to the shuttered upper-storey windows. A white flag hung from the building, no one showing themselves. Dickie visibly relaxed, lowering his rifle, turning back to face the advancing troop.

'They're surrendering,' he said, relief in his voice, across his face.

Silence.

Jimmy stopped, felt his scalp crawl, itching as if insects were crawling. He noticed a slight breeze, fresh, sharp, draining from the sea.

Silence.

He heard a slight rattle, a latch undone, a shutter released, looking up to where the white flag, a dirty sheet, fluttered against the light breeze. He caught a flicker of dull metal in the growing light, thin, tubular, deadly.

'Run!' It was all he could say.

Dickie stopped his stroll towards the station door, looking back to Jimmy, confusion passing across his face.

The bullets slammed into Dickie's back, pitching him forward. Jimmy, Joe, the troop ran, hurtling towards the building, the last yards scrabbling on hands and knees. Jimmy looked back as he found the protection of the building eaves. Dickie lay sprawled in open ground, exposed, abandoned, a seam of dark fluid draining into pools in the uneven pavement. No one would rescue Dickie – they had work to do inside this accursed place.

Jimmy renewed his grip on the bayonet, the weapon he had honed for such an occasion, turned to the stout wooden door, nodded to Joe, the troop clustered around the entrance.

'Reckon we'll have to knock this fucking door down,' he said.

Ten men leant against the structure and heaved – the door stood firm.

A deep breath, a collective lungful of hate, revenge, vengeance. Ten men working together, their heads throbbing, sinews stretched taut, faces red with rage. The door shifted slightly, a scraping sound – something barricading the entrance.

Another mighty heave, the opening now wide enough to admit one man at a time – no one inclined to enter just yet; they needed something to dissuade retaliation from within.

Jimmy looked back again at Dickie's prostrate body, saw the

revolver harnessed to his waist – that would do it. He gathered his legs together, sprang forward, reached Dickie, desperately releasing the weapon, expecting the lethal volley that would end his days, just as it had with Dickie.

It didn't come. Jimmy clawed his way back to the door, steadied himself before the portal.

'Reckon they're wait'n for us behind this fucking door,' he said to the crowd. Without explanation, deprived of any plan, Jimmy leant forward, cocked the gun. 'Push this fucking door open when I start fire'n.'

The pistol made an awful noise as Jimmy loosed off four rapid shots around the gap, the door flung open under the collective weight, a narrow corridor leading to stairs at the far end, rooms either side withholding their treasure, targets of their rage.

A figure lay bleeding at the base of the stairs. Joe rushed forward and drove his bayonet deep into the soldier's chest, pulled free, did not linger over the man's fate, clambering desperately towards the building's lofty heights. Jimmy darted from the corridor into the first room, almost collided with its group of defenders. His lance flashed as he cut, stabbed, skewered, one, two, three figures; a blur as they went down under his knife. Sticky, red fluid flowed down his arm, he lost count, crushing the vanquished underfoot, as he clambered forward, lusting for their destruction.

He reached the far wall – this room was done – a feeling of success, a curious sense of achievement washing over him. He turned to survey his handiwork, to proceed to fresh fields, when a body hurtled into him, knocking him backwards, a stunning blow. The weapons flew from his hands, falling with a clang to the floor, fists pummelling him desperately.

Jimmy had grown up fighting, dirty fighting, never clean, a winner at all cost. He had learned the hard way that kindness, latitude, lassitude in a fight gained nothing, that even when the result might be unimportant, a killer stroke was necessary, and it had to be swift. This brawl was different though the technique was the same. It was a matter of life and death.

He caught a glimpse of his bayonet as the man's fist pushed his head to the floor. It was beyond his reach!

Jimmy managed a quick glance upward as the flailing fists tired. Blood dripped onto him from the soldiers battered face – Jimmy's brutal responses were having a devastating effect – a fetid smell from the man's decaying teeth now coming in short, concentrated bursts. Jimmy squirmed slightly sideways, felt the lost pistol as it dug into his back. He wriggled again, grasping the butt, swinging it in a wide arc, striking an exposed temple. The man reeled back, clutching at his head, Jimmy brought the pistol to bear and fired. The rear of the head exploded – blood, bone, skin, hair showering over the prone bodies of Jimmy's victims.

He lay quietly on his back, eyes closed, dreaming briefly of home, of spring flowers, the lush fields of the Warrumbungles. Slowly, he registered screams, the occasional gunshot. The business of conquest was being played out with brutal effect. Victory now seemed assured.

29

The Present Day

At Pennant Hills Road, Harry turned right, into the stream of cars and clattering, hissing trucks venting air brakes, all heading north to the Central Coast and beyond, all seeking some sort of nirvana, escape from the pressure of a city out of control.

The weather had turned bleak, a shiny film of moisture deposited on the road, portend of the lurking storm, of an evening deluge so typical when the southerly winds beat back the warm air from the hinterland.

Harry wanted this to be simple. He knew though, that his mother would try to complicate things, would twist the logic, allocate blame, offer her opinion, specify the necessary solutions, apportion remedies she deemed appropriate – responsibility, guilt for the mess would fall heavily upon him.

Was that fair? Was he responsible for it all – the flaws, the broken relationships that seemed to permeate the family, the wounds that appeared to have their genesis so long ago?

The turning lanes at the Comenarra Parkway were stacked with cars, headlights shining now in the fading light, the wiper blades

277

slapping against a steady drizzle, almost beating in time with blinking indicators – the repetition hypnotic, engrossing, so absorbing he almost missed the movement forward of the stream.

He expected his mother's derision – maybe it was justified, perhaps he had allowed the past too much authority, too much influence?

As the traffic stream wound down into the valley, Harry felt his mouth dry, a sour taste, his tongue catching against the back of his teeth, a rasp in his throat.

He turned right once again, accelerating fast, dodging reckless traffic that hurtled down the hill along a slippery road, the rain now beating against the windscreen.

Typical bloody Sydney, he thought, *fine one minute, a deluge the next.*

Anika flashed into his mind. She would be enjoying an evening drink at the club in Dhaka, warm, the evening approaching, planning her next project, tempting the next donor with one of her ventures. Harry pushed the image from his mind – he needed to brace himself against the coming onslaught.

He drew the car to a stop on the driveway. Two vehicles parked already: one, his mother's old canary- yellow Corolla, the other unknown. What traps was his mother laying? Conversion or exorcism? *A ritual casting out of the demons*, Harry thought. *That will fix everything.*

Deep breath, the car door open, Harry squeezing past the rampant yucca, the lethal spikes prodding at him as he edged towards the gate, through rain, drops of water smashing against his head, beating against the vehicle's roof, rattling against the corrugated tin roof of the house.

Harry ducked through the gate, into a narrow, covered passageway, shaking himself free of the drenching, brushing tousled hair away from his forehead. He stood for a moment, invisible in the dark of the alley, his mother's voice, loud, emphatic, purposeful, striding towards him. *I could leave now*, he thought, *I could just disappear, off to Andy's next job, and avoid the repercussions of the past.*

Harry stepped forward into the light of the kitchen. Two women – his mother, tall, weathered, tense, standing at the edge of the kitchen talking to a lithe, dark-haired woman. As he slid open the large glass door, his mother turned towards the movement.

'Harry,' Ruth said. 'You're here at last. I'd almost given up hope.' Never one to let a criticism go through to the keeper.

'The rain,' said Harry. 'It slowed everything down. All the way from the city.' An exaggeration, but it would pass.

'Harry, this is Jessica. Jessica, my son, Harry.'

The woman smiled, a smile that stopped Harry's breath, a smile that amplified the fine structure of her face, a smile that shone beyond her face, that animated her entire body, that surrounded Harry with a sense of peace.

Harry stepped forward into a place he had not expected.

'Nice to meet you, Jessica,' he said.

'Jessica is the person I told you about, Harry.'

Harry remembered his mother's plea for help with a tinge of guilt that he hadn't found time to contact the woman. 'The person ...'

'Yes, the person who contacted me through that DNA testing place.'

'Right, that person.' Harry smiled. 'We're related, it seems.'

Jessica sober, the remnants of the smile still playing about her beautiful face. 'Yes, same great- grandfather.'

'Old Angus,' said Harry. 'I met him when I was just a small kid. Seen, not heard. That was his philosophy on kids. So, I can't say I have a detailed memory of him. Mum knew him well, though.'

'Yes, your Mum has been really helpful.'

'What more can we help you with?' Harry said, moving towards the old lounge. He walked to the door, the entrance to the verandah where the television, volume high, all-day news, pronounced another crisis. He closed the door.

'It's my mother,' Jessica said.

'Your mother?'

'Yes, my mother, Gima.'

Harry had an image of a beautiful, old woman – beauty through the generations. Maybe another of his fantasies, but it had to be that way.

'She wants to meet you. And your mother,' Jessica said.

'I've told Jessica I can't go,' said Ruth. 'Your father. He needs me here.'

A lame excuse, thought Harry.

Harry ignored his mother. 'Why does your mother want to meet us?'

'Gima is old, not well,' Jessica said. 'She hopes you will know something about my grandfather, Jimmy.'

'I won't be able to help her there but ...'

'I know, but Gima can see many things from the people she meets. She says it's in their aura, the way they stand, hold themselves, their presence.'

The vague image of a pale horse, the one Harry thought he saw in Israel, passed through his mind. Where did that thought come from?

Harry sighed. Many things were pressing him, the move to Tunis, Frances, he needed to clear the ground with his mother, the mess of his life. This seemed an unnecessary diversion.

'Your grandfather, Eiric, was Jimmy's close friend,' Jessica said.

'Where is your mother?' Harry hoped she maybe lived some distance away?

'Redfern. She lives with us in Redfern.'

Harry sat, considering excuses for a refusal. He could find none. Ruth obviously had given it some thought, had manufactured a reason, was running from any commitment. They were the same it seemed – running at the first opportunity.

'When can we see your mother?' said Harry.

'The morning,' said Jessica. 'First thing tomorrow.'

Harry sat, quiet for a moment, considering diverse paths that shifted before him, decisions intertwined with actions, flawed choices, blind alleys. Where would this lead? He had a feeling there was something, some insight associated with this woman, with her mother, with their past. It was an opportunity he could not refuse.

'Give me the address. We'll be there,' he said.

Ruth started forward, mouth working in protest. 'I can't …'

'We'll be there, Jessica, both of us.' Harry's voice carried a warning. Ruth stopped. A sharp glare from Harry, Ruth remained silent. She needed to accept her part in his turmoil. Any confrontation here, now, would only lead to recrimination, accusations that merely shifted the blame, nothing solved.

Tomorrow, Harry hoped, a piece of the puzzle, the enigma of their lives, would be found. Ruth had to be there. Harry knew it in his bones. How often had he acquiesced to his mother? How often had he run from the discomfort of confrontation? How often had the weakness of his soul resulted in decay, and erosion of his hopes?

Harry felt a shock; it passed from his guts to his feet, along his spine, scattering through his scalp, his vision briefly blurred. He shook his head, a dull pain behind the eyes, looked up, saw the two women observing him.

'We'll be there, Jessica, both of us.'

*

Harry chose the Harbour Bridge, remembering those wild motor-cycle days, the early morning rush to the first lecture, the treacher-ous slip and slide as the first rain mobilised the grease and oil on the road at the tollbooths. The booths were gone now, the traffic lighter since the advent of the tunnel.

He veered left across the Cahill Expressway, the ugly barrier that tore Circular Quay from the city, witness to a departed New South Wales premier's folly, or was it corruption? They headed south.

'You should have taken the tunnel,' said Ruth.

'I wanted to see the old way into the city,' Harry said.

'You can't live in the past, Harry.'

Harry turned down the ramp onto the Eastern Distributor. They had such romantic names for their roads these days. The traffic crowded along the narrow lanes – Bangladesh flitted into his mind.

'You can't forget it either, Mum.'

'Turn off at Lachlan Street,' she said, hands gripping the door handle, ready to abandon ship if things deteriorated. Sydney traffic seemed to have that effect on passengers.

The furious pace melted away as they entered the suburb.

'Where are we going?' Ruth was looking increasingly nervous.

'Redfern Street.' Harry glanced at the plethora of new high-rise apartments. 'This isn't what I remember of Redfern.'

'Times change, Harry.' Ruth seemed to shrink into her seat. 'There are still parts you shouldn't walk through.'

Convincing Ruth that she had to make this journey had been difficult. First, a flat refusal, then an ultimatum – a feature of his life now it seemed – fatigue, exhaustion, want of plausible excuses, capitulation. Harry was surprised that he could wear down his fractious mother.

Redfern Street, a mix of new and old, a row of semi-detacheds. Harry stopped the car.

'That one,' he said, pointing to a front yard filled with a jacaranda, blue window frames and door. 'Reckon we're here.'

As he levered the car into a tiny space opposite the house, he saw the front door open. Jessica waving, walking to the spiked, iron, picket fence, standing, waiting.

'I told the neighbours you were expected. They left the parking spot free,' Jessica said as they approached.

'Lucky no one else took it before us,' said Harry.

Jessica laughed. 'They would have been moved on. This *is* Redfern.'

They moved through the door, into a narrow hallway, living

room through a wide door to the right, narrow stairs angling sharply upward, a shaft of light from the house rear, presumably the kitchen.

'In here,' said Jessica, swinging her arm to the right, the room filled with a textured couch, a large padded chair meant to lift the infirmed, an assortment of richly coloured rugs. 'Mum will be here soon.' Jessica turned, walking towards the light.

Harry sat, sinking back into the old cushions, listening to the muted hiss of the traffic beyond the large bay window, smelling, almost tasting the slightly musty odour, probably rising from the floor – these old houses usually had poor foundation drainage, draughty floorboards.

Ruth perched at the edge of the lounge, tense. What was she expecting, the attack of a troll?

Harry laughed to himself. What did *he* expect? An old woman, certainly not an ogre, someone from their past, a link perhaps, to the genesis of this disorder that seemed to swirl about, driving him to the shallow, the ephemeral, to separation in a crowded world.

A faint knocking beyond the door.

Ruth lifted her head, focusing on the exit to the hallway. Was she about to run?

A faint breeze fanned Harry's face; a door slamming shut – the knocking closer now.

In his mind, Anika lying quietly on the bed. What had she said? *I've come to terms with my past, the sins of my father, you might say.* Harry didn't understand. She tried to explain. *Not my actual father, but way back, back when the States was a wild place, when the Europeans, the white men in all their treachery, almost destroyed the last vestiges of culture and respect in the Indian tribes of America*. Harry still couldn't understand. She lay back on the bed, exposing herself to him, her inner self. *They killed men, women, children. It was brutal. Some survived, some tried to hide their origins. I had to force the admission from my mother. He was an Indian, a good man, though he passed on to us all the bad, tangled stuff that came with that sad, cruel history. It wasn't 'til I understood his journey that I could understand where the destructive part of me came from.*

Harry looked up. He sensed a presence before she appeared.

An old woman, small, straight back, dark skin, short, black hair, stood in the doorway, leaning against a stout walking stick. Harry could see the granddaughter, Jessica, in her vibrant face. She stood for a moment, surveying the room, appraising Harry. Ruth shuffled uncomfortably on the couch.

'Harry, Ruth,' Gima said. 'It's so good you came.'

Harry immediately stood, moving to help Gima to her chair. She waved him away.

'A bit of gout today,' she said. 'I can usually walk better than this.'

Harry watched her move across the room – slim, lithe, athletic, despite her years, confidence that seemed to elude the aged. *She had to be very old*, he thought, *in her nineties at least.*

Once seated, Gima looked at them for a while, a calm descending upon the room. Harry felt a lethargy, drowsiness filling his mind, his body. He shook his head, glancing briefly at his mother. Ruth reclined calmly now, amongst the soft cushions.

'You look like your grandfather,' said Gima. 'He was such a vibrant man.'

'You knew him?' Harry said.

'Oh, yes, though I was very young.' Gima smiled a smile that drew Harry to her. 'Jimmy loved Eiric, saw in him a kind of saviour, I think. A man who could carry forward the fortunes of the family.'

'You knew Eiric was Jimmy's brother?'

'No, not in so many words. They were close, a closeness that had to come from somewhere, something I didn't understand.'

'Eiric didn't live up to expectations,' said Harry. He felt the failure.

Gima fixed her gaze on Harry. It could have been minutes before she responded, Harry lost any sense of time.

'I see him in you, Harry,' she said finally.

Harry silent.

'It wasn't failure,' she said. 'He went another way.'

Pause.

'My mother, Gurley, always said he took Jimmy with him.' She continued to search Harry's face, turning finally to Ruth. 'Your father, Eiric, carried a great burden.'

'He abandoned the family,' said Ruth. The old bitterness was surfacing.

'It was the same burden that Jimmy carried, Ruth. The weight of what they did, what they had to do. They couldn't avoid, couldn't prevent the cost.'

'What happened to Jimmy?' Harry recognised the significance of his question.

'He abandoned us, his family, too,' said Gima, no bitterness, no regret in her words.

Silence once again.

'He lost so much in that place. I think he lost his soul, or at least his belief in all the good things, the spirits that make this land.'

'He lived with Eiric and Rose,' said Harry.

'And me,' said Ruth. 'I remember him so well, even though I was very young.'

'Yes, when he left us, he was convinced he could restore it all, and together with Eiric, could bring back all the good things into their lives.'

'Eiric failed to live up to that hope. The whole thing disintegrated.'

'Everything fell to pieces then,' said Gima. 'We only saw Jimmy once more after that.'

'He left the farm when dad walked out.' Ruth engaged in the memories now.

'I see Jimmy in both of you, especially you, Harry.' Harry was held by Gima's eyes – intense, unfathomably deep, penetrating. 'You regret so much but are unable to see a way clear of all the troubles.'

Harry said nothing.

'Jimmy had a special connection to the land. He said that of Eiric as well. I see some of it in you, Harry.'

'I'm not sure I can handle responsibility for the land,' said Harry. 'I can't understand myself.'

'You will soon.' Gima rested gently against the back of the chair, closed her eyes.

The memory of an old lady in Tel Aviv came to Harry. Were these linked messages, warnings of the dire need for restoration, the repair of his life, essences that begged discovery?

'Mum is tired, Harry.' The words came from behind. 'I think we should let her rest.' Jessica stood in the doorway.

Another connection he could not ignore?

They stood to go. As they reached the door, they heard words from behind. 'When you decide how you will find yourself, Harry, take Jessica with you. She will recognise Jimmy, wherever, however, you find him.'

Harry nodded and went into the bright day. The breeze was from the north-east now, bringing a slight saltiness from the warm northern ocean.

30

THE ROAD TO DAMASCUS

Early Autumn 1918

Dickie Blomfield buried. Nothing but grief. The troop was submerged in grief. Tubby Matthews couldn't hide his grief, would transfer the grief to paper. The family would be informed. The nation would mourn another casualty.

Jimmy stood next to Horse.

'Freddy's got all his stuff, Tubby,' he said. 'In a bag, with his 'orse.'

'We have to move.'

'What? Leave his stuff behind?'

'Send it back with my next report this afternoon.'

'Home?'

'Yeah.'

'Thought we was headed that way after this lot.'

'We've been told to pursue what's left of the Ottoman Army north to Damascus.'

'We lost Dickie!'

'Yeah, and you need someone to lead this mob.'

'Who?'

'Not many options, really.'

'Right about that. Who?'

They stood for a moment.

'You.'

Jimmy took a step backwards.

'Hang about, Tubby! 'Case you've missed it, I'm a blackfella.'

'Yeah, but the men listen to you, watch what you do, follow you.'

'Only 'cause they got noth'n else to do.'

'Yeah, well, it'll do for now, until we get someone permanent.'

Tubby turned, walked away.

Jimmy remained for a while longer, looking northward. He wondered what was in those mountains to the east of this sea, beyond the barren scarp that dominated everything. *What kind of arsehole would put him in a position like this*, he thought. *A blackfella running part of this awful mess, with more to come!* The reaction of the troop didn't worry him – what awaited them at the rear of a desperate Ottoman Army brought a clamminess to his hands, beads of sweat to his forehead despite the cool breeze wafting from the surface of the lake.

'When are we off, then, Boss?' Joe's lively voice broke Jimmy's reverie.

Jimmy swung about to face his responsibility.

'Tubby was desperate,' said Jimmy.

'Yeah, reckon he was, picking a fella like you.' Joe smiled. 'Still, can't think of anyone else stupid enough to do the job. None of us can.'

'Thought we was head'n home after this.' Jimmy swung his hand across the scene, tired horses, tired men, newly filled graves.

'None of us wants to go on without Dickie, but Tubby says we've got orders.'

'To follow them Turks all the way to Damascus. Yeah, I know.'

'Well, I'm ready,' said Joe, the familiar gleam returning to his eyes.

Jimmy wondered when this lust for killing would cease.

*

The troop climbed, winding up to the high plateau of the Golan Heights.

'Whores,' said Joe.

'What?' Jimmy glanced sideways at a recumbent Joe, reclining in the saddle, eyes fixed on the wispy cirrus fleeing across the sky.

'I mean, Damascus should have them, right?'

'We're not there yet, you tosser.'

'Yeah, but, when we get there, it'll be over, right?' Joe heaved himself upright. 'We can get some horizontal recreation.'

Jimmy sighed.

'Don't get ahead of y'self, Joe. We still got a bunch of Turks between us and bloody Damascus.'

'Yeah, but they're fucked, aren't they?'

'Still got guns.'

Joe descended once more into daydreams. *Lustful imaginings,* Jimmy reckoned, *of victory and the spoils of war.*

Damascus. Jimmy recalled some of those tedious Sundays.

Behold, Damascus is taken away from being a city, and it shall be a ruinous heap. Jerusalem, Gaza, Jaffa, Nablus, Megiddo, the Turks had usually left things intact. Allenby, the British, defenders of the faith, said the enemy should have withdrawn earlier, destruction inevitable in the face of their careless ignorance of the cultures they had enslaved. Jimmy pictured Damascus as a golden city surrounded by impregnable walls, a place of art, music, and literature. *The barbarians*, he thought, smiling, *were about the invade.*

'Philistines,' Jimmy said, remembering the label he'd received from the priest.

'What?' Joe shook his head, stirring from his reverie.

'We're the bloody Philistines, and we're just about to 'ave a go at Damascus.'

'Don't reckon the Philistines had much to do with Damascus, Jimmy.'

Jimmy knew Joe was right, though he couldn't rid his mind of the image, a jumbled mixture of ecclesiastic torture, barbarians at the gate, crumbling walls, ruin.

'Them Turks are on the run, Joe,' he said. 'Might be crazy fight'n if they're desperate.'

'We'd better hurry up then, before they reach Damascus.'

There he goes again, thought Jimmy. *Always the need for punishment; guts full of vengeance.*

Joe kicked his horse into a trot, moving forward in the long column of horses, men dozing in the saddle, the cloud of dust brushed clear by a growing breeze rising against the scarp of the Heights, Lake Tiberias a fading silver splash behind, far below.

Jimmy looked ahead, eyes squinting against the glare, saw a small dot of dust approaching from the north, a horse, full gallop, rider crouched low against the saddle. 'We've got company,' someone said.

The horse was agitated, rider fighting to quiet the mount, a discussion. Tubby turned about, moving down the now stationary line to Jimmy and the troop.

'You need to go with this fella.' Tubby pointed over his shoulder. 'They need you and your men at Barada. And you've got to move fast.'

'Why us, Tubby?' Jimmy had to ask.

'Because you get things done, no fuss, no regrets.' Tubby smiled. 'And you've done it before.'

'Done what, Tubby?'

'Broken their will to fight.'

Jimmy had a premonition: this was the last battle, his Armageddon, the culmination of all his fears, the revelation of a recurring dread, the end of things.

'Right. Well, we'll be seeing you, then.' There was no purpose in an argument, in the clarification of his weariness, for excuses.

'Four troops, you, you and you!' Tubby pointed down the line. 'Get going. The rest of us will catch you shortly.' He moved aside to watch them leave.

It was thin reassurance, and he saw hollowness in Tubby's eyes, he felt the weight of being an executioner, an assassin, the dark cloak of the cursed twisting tightly about his shoulders.

He waved to his troop, they tore themselves from the column, moving quickly to a gallop, following the dusty tracks of the harbinger, to an end shrouded in uncertainty. Jimmy could only dream of a release, an undoing of the web that seemed to tighten with every step along the road.

'Who was that fella on the road to Damascus?' Jimmy had to shout.

'Paul,' Joe called, after a moment's thought, over the rush of the wind.

'Yeah,' said Jimmy, remembering the drone of the priest, another of those obscure stories that seemed so irrelevant to a boy. Jimmy suddenly felt as blind as the apostle had been, a sad pawn in someone else's game.

They rode hard for more than an hour, a squadron of men and horses, across flat country, pace slackening only as the ground started to climb. The steep hills closed about them at last, Horse labouring against the uneven ground, the entrance to a steep-sided gorge, a fast-flowing river.

Their guide called a halt, pointing upward. 'You need to climb up there.'

'Why?' said Jimmy. 'What's up there?'

'Just get going, leave the horses, the Colonel will be waiting for you on top.'

Jimmy waved the men from their mounts, briefly caressing Horse's nose, turned and walked briskly up a rocky path, the crumbling face of the hill making his footing treacherous. Head down, thighs aching, he felt gradual relief as the gradient softened, a noise above, a voice.

'Need you fellas along the ridge,' said the voice. Jimmy glanced up at a young officer. 'Know how to fire a machine gun?'

Jimmy stood a moment, caught his breath. 'Yeah, used one once at target practice.'

'That'll do. We got the guns, but are missing the men.' The officer paused. 'Move along the ridge.'

Jimmy walked along the narrow, stony track, found the cache of weapons, wondered where all the men, the machine gunners, had gone.

'No men, just guns,' said the Lieutenant, as if he could read Jimmy's mind. 'And plenty of ammunition.'

'Strange,' Jimmy said. 'No gunners?'

'Got ahead of ourselves.'

'What?'

'Heading for Damascus.' The young officer was visibly peeved. 'Almost got there too …'

'So, what do y'want us here for?' Jimmy glanced back along the path, at the crowd of tired soldiers trudging along the small track.

The man pointed, index finger slightly crooked, boney, a slight nervous tremor. Jimmy followed the finger into the gorge below.

'Get your arses along the ridge!' A shout. 'And pick up a bloody gun before you go!' The Colonel had arrived.

Jimmy couldn't remove his eyes from the scene below. Deep within the shadow below he saw movement; movement resolved into a crawling mass of wagons, horses, vehicles and men, soldiers hurrying forward, desperation in their haste, pushing through a tight gorge beside a swift stream.

'Pick up a fucking gun, you bastards!' The Colonel shouted, sweating profusely, madness infusing his face. 'They have to be stopped!

Jimmy swung around, for the first time contemplating disobedience. He had done terrible things, witnessed awful things, accepted the unspeakable; this took him to another place, a level of degradation he refused to accept.

The men marched forward; he heard the metallic clink of

tripods against the stony ground. Joe stood with him, a vacant stare, the zealous gleam fading.

The firing began.

*

Before the war, the gorge had been a peaceful place. The stream flowed almost all the year, through the cold winter's months that sometimes brought snow and ice, to the long, baking summer; a quiet route west to Beirut. Travellers mostly moved through the gorge early, even at this time of year, because towards midday, without the wind, it could get close, almost suffocating.

Today, the remnant of the Ottoman host had no choice. Men, horses, carts, vehicles crowded the narrow road, heading west, towards their only hope, the Mediterranean, Beirut, and a chance of rescue.

Jimmy felt the air vibrate with the constant percussion of the guns, the distant screams of dead and dying animals, shouts from those still alive, saw the maddened scramble, men clawing over the dead only to be blown apart by the constant barrage from above. Those lucky enough to escape the initial volley were caught further along the canyon by another group of guns. The Colonel was thorough; he had anticipated escape.

'Jesus Christ!' Joe said, a moan rather than an exclamation. He went to the edge of the scarp.

The guns close by ceased their rattle.

No movement below, an eerie quiet, just the distant knock of the guns further along the ridge.

A figure below staggered to his feet from beneath a pile of bodies, miraculously saved from an appearance in Cennet, the garden of his creator.

'Jesus!' said Joe. 'How'd he survive that lot?'

Jimmy held the vision.

A brief staccato clatter.

The man stood motionless for a brief moment, arms spread wide, a dark stain erupting from his chest, finally toppling backwards into the swiftly flowing stream, carried away as a tumbling, ragged lump.

Jimmy stared.

'Where are your guns?' The Colonel renewed his supervision.

Jimmy turned, stared at the man.

'None left, Boss.'

'Plenty. Go get one, there's more of these buggers coming.'

Jimmy wondered what had happened to decency, compassion, mercy, wanted to batter this bastard, show him the evil that had been done. He dropped his gaze to the ground, spun on his heel, walked back along the rim, down the steep path, in a daze until he felt the soft nose of his friend.

'What do we do now?' said Joe.

Jimmy turned, surprised that he was not alone. He stood for a moment, looking at Joe. Perhaps he had misjudged, maybe there was hope, a chance that this conflict had some sort of positive outcome. 'Wait 'til they're finished, I guess.'

'Deserting our post, they'll say.'

'Maybe. Maybe not. But I reckon that bastard up there will make us pay, somehow.'

Jimmy felt a nudge at the shoulder, reached out, touched Horse – a head lowered for an ear scratch.

'Horse says we'll have to clean up the bloody mess,' Jimmy said. He expected they would be forced to do worse. Still, thinking about it, he saw the rationale, a predictable response to his undisguised loathing would probably be superiority; superiority would lead to contempt – they were in for a hard time.

Silence finally filtered past his thoughts, the guns all silent, the work no doubt concluded, the toil of thousands at an end. They waited with the horses for the exacting of revenge.

They waited.

The first of the men clambered down from the ridge-top, an hour after cessation of the gunfire, blank faces, rounded shoulders – they bore the weight of condemnation, of self-loathing. Freddy walked close, Jimmy didn't look at him, that provoked a declaration.

'It's a bastard, this fucking job,' he said. 'Ever wonder why we do it?'

Silence between them for a moment.

'Been asking myself, every day now,' said Jimmy. 'Just gotta get to the end.'

Get to the end.

Advice to himself. So many willing to command, direct, lead to some sort of end, dead ends most of the time, without value or purpose. For the first time in ages, it seemed, he thought of Gurley. Gurley, Uncle Henry, the old folk that survived the ravages of the whitefella, those in his life who refrained from instruction, preferring subtle observation.

Had Gurley ever capitulated? Abandoned to the whims of a

tyrannical Angus, subjected to whitefella law, far from her beloved Black Hills, was she laying down, whining, asking to be trampled?

Jimmy couldn't see it.

'The end?' said Freddy.

'They're almost beaten, we just gotta stick at it for a while longer.'

'You didn't stick around up there.'

'They were beaten.' Jimmy felt the burden of his desertion. 'They just wanted to escape.'

Freddy stood silently, nodding his head.

'Yeah. But orders are orders.'

Jimmy turned to a shout from the path leading to the heights above the gorge.

'You lot!' The Colonel gesticulating wildly at Jimmy and Joe. 'Pick up your bloody shovels!'

Jimmy felt Horse – a slight pull, rigidity, irritation. Joe braced his feet against the ground. Was this to be their last fight, their disgrace?

'Seeing you couldn't kill the buggers, you can bury them!'

Jimmy acknowledged the order with resignation, retrieved the tool, walked steadily into the jaws of the canyon, followed by the men of his troop, all volunteers to the grim task of sorting the dismembered from the whole, the living from the dead.

31

NEW ENGLAND – NEW SOUTH WALES

Early Autumn 1919

Low on the hillside, Jimmy saw the gate and his chance. He took it and rode beneath the iron portico, *Kempton: Hereford Stud.* It seemed things had become more grandiose in the years since his departure; prosperity snatched from the grip of war, the fallen a memory, the foundation of new wealth.

He lingered a moment along the broad avenue, the trees shorter, less majestic than he remembered, still providing though, a bulwark against the rough ground and the sparse, late-summer pasture. The autumn rains had not yet arrived. The one anomaly in the good times?

Easing himself slightly in the saddle, he remembered the arrival, the sparse crowd pressed against the Woolloomooloo dock, the walk into the city with Joe, the brief rest at a pub. They wouldn't give him a beer! Joe bought him one anyway, telling them to get fucked. Did they have any idea what they had endured in that godforsaken place? He released the reins for a moment, held his hands, palms upward, before him. He still saw the blood. It made him shudder. He ran his thumbs across the tips of his fingers, as if, somehow, that would wipe it all away, the sticky, caked, deep-red mass, lives, a reminder of those years of madness.

Damascus hadn't been the end of it.

Should he have just turned about and ridden away? There would have been ways Horse and he could have made it home, a home without the tragedy that enveloped them all.

Renamed, exiled, disowned – they would, at least, have been together.

He laughed, a strangely bitter laugh from someone so used to believing in compassion, hope, integrity.

Damascus hadn't been the end of it. They rode through deserted streets, took the surrender of that enlightened city, lingered only long enough to admire the golden dome, Aleppo drawing them through the northern gates.

What gullible fools they were, to believe the ultimate perversion had been that horror in the gorge.

Jimmy recovered the reins and walked the horse along the neat road.

Horse. They never called it murder; they said that instructions from above forced their hand. Some god maybe? The same deity that had forced bloody death on so many, that still consigned prejudice to the pubs and bars?

The pillar of his belief, loyalty beyond belief, all without foundation.

The arid lands of the Negev. The rattle of the dry desert bushes, the wind from the south, hot, burning. As Jimmy led his friend into the rough country, it clawed at him: sand, grit, heat, anger, futility, despair. A war fought for dubious reasons, waged for wealth, privilege and rank.

Horse knew, was resigned to the cost of his loyalty, accepted that Jimmy could not abandon him to the whims of Palestine. He lay down, deep within the fold of a dry watercourse, lay quietly, refusing to catch Jimmy's eye until the very moment, the second before the bullet entered his brain. The sound of the light breeze, the light buzz of insects disturbed by their passing, the cry of distant birds about some hidden water, faded for Jimmy, submerged forever beneath the crack of the gun and the loss he knew he would never be able to understand.

Horse was gone, a tragedy that could not be reconciled, no matter the outpouring of bitterness and recrimination against those gods; they had spoken, the divine law had to be obeyed, loyal friends died to save the cost of their passage home.

Jimmy folded into himself after that day; not even Joe could rouse him from a melancholy that swept across his beliefs. He abandoned his task; the fighting was done, home and the only chance of salvation beckoned: home, family, his people, the land of his ancestors.

The horse ambled forward along the road, dumb, uncommunicative, sullen. Borrowed by Joe from stables in Glen Innes, Jimmy needed time to re-gather himself, to set his defences against the demands of his family, against their recognition of the person he had become.

The road curved gently around the contour of the hill, the tip of the homestead gable visible against the pale-blue sky. Jimmy wondered if the old man had beaten him home, whether the business he had dragged Joe away to in town had merely been a ruse to get rid of him.

The road continued to curve, the house now in full view.

A small girl ran along the road towards him, a dark girl, shouting something over her shoulder. Kamilaroi. She stopped abruptly, turned a delicate, broad face, fixed dark eyes upon him, suddenly uncertain. Jimmy was the stranger here, the threat, the butcher loosed upon the land, the invader – he felt the weight of his role.

Jimmy slowly swung down from the saddle – he didn't want to frighten this sprite, her long, brown, threadbare skirt swinging slightly in the light afternoon breeze, apprehension evident, hand-to-mouth. There was something here that he could not explain, a vague familiarity, a lost past, forgotten dreams. Gravel crunched beneath his boots as he took the first tentative steps forward.

Alarm!

The child turned and ran.

Jimmy reached for the reins, walking the horse to the homestead, the memory of this place slowly seeping into him. The house, its yard and hedges neat as always, the red bougainvillea still blooming despite the encroaching winter, the stables nearby, where an age ago, Angus had bound him to his cause, the devil's bargain. To have his life stolen by this man, to years of purgatory, ending in this weight, was a load he seemed unable to shift from his shoulders.

He strolled forward to the stables, swung open the heavy, timber door. Horses, snug in narrow stalls, glanced up at the sound of the latch, the squeak of the hinges, his heavy, booted footsteps across the straw- laden floor. He almost caught sight of Horse, always glad to see him, always ready to talk, to see things from a new perspective, the correct viewpoint, it usually turned out. He had been naïve; Angus had made a fool of him. He wondered what would come next.

Angus had been short with him in Sydney – handed him a train ticket, told him when and where – that was it. He whisked Joe away. 'The Redmans are waiting to welcome Joe home,' he said. He was grateful for the desertion, it gave him time alone, time at Central Station, watching the crowds, imagining his reunion with Gurley, Cara, the family, so close now.

The sound of feet on the stable's back verandah.

The door burst open, a crowd, familiar faces, older now, rushed to him, smiling, hugging, laughing.

'Ya home!' A collective shout. Despite Jimmy's sturdy bulk, the buffeting crowd pushed him backwards, people whirling about him.

'Never thought we'd see'ya again!' Henry pushed through the mob.

'Survived.' Jimmy could say no more.

'All them reports com'n through. Thought you was dead or dying somewhere.'

'Nah. We made it, Joe and me.'

'Joe? Where's he?'

'With the old man in Glen Innes.' Jimmy reflected a moment. 'Ted didn't make it.'

'Yeah, the old man told us.'

'Didn't get to him soon enough.' Jimmy still saw it as his failure.

'The old man was pretty bad for a time.'

'Yeah, knew he would be.' Jimmy looked across the gathering. 'Gurley?'

'Gone, Jimmy.'

'What? What do'ya mean, gone?'

'We didn't know you was com'n, thought for ages you was dead.'

'Where is she?'

'Gone. Took off for the caves when we heard about all them dead fellas over there.'

'Alone?'

'Nah. Went with Cara. And her cousin. That short fella from them people down south.'

'When?'

'Ages ago. Like I said, we thought you was dead. The old man said you was lost around some place called Megiddo.'

'Took Cara?' Jimmy needed to confirm the details.

'Yeah,' said Henry. 'But she left the little one with us.'

'What?'

'Yeah, left Gima with us.'

'Gima?'

'Gurley was pregnant when you left.' Henry smiled. 'She didn't want to tell you, case y'got inta trouble, desert'n like.'

'Where is she?'

'Right here.' The crowd parted to reveal the little girl from the road, the dark beauty. Gurley was written across her face, across her resilient body, in the curls of her hair.

A little mouse, Jimmy thought, *a little mouse with the look of her mother.*

'Come here,' he said, waving a hand at the little girl. She shrank back, almost falling into the arms of a plump woman. Jimmy waited then, waited for the little mouse to be delivered into his arms, sure now that he would have to find a way to free himself from the past, wash clean of the blood in which he bathed.

'The caves, you said?' He was already moving. 'I need a horse and wagon.'

He headed for the door with a vision of fresh mountain water, clean air, tall trees brushed by a crisp breeze from the south. *Fine,* he thought, *but how the hell can I get rid of all this shit and my damn failure to save a friend?*

*

Eiric smiled broadly, stepping forward, embracing Jimmy.

'Thought I'd never see you again,' he said.

'Yeah, there were times,' said Jimmy. 'Joe was a handful as usual.' He looked at Eiric, pitifully thin, so thin the bones of his arms, elbows, wrists, seemed ready to burst through the transparently delicate skin, moulded precariously about his jaw and skull.

A moment of silence.

'The old man's not back yet?' Jimmy needed the wagon, supplies, wanted to be away.

'Still away.'

'Left him and Joe in Glen Innes.'

'Yeah.'

Silence.

'Y'look'n like shit, Eiric.'

'Gurley left soon after I got back.' Eiric clearly didn't want to talk about his appearance. 'Took the young fella with her.'

'Know where?'

'South.' Eiric swaying slightly on his spindly legs. 'Probably those caves of yours.'

'Yeah, that's what Henry said.'

'She thought you were dead, Jimmy.'

'Take more than a war to knock me off,' said Jimmy. He laughed.

'Left a little one behind.' Eiric looked apprehensive, Jimmy nodded.

'Yeah, I've met Gima.'

'I think she didn't want to believe the reports ... that you were dead. Said she couldn't stick around here any longer. Said she'd be able to work things out, be able to tell when she got to the caves – whether you were dead or alive.'

They stood silently for a moment, looking at each other.

'It was a bad time, Jimmy,' said Eiric at last.

'Yeah, it was.' Jimmy wasn't sure which times were in Eiric's mind.

'And, right in the middle of it, I fucked off.'

'Not your fault.'

'Yeah, it was!' Jimmy could see the pain in Eiric's eyes. 'I should have prepared better. That medical officer was ready to let me go.'

'Better you didn't, *Buralga*.'

'I could've made it.'

'It got worse.' Jimmy looked down at his hands. 'We did some terrible things.'

'Still, should've been there.'

'Even Joe couldn't stomach it at the end.'

'The old man can't get over Ted.'

'Yeah, that's part of it.'

Again, they stood silently for a moment, looking at each other.

'You taking the little one with you?'

'Nah, she's safer here right now.'

'I'll make sure she's right, Uncle Henry, everyone.'

Jimmy nodded.

'Horse,' he said. 'Couldn't leave him behind ...'

'They wouldn't ship them home.'

'Nah, said goodbye to him in the Negev. Slapper had Tuppence after you got sent home. Did the same as me. Almost threw us all in the clink. Said we destroyed their property. Just couldn't leave them behind.' Jimmy felt a growing despondency, a pall that lurked close, threatening to overwhelm him. 'You saw how them Arabs treated their horses!'

'Yeah.' Eiric silent, head bowed. He stepped forward, hand reaching out for Jimmy's shoulder. 'Slapper wrote me a note, told me. Didn't know he could write.'

They stood for a moment, mute.

'Gurley will be at the caves,' Eiric said.

Jimmy raised his arm, felt the shoulder of the wasted man before him.

'Take what you need,' Eiric said.

'Wagon, horses, a few supplies.'

Eiric smiled. 'Get going before the old man gets back. Mum will help us get some stuff together.'

Jimmy looked up then, saw Doreen on the house verandah, her face creased with concern. He released Eiric, walked carefully along the path to the house. 'Nice t'see ya, Mrs O'Sullivan.'

'Jimmy! Never thought to see you again, what with the reports of casualties and all.' A wan smile passed across her face.

'Tough old bastard I am,' Jimmy said.

'Jimmy needs to get to Gurley, Mum.' Eiric had followed.

A pause. Doreen's gaze intensified for a moment. 'Then we'd better get you going ... before Angus arrives.' She turned, darted inside the house, returned with a purposeful stride. 'Flour, a few hens for eggs ...' Doreen continued with a list as they moved towards the barn.

'And what about your little girl,' said Doreen when she had completed the recitation. 'You won't leave her behind, will you?'

'Gima's too young, safer here.'

'No, you must take her. Uncle Henry will go with you. You mustn't go alone.' Her insistence was overwhelming.

'It's a long ride.' Jimmy felt he was fighting a losing battle against a determined foe.

'Gurley cried and cried before she left! No, you've got to take her.'

Jimmy fell asleep that night on the trail, dreaming of Horse, of their final moments, the flood of blood, of raising his eyes to the bleak horizon in the Negev, looking up to the fleeting glimpse of a winged Pegasus, a snow-white horse tossing its head defiantly, seeing Horse with hope in his eyes, master, as always, of this earthly realm.

32

The Present Day

The photograph sat on the table. Harry examined it again.

A crowd, men and women, were posing for the camera.

A picnic. A mix of headdress – flowery bonnets, trilbies, work-stained hats.

Angus, at the centre of a crowd – suit, the squire – at least twenty people spread out on either side of him.

The eldest brother, Ted – lean, fit, standing proud, the anointed – close to the old man.

Joe, four away from the epicentre.

Eiric at the margins of the group, eyes turned away from the photographer. Where was he looking? Harry traced his gaze with a finger. His finger stopped. Medium height, muscular, dark, sober lines cutting deeply into his forehead. Jimmy? He saw the possible match with the photograph he'd been shown in Jaffa. Harry wasn't sure – work dungarees, loose, flannel shirt cast a different hue, unlike the khaki uniforms of the horse soldiers.

Harry's finger slid one person further sideways – a radiant face, stunningly beautiful, a vitality that a faded image could not dim.

Lissome, athletic, calm.

'Who's this?' Harry said.

'It's Gurley,' said Ruth. 'I think she was only about thirteen or fourteen, then. I wasn't even born.'

'And Jimmy?' Harry needed confirmation.

'Next to Gurley.' Ruth leant over Harry to peer at the old image.

Harry saw the resolve in the man; Gurley standing so close, she seemed to be drawing energy from his steadfast frame, a structure rooted deep in the ground.

'It's incredible how alike Jessica is to the girl in this photograph,' she said.

Harry wondered at the immutability of Gima, the peace that pervaded the space about her despite the trials, judgments, the suffering that had no doubt assailed her, the inescapable damage that she must retain. And Jessica's part in the continuance? The resemblance was testimony – Jessica was the living image of her grandmother. He remembered Gima's prophecy. 'She will recognise Jimmy, wherever, however, you find him.' How could that be? Jimmy would be long gone, Jessica far removed from past events – or was she?

The obstinacy of life against all judgement fascinated Harry. He felt the irresistible pull of their history. They were all bound to the past, but how?

'I found someone in Tel Aviv,' Harry said, looking up at Ruth.

'Found someone? Not another of your infatuations, Harry.'

'No, Mum.' Harry was irritated. Would she never cease her pathetic prodding? 'Someone connected to the family.'

'What? In Israel?'

'Like Gima,' he said. 'Very old, tied to Grandpa, Eiric.'

Harry felt the heat of Ruth's appraisal.

'Who, Harry? Dad only went overseas once; they fought the Turks most of the time.'

No point in disguising the news. 'The old man left progeny in Palestine.'

Ruth silent.

'You've got a half-sister in Israel.'

Ruth stood for a moment, silent, the only sound the distant hiss of traffic along a wet Comenarra Parkway.

'She's pretty well-off, lots of family, no real desire for any connection.'

'How can you be sure?'

'She looked like an O'Sullivan: same nose, same mouth, eyes, commanding presence; a female Angus, really. I wouldn't mess with her despite her age.'

Ruth was quiet for a time, thinking, then a half-smile. 'Jesus, I never thought he had it in him.'

'Grandpa never knew,' said Harry. 'Joe kept it from him.'

'What?' Ruth looked startled.

'Joe never said a word, even though he knew. Jimmy as well. Seems they found out about it after Eiric got shipped home. Her mother thought Eiric was dead. Joe lied about it.'

Silence. Harry saw emotion in his mother's face.

'Maybe I should contact her?' Ruth said, finally. She was fishing for a way forward.

'I really don't think she wants that.' Harry saw relief in the relaxation of Ruth's shoulders.

'Was that what you were doing in Israel?'

'Andy wanted me to start a negotiation with some of the locals,' said Harry, wondering if his mother would accept such a bland explanation.

She didn't. 'So, how did you find her if you were tied up with business?'

'I visited some of the places where they fought, the Jordan Valley.'

'That's pretty deliberate, Harry.'

'I wanted to see some of the places they had fought through.'

'How did that lead to, what was her name?'

'I didn't say. It's Francine.'

'Francine. How, why did you go looking for this woman?'

Harry closed his eyes, felt his energy drain away. This was never going to be easy, with more revelations, more confrontations to come.

'I just had a feeling there was something, someone there who could fill in the missing bits of Eiric's life.'

'A feeling? Harry, they saw you coming,' Ruth said, doubtful now, a cynical tone.

'No!' Harry had to defend his exposé. 'It all fits. She had a photograph. Joe, Jimmy, Eiric, her mother, all of them, all there together.'

Harry felt a closeness about him as if the room were attempting to squeeze admissions from the occupants. A thought came to him as he watched the play of emotion across his mother's face. He rejected it. It filtered back gradually. He sat in the nearest chair, his body suddenly charged, the tingle of electricity. He looked sharply at his mother.

'I just knew it, Mum.'

'Knew what?' Ruth irritated now.

'Knew I had to look, knew I was close to something, just like I knew we had to talk to Gima, like I was, am, close to something that explains why all our lives are so messed up.'

'Speak for yourself.' Ruth angry now.

'Mum, admit it. You haven't got a bloody clue why you have spent so many years being unhappy with everything.'

'No, I haven't.'

'You, me, the whole bloody family, we're thrashing around, running away the moment things get personal, the moment anyone gets close.'

'I'm happy with your dad!'

'Mum, you haven't talked to Dad for years, except to ask him if he wants a cup of tea.'

Mouth forming the words, Ruth nevertheless silent.

'I've located grandpa's half-brother, your half-sister, all on some sort of hunch.' Harry drew a breath. They're pieces of a puzzle, a riddle that involves me, whether I like it or not.'

'A puzzle? It's simple,' said Ruth. 'Two randy buggers who couldn't keep it in their pants. And you're the same. What about Frances?'

Harry sat still. The truth had launched itself forward. He remembered the Sunday School quote: *The Lord is long-suffering, and of great mercy, forgiving iniquity and transgression, and by no means clearing the guilty, visiting the iniquity of the fathers upon the sons to the third and fourth generation.*

Forget the religious connotation. He had found the cord that bound them to each other. Now, he had to break its influence.

The sins of the father should no longer be laid upon the children.

*

'Frances doesn't want us together again,' he said.

Ruth sighed. 'Harry, she's just tired of your shenanigans.'

'No, she's told me she wants out.'

'You've got a responsibility there. You can't walk away.'

'She's adamant, Mum. Says it's final.'

'When did she say that?'

'I went to see her, and I've talked to her on the phone.'

'It can't be final, Harry. The baby!' Ruth said, harshness in her voice.

Harry didn't want this conversation; he knew the extent of Ruth's investment in Frances, the baby, in continuity. She feared the collapse of all that was safe.

'I've told her I'll support Sofie.' Maybe that would calm his mother's fears.

It didn't. 'You are deserting a good, stable life!'

Stable life? He couldn't remember when a good, stable life was a recipe for happiness. A good, stable life had done nothing but lead him into self-doubt, confusion, and an enduring sense that something was missing, something misunderstood, a life misread.

'Frances wants it,' he said, as if that was the final statement, nothing further to say, nothing else to add.

'You've got to work at what's good, Harry.' Ruth was fighting on. 'You can't just walk away from it all.'

From it all? What was 'all'?

'Mum, your "all" is just a misguided dream. What good is it at "all", if you can't deal with yourself, understand the drivers ... and the brakes.'

'You're talking nonsense, Harry. We've all got things we have to deal with. Nothing's perfect. You just get on with it. Stop grumbling.'

'I'm not moaning about my life. It's just ... there's something I need to find. I know it's there. I'm almost on to it.'

'Harry, you've gone bonkers!'

Harry breathed out slowly. Frustration? He always knew it would be difficult, probably impossible to bring his mother with him on this journey. What had Anika said about those who wandered through life resisting change? Overripe fruit? *That describes Mum*, he thought. *Overripe, kicking and screaming against change.*

'Mum, you got it perfectly when you connected Angus, Eiric and me. That's the thread. And unless I can somehow cut the link, I'm not going to survive.'

Ruth stopped short, mouth trying to form a response.

'And,' said Harry, 'Jessica has got some leads on her grandad, Jimmy, that we're going to follow up.'

'What earthly good will that do?' Ruth said, turning away, exasperated, throwing her hands in the air.

'I don't know.' Harry already abandoning any attempt to enrol his mother. 'But I've got a feeling that Jimmy might have some of the answers.'

'He's dead, Harry. How can he have any answers, for God's sake?'

'I don't know.' Harry turned to leave. 'But it's worth a try.'

Harry left the house. He stood for a while on the street, the blustery wind tugging at his hair, his coat, his trousers. He stood and remembered the photo of three soldiers and a small, pretty woman and marvelled at how intertwined their lives really were, at how the disturbances of the past survived and flourished with such intensity in the present.

33

NEW ENGLAND – NEW SOUTH WALES

Spring 1932

Jimmy stirred, the sun not yet above the horizon, the pulse at his temple like a hammer, a peculiar scent in the air, a reminder of those half-forgotten days at the edge of the Palestinian desert. He stayed, reluctant to rise, loath to admit he was wrong, that the path he had taken was a dead end, an error of monumental proportions.

He didn't understand why he had arrived at this place, this state of mind, this predicament. The how? It was only too evident. He turned it over in his mind every day, dwelt on his mistakes, tried to analyse the significance of each step, the rungs of a ladder downward, into this miasma of befuddled dreams. The why – he could only guess.

A soft, slightly quivering object worked cautiously at his ear. He forced his eyes open, looked upwards into the light brown, the finely bristled nose of a horse. The nose lifted as Jimmy brushed it gently away. He forced himself upright, scanned his surrounds, tasting the excesses of the previous night, the sourness drifting through his body, robbing him of the will to stand. The horse, tethered to a small cart, watched him as he eventually struggled to his feet, staggered, then steadied himself.

The rough track descended, leading to the valley and a small stream, where early morning mist swirled, punctuated by a column of rising smoke; Eiric was awake, the tasks of another day would begin, and Jimmy would need to maintain a balance, steadiness that too often seemed to drift, to fall into a chasm of their self-loathing.

Jimmy hadn't correctly measured the real impact of that war, the years away, the separation, the loss, the chaos it had created within every grain of his life. He joined Gurley, the Black Hills, the children, determined to return to his origin, to the garden. Unreserved at first, they revelled in their combination. Gurley planned, he provided; an essential blend, a celebration of freedom, of their suitability, their desires.

Jimmy watched as the mist rose, revealing the small house, roughly-hewn timber walls, broadly covered verandahs, crude, stone chimney – the product of their combined labour – now the residence of Eiric's city-born wife. He turned to the horse and cart, fondling the willing nose for a moment, the softness redolent of Horse, of loss, pain, the dissolution of commitment. Jimmy shook himself, like a dog removing water from its coat, climbed aboard the old cart, urging the horse, with sharp clicks of the tongue, into a brisk trot along the rough track. *Need to do some work on this road before the winter rains arrive,* he thought. *Though, plenty of time – they are still a long way off.*

They tried everything, committed their whole being to the union, the world irrelevant beyond the boundaries of the hills. They didn't see anyone for weeks, even at a distance, didn't want to, wasn't necessary. The days marched into months, the months to almost a year before Jimmy's subterfuge began to unravel.

He hadn't wanted it all to catch up with him, the blood and death, the bitterness, the loss. Those days before departure from Palestine rattled like a tram through his mind, when a thousand horses, friends, mates through such savage times, were victims of a callous decree. Gurley could not understand, would not understand the depth of that bond, the horror of desperate survival in war.

Jimmy drove the cart into the crude stockyard, angling close to the stable door, trying for a quick release of the horse – he hoped his overnight absence would be missed.

'Home late?' The words from the corner of the building. 'Or are you up early?'

Jimmy turned to the voice. Eiric smiled.

'Late.' It was not the first time. 'Slept in the cart.'

'You've got a good horse there,' said Eiric. 'All that way from the pub, without your help.'

Jimmy looked at Eiric, still thin after all these years, swaying slightly, even in the light breeze.

They didn't mention those days, just dealt with the abyss, the nightmares. Eiric's blackouts, the descents into a fury, had receded; his own inner hell dulled by alcohol, binges that caught him unawares, he seldom chose them or saw them coming. To last a week without that dull weight draped about his shoulders meant virtually tying himself to work on the farm, no excuse to venture into town, no opportunity to disappear on some errand. Eiric could usually organise appropriate distractions. This time, Eiric committed to family, Jimmy ventured into Guyra for essential supplies, urged to hurry back.

Three hotels, four stables, a general store, not much else. Jimmy, not enough money, even for a beer. That might have been the end of it, home, safe, sober, but the publican had found a dead dog jammed between the logs of the woodpile at the rear of the hotel. Jimmy saw his chance, offered to dispose of the stinking carcass for five quid, received his reward, walked to the second pub, hid the putrid remains in the hotel yard and waited.

Three hotels, three dead dogs and fifteen quid. Enough to drink his fill and more.

Jimmy ran his fingers across his forehead. The sharp pain behind his eyes was receding now, leaving a numbness, the advancing day promising respite from the visions of his failure, his abandonment. The nights, he found, were the worst – alone, cocooned within the blackness, rejected by those ancient powers, lost, separated.

Eiric waved an arm towards the hillside above. Jimmy shook his head, the sound of Eiric's voice a sudden lance into his forehead.

'What was that?' said Jimmy.

'Sheep need moving,' Eiric said. 'From the south paddock.'

'Yeah, I'll get right on to it.'

A moment.

'Red's threatening to leave,' Eiric said. Jimmy saw the distress in his eyes. 'Take the kids, to Sydney.'

'Yeah, she's been pretty quiet lately.'

'Not with me, she hasn't.'

Jimmy didn't want to delve further – it reminded him too much of his own story.

'She's got tons of spirit, *Buralga*. Whatever it is, she'll get over it.'

Eiric stood quietly, shaking his head, swaying slightly as he always did. Jimmy gathered together the discarded harness, turned towards the stable door, and stopped. 'I'll fetch them sheep inta the creek pasture,' he said over his shoulder, pushing through the stable door.

He fought to control the vision of his own failure.

The Hills were seen as his return, their homecoming, renewal of a bond with the realm of their ancestors. He thought they could make it work, build anew from the bankruptcy of the war, his betrayal. Gurley's rejection of everything associated with the whitefella was positive at first, the problem of his nightmares incidental to her main aim – the restoration of Jimmy's soul, their recoupling.

She had prepared well. Jimmy recalled the first sight of the camp: shelter, warmth when the south wind blew cold, happy, healthy children, standing at the edge of the scarp, listening to the fall of the water, the rustle of the wind in the tree-tops, the garlanded cave beckoning him, its stories piercing the dull fog of his shame, promising redemption.

In time, he could fall asleep clear of the torment of those years of destruction, free of his final moments with Horse, of the grasping, biting, clawing images that invaded his waking, his sleeping, the tormented half-world that he had inhabited.

Almost a year into his recovery, in the hours before dawn, a noise, the stamping of feet woke him. He walked to the edge of the camp, peering cautiously into the dense foliage – no smell, no movement, no life. Another sound, this time from within the cave. He assumed *a dingo or some other scavenger – they're after the food within the caves.* He approached the entrance, retrieving a stout branch from the smouldering fire as he passed.

The interior of the cave should have been dark, resilient, even to light, of those celestial bodies, the Milky Way, the stream of the great emu. He braced his feet against the dusty floor, a luminescent haze trembling at the far end of the cavern. It floated, dilute, gathered eventually to form a shimmered image, a crude remnant, indistinct yet familiar.

This was no scavenger.

He planted his feet firmly against the ground, blinked, a brief relief from the penetration of the light, an invasion into the very heart of his being – the image had steadied, resolving itself into a blurred form, an abandoned comrade, a statement of his culpability – the message was clear, he could not be free of his guilt. The apparition brightened briefly, flickering, seemed to implode, disappeared.

Jimmy stood in darkness for a moment, then turned, finally bursting breathless into a world showered with the pinpoint light of a billion stars.

He stood, surveying the camp, realising that his recovery had been a sham, a delusion, the futile hope of desperate souls. The past would always be a millstone, ultimately distorting his and the lives of those he loved.

*

Jimmy helped the boy as he reached upwards, small hands, fingers grasping for the round, ripe fruit. The boy, though tall for his age, still couldn't reach the upper branches, trees grown lofty in the fertile river flat soil, bountiful even this early in the season. A successful grab, Jimmy carefully dropped Eiric's boy, Jamie, to the ground, hands grasping the bounty, smiling, laughing at his success.

Jimmy enjoyed his time with the boy, another character to mould, another mind to introduce to the world of creatures, to the workings of the earth. Jamie reminded him of Gima at a similar age, the same curiosity, same resilience, determination. He watched Jamie drop the prize into the wooden pail, almost full, turn to the line of trees, consider the next target, shift his gaze back to him, finger pointing hopefully towards the high branches.

Jimmy stood quietly, his mind wandering to half-forgotten times. He seemed to be drifting in his mind a lot these days, meandering across a plain of memories, recollections good and bad, often jumbled together with no coherence, merely sifting through the confusion of his life, indiscriminate, random.

He started, absently, towards the trees at the end of the line, branches overhanging the fence, the fruit there for the picking by the odd cow straying to the boundary. Walking through the spring grass, long against the wire fence crowned with a barbed strand, he could see the remains of the defences, the bodies draped, limp, smashed, dissected. The boom of the guns was curiously absent; yet, he could hear voices, distressed, shouting, pleading – soldiers were dying out there, Strepford one of them, his body cut in two by enemy fire, a look of surprise, of shock, peeling away that forbidding, cruel, malicious, grim countenance. Jimmy never wanted such an end for the tyrant, yet such conclusions seemed to arrive without discrimination.

Voices penetrated the grim scene – strident, harsh, damning.

He felt something soft slip carefully into his hand, but he couldn't tear himself away from the scene, smelt the sweat rising from Horse, the wheezing breath as his friend laboured desperately to get clear of the worst of the battlefield; he knew Horse could do it, entrusted his life to the magic of his companion, his saviour, his deliverer.

Jimmy's hand shook, then his arm, insistent, urgency that broke the thrall. He looked down. Jamie, hand now tightly grasping Jimmy's large, calloused fist, looked up with worried eyes, pulling him around to face the house. The shouting came from the yard, the front of the house, the avenue to the stables.

'There's no point! It's just talk!' The words cut through the air. Jimmy heard the bitterness.

Indulgent tones in reply. 'Come back inside, please, love ...'

Jimmy felt the vibration, the shifting of the ground. 'You don't listen; you always know better.'

The slam of a door.

The finality.

Quiet.

'Go inside to your mother,' said Jimmy, gently pushing the boy towards the house. He watched the boy reach the verandah; then he went in search of his friend.

*

He wasn't a counsellor, didn't have the skill to find solutions; his own failure with Gurley was evidence enough of his ineptitude.

What could he say?

That it would be all right?

That Rose would come to her senses?

He did that, even though he didn't believe it, couldn't see any way back for Eiric. The die had been cast. The last words had been uttered.

Eiric was broken. The amalgamation of their lives had dissolved.

Rose complained bitterly during the months after Eiric's departure, trying to bolster her own part, protesting her innocence, Eiric's incompetence, stupidity, folly. Jimmy, while sympathetic to the task of running the farm, grew tired of the incessant carping, felt he could no longer stomach the destruction of his friend's character; he had been witness to the strength of Eiric's resolve, to the man's ability to press forward against overwhelming odds, in the face of lethal fire.

Jimmy simply packed a swag and left. He intended to search for his family, they had moved south, to the high, snowy mountains, he'd heard.

It was full summer. Many properties were shifting their cattle to clean pastures – he would make his way as a stockman once again.

34

The Present Day

In the old house, metres from the beach, Harry listened to the crash of the surf, the lingering hiss of the waves as they foamed to the beach. He sat, deep in the old couch, feeling the chill on his face through the leaky glass louvres. It was a cold morning, too cold to budge for an early morning surf. Perhaps, twenty years ago, Harry would have ventured across the frosty dunes, plunging into the water, into the rip that would scoot him beyond the breakers, to the watery walls peeling off the point, eagerly abandoning himself to their power.

Now, Harry sat watching the magpies in the trees struggling with the cold, the wrens flitting, foraging, fluffing their feathers to retain what heat their small bodies could generate.

He stood, rubbing his hands together, lifting a small log from the pile, swinging the stove door open, placing it carefully on the fire, grateful for the warmth, for the peace that he had found in this place.

A noise. Was it in the house or beyond?

A light, distant thump, as if something, someone had fallen out of bed onto a timber floor.

Harry looked across the richly textured room, walls decked with books, timber floors layered with rugs – the product of his travels – to the stairs, the portal to this lofty space.

The thump became a clatter – boots on stairs.

Harry caught a glimpse of the grey, winter ocean through a veil of leaves, branches, sturdy trunks. *I should have more fortitude*, he thought, as a vision shot by on a wave, the twist and turn of an early morning surfer.

He swung around from the window to the figure emerging from the stairs, the footsteps fading to a brief echo.

'You're ready?' he said.

Silence. It seemed they didn't often need words. He felt desire, warmth, veracity radiating at him, understanding that he never thought possible, not between two people, not in his life.

'Yes, all ready,' she said, walking towards him, opening her arms, holding him in a tight embrace, her cheek pressed against his chest. 'I'll miss you terribly.'

What could he say? That he would be busy, too busy to worry about missing her, that she would be the same, both of them caught in whirlwinds of their own making?

'I'm missing you, already,' he said. 'I missed you in bed when I woke up. You'd already gone to pack.' *I couldn't have said that only months ago*, he thought. *It's not needy; it's how we both feel.*

'It's only for a couple of weeks,' she said. 'We'll both be flat out.'

Harry reluctantly pushed her gently away from him, studied her face – the angular facets of her cheeks, the broadly spaced eyes separated by a stylish nose.

'Anika, if you're going to catch the plane, we'd better go.'

'Not sure I want to,' she said. 'You're heading bush with another woman. It doesn't seem right that I'm not there, too.' He marvelled at the reversal of her tone.

'Jealous?' Harry said.

'No, no, I'm not. I just want to be part of it all.'

'Bangladesh is only a few hours away. I'll call you every day. Report in.' Harry laughed.

'I'll be in the Sundarbans most of the time,' she said. 'With Andy backing you up on the aid you promised, despite the companies' pull-out, I can afford to appoint some really good managers.'

They went to the car. To Harry, it was like the last walk of the condemned: his parting from life, from all the world's goodness, from any future hope, from any chance of redemption.

That's a bit dramatic, he thought, pushing away the emotion.

He gripped the steering wheel, knuckles white, arms rigid.

No! The feeling of loss at Anika's departure was real, right, immutable; it was their bond.

He looked sideways at Anika; her gaze was fixed on him, the first flood of tears watering her eyes.

'You'll find what you're looking for, Harry,' she said as she reached out to touch his face. 'I know you will. Jessica will help. She's looking for the same thing.'

Harry smiled. He drove the ten kilometres to the small, country airport, reluctantly releasing Anika to her cause, feeling for the first time in his life, the power of his commitment, of their bond, belief that he, at last, had control, could feel confidence in his choices.

*

In the afternoon, Jessica arrived. Harry had satisfied his urge for a surf, and the last of the cold was banished from his feet and hands.

'It's not a long drive, Harry,' she said.

'Where do you want to start?' Harry was reluctant to leave the beach house.

'They're expecting us in Tumut tomorrow. Mum set it up.'

From here, just a few hours. Harry was relieved that their first day wouldn't be a long trek.

Harry suddenly wanted to say *no* to the trip, to delay the start of the search, rest in the comfort of familiar surroundings, lose himself in the simplicity of the beach, the ocean, isolation, but he knew that would only delay the inevitable. He had to carry it through, no matter the endpoint – success or failure. The fate of Jimmy, the tie between Gurley, Gima, Jessica, Eiric, Ruth, all of them to himself beckoned, drew him forward, promised resolution, and gave him purpose.

'We can leave this afternoon,' he said.

Jessica stood motionless for a moment, looking intently at Harry. By the time Harry had pulled himself free of his fading doubts, she had moved to the large window overlooking the beach. The headland loomed in the distance, the old wharf teetering on the edge of the rocky cliff, grey puffy, billowing clouds, waves building during the afternoon to white crests brushing the old jetty boards.

'Great place you have here,' said Jessica.

'Yeah,' said Harry. 'I love it, sitting here inside the banksia forest, the ocean only a short walk away.' Harry felt a surge of love for the place, a longing for Anika.

'This was once a great place for the Aboriginal people around here, maybe sacred even.'

Harry listened.

'There are middens along the beach, all the way to the river-mouth.'

Jessica wrapped her arms close about her body, her gaze beyond the large window, beyond the confines of vision.

'Then the white settlers arrived,' she said. 'They built wharves because there were no roads. It was close to where the gold was, a good jump-off spot to the goldfields.'

'What happened to the local people?' Harry had to ask.

'Don't know,' she said. 'They just disappeared in the end. The settlers brought sheep, cattle. The local Aborigines saw them as fair game. There was trouble. The local people lost.'

And? Harry wanted to ask, but Jessica continued, a wistfulness in her voice. 'They shot a lot of them, poisoned them.'

'We never hear those stories,' Harry said.

'No, like you never hear about how they treated people like Jimmy or Gurley.'

'Different time.' A mollifying statement, though Harry didn't want to excuse the past.

'I remember my grandmother, Gurley, telling me how Jimmy came home from the war, years fighting for this country, and they cut him off. It was fine for him to defend this country, kill the enemy, risk his life, but when he returned he wasn't even treated as a citizen.'

'And the old man, Angus, he must have known who Jimmy was.'

'Yes, and I think Jimmy knew too, though nothing was said. It explains his commitment to Angus' boys, his brothers.'

'And your Mum, Gima?'

'She doesn't care, except she saw something in you, something from both Eiric and Jimmy.'

'There must have been a lot of sadness.'

'Gima? Sad?' Jessica smiled, pensive. 'Gima's never sad. Always determined, never sad. She just wants to know, hear words from her father, Jimmy.'

Harry thought about their prospects of uncovering the facts. 'He's dead, Jessica, or he's some sort of dried-up Methuselah, living in a mountain cave we'll never find. How are we ever going to find him, now?'

'Not him, you wally!' Jessica turned, smiling again, heading for the stairs. 'We'll find his spirit. People like Jimmy never die, not completely. His spirit is out there. And Gima said we would find it.'

Harry smiled at the thought, grabbed the car keys, strode to the vehicle, Jessica close behind. The cord had been cut. Now they had to lay bare the chain that had always dragged them low, into the mire of uncertainty and despair.

*   *   *

www.ingramcontent.com/pod-product-compliance
Lightning Source LLC
Chambersburg PA
CBHW060740190726
48285CB00001B/287